NIGHT SHIFTERS
II

LEGEND OF SUHNOYEE WAH

CHERYL LEE

 www.trafford.com
North America & international
toll-free: 1 888 232 4444 (USA & Canada)
fax: 812 355 4082

Contents

Special Thanks

I would like to take this time to say thanks to all of my family and friends for supporting me. I would like to give a special thanks to my friend Chrissy Kunz for inspiring me to write what I thought was my end but it turned out to be my beginning. I would also like to thank my "Olive Garden" girl friends Samantha, Tiffani, Melissa, Amy, Kristin and Laura. Thanks girls I love you all.

And a special appreciation to Joycelyn Arnold, thanks for all of your hard work.

Chapter One

RECOVERY

The beeps were getting louder; the faint voices in the distance were getting closer. My eyes were blurry and I could not make out the faces around me. I had no idea where I was. The images were coming and going. The jumbled languages and muffled sounds were as if I were inside a tunnel.

I must have been between both worlds.

My head was pounding and my back hurt terribly. I could not remember what happened to me or why I was here. I was not sure who these people were either. Both my arms were hooked up to machines and there were tubes everywhere.

I blinked several times; my vision was still a little blurry though. I heard a sound as if someone was crying. I opened my eyes to see a woman sitting in a chair, her face buried in her hands. I tried to communicate but, I could not speak, my throat was too sore. I just stared at her. I forced air through my lungs and made a noise. She slowly raised her head and looked at me with great relief.

"Kyle, son, you are awake! We thought we lost you!"

I still could not speak but, I looked at her. She laid her head on my chest and cried. I pondered in my mind what had happened to me. The woman looked at me again.

"You're in the hospital, you had a terrible accident."

She continued.

"You were searching for Elsha and, when you found her, you ended up trapped inside the cave too. You tried to escape but, rocks hit you on the head." She explained.

She also said one of Elsha's horses got loose and wondered off. Somehow, I managed to pull myself onto him, it saved my life. Then, she had this grim look on her face, she said something else happened.

"A wild animal must have picked up the scent of the horse and tried to attack it but, it injured you instead."

I wished I could remember all of this, but I just could not. I could not respond to her at all, I could only stare at her. She gently stroked my forehead with her hand and told me everything would be all right.

She continued telling me more about that night.

"Chief Spearhorn urged us to bring you to the hospital on the reservation,"

She went on to saying.

"He told us that your life depended upon it and he was right."

She was about to speak again but her cell phone interrupted her. She walked to the other side of the room and spoke softly; but, I could hear her telling someone that I was awake and I could not talk yet. I also heard her say, according to the doctor, I had short-term memory loss and that I should regain my memory soon.

I have short-term memory loss; no wonder I did not recognize anyone. Well that sure explains everything. It all makes sense now I must try to remember. I tried to make myself think but it only gave me a headache.

A nurse came in and said visiting hours would be over soon. I needed to know more about what happened to me.

"Your father will be here in the morning to see you,"

She said as she held my hand and told me she loved me. This woman must be my mother.

"Elsha is doing better,"

She stated calmly.

"She had suffered a concussion and she will be going home soon."

At that, she kissed me on my forehead and told me to get some rest. After she left, another nurse came into check on me. She introduced herself as Me'omi and told me she came to look at my back. She handed me a bell and told me to ring it when I felt pain anywhere. As she checked the bandages on my back and I rang the bell quickly. I screamed inside my head.

"Ouch! Hey take it easy!"

Carefully she removed her hands.

"Still sensitive to the touch I see,"

"I will gently remove your bandages and replace them with clean ones."

She continued.

"You're doing well. It will take some more time for you wounds to heal though."

Then you will be back to normal.

It was funny, I did not feel normal. It was a feeling I could not explain, I was myself only different somehow. The nurse told me to press the call button if I needed anything. I nodded to her and she closed the door.

That night, I dreamed a peaceful dream. I was standing in the middle of an open valley with rolling hills. I could feel the wind blowing in my face. Looking around, I watched the birds fly in the sky while some of the forest creatures were running around looking for food.

The tall trees were swaying back and forth in the wind as if they were rejoicing. I heard a sound coming from over the hill so, I ran to it to see a gorgeous white stallion running through the meadow.

It stood up on its hind legs and neighed. With its front legs in the air, the horse appeared to be dancing almost. It was the most beautiful creature I had ever seen. I wanted to move closer but, I decided to wait. As I watched it running around and jumping, the horse showed great strength.

As I sat down on the ground, I could hear eagles flying high above me. The sounds they made were as if they were communicating to each other. I thought I had died and gone to heaven. This place was so peaceful. Just listening to everything around me was like music to my ears. I could hear the sound of a babbling brook not too far off in the distance.

I wanted stay here and never wake up. I felt such a connection to this place. It felt like home to me. Now, this is a dream, no disturbances at all nice and pleasant.

The next morning a doctor came into my room. He was tall, had a very slender build, as well as long, black shiny hair. His eyes were an emerald green color and he had high cheekbones.

"Hello Kyle my name is Dr. Gregory Spears."

He sat down next to my bed.

"How are you doing?"

I wrote on my notepad given to me that my back was still sore but, otherwise, I was okay.

"Good. I need to do an exercise to test your thinking ability."

He held up some cards and asked me to point out differences in the pictures. I felt like I was back in elementary school again. After this exercise, he had me play a memory game just to test me a little bit more.

"You're showing signs of improvement and swelling in your brain has gone down; trauma can sometimes affect other parts of the body." He went on to tell me that he was sending me to therapy and that I had to remain in the hospital a few more weeks. I wrote on my notepad again asking him how long had I been in the hospital.

"You were in a coma for about a week," the doctor told me.

I still could not believe this was happening. I could not remember anything at all. Since I was awake and could understand, he felt it best they keep me for a while.

"You're a brave young man to have survived such an ordeal," he told me, "you lost a lot of blood and needed a transfusion."

He said I had a very rare blood type none that he had ever seen before. Luckily, they found a donor whose blood, though not a completely, was a close match. My heart stopped a couple of times but, they were able to revive me.

"Can you remember anything?" he asked me. I nodded no. "It will come back to you soon."

I spent weeks in the hospital going through therapy treatments. I was afraid I was going to be like this for the rest of my life.

As the days progressed, I got better. The doctors and nurses on the reservation worked with me to help me maintain my strength. My parents came to see me and shared more information with me about my accident.

They told me how the tribal council had a meeting to seal off the cave and no one was to enter it. The cave was now a national landmark and considered private property of the Tribal Union.

Since Elsha's dad owned the land, he made an agreement with the council members that the cave was now their property. The police department placed "No Trespassing" signs around the area to keep people away.

Slowly but surely, some of my memory came back. I was able to talk again, which made things easier for me. There were still some events I could not remember but, the doctor said that in due time, I should regain them.

I would be going home soon; it felt like I had been here forever. A nurse brought me an envelope with my name on it.

"Do you know who sent it?" I asked.

"I don't know." she said. As she did, there was a knock at the door, it was Tony. I was glad to see him.

"How are you doing?"

"Well," I told him.

"Can you remember anything that happened?" he asked.

"Vaguely."

Some parts I could not remember and it irritated me a little. Tony was just glad that I survived. He went on to explain to me what happened when Elsha and I were trapped inside the cave.

"How is she doing?" I stopped him for a moment to ask.

"She had a serious concussion but, she's back home. She spent a week in the hospital recovering. Her father said that if you had not helped her get out of the cave, her condition would have been much worse."

He told me that she would have suffered without treatment. Therefore, I am quite the hero back at home. On the other hand, her father has probably grounded her for the rest of her life.

"She has been very worried about you and she wanted to come see you so she sent you a letter," Tony told me.

Then I thought to myself for a moment. I did receive a letter from someone. Perhaps this was her letter.

"Hand me the envelope on that table," Tony did as I asked.

I opened the letter and it was from Elsha. She started out by apologizing for getting us both trapped in the cave. She said she did not know what would have happened to her if I had never found her. She went on to say her uncle was very glad that I lead them to the cave. He was probably going to ground me for the rest of my life.

"Yep I was right." I softly said.

Her letter was short but, she stated that she would see me soon.

Of course, Tony was being nosy. He just had to know what the letter said.

"She wanted to let me know that she was doing okay" I told him, "And that she thanked me for saving her."

"Are you going to be released from the hospital?"

"As soon as more test results come in."

"I was hoping it would be today so I could drive you home."

Another knock was at the door; Big John came in with a few others they came to see how I was doing. I told him that I was much better.

"A couple of the people got together to sign a card and brought some of your favorite music." He told me as I thanked him.

"I will come back to see you again." He went to leave but, turned around and said, "Oh, by the way, I have an envelope here for the both of you."

Tony and I both opened our envelopes. We had both received new invitations to the Summer Bonfire. Big John told me

"As soon as the doctors release you from the hospital, I'll make sure you two have a good time," he told us. They had to resend the invitations because he did not want me to miss it.

"You don't have to go through any trouble because of me."

"It's no trouble at all." Tony and I both thanked him. "I will see you soon." Tony was very excited. Big John pointed at me and said, "You just work on getting better; we need you." Then he was gone.

"What does he mean by that?" Tony asked me.

"I'm not sure."

That is what I told him; however, deep down I had a feeling I did know. Tony and I sat and chatted for a while as he explained more of what happened to me.

"The lightening was so bad that everyone had to seek shelter. The ranch hands had to quickly move the horses inside but, Wind Star ran away." Then he started the story.

"Elsha's dad did not want to give up though, neither did your dad. Police Chief Morgan had no choice but to order everyone away from the cave. The storm was like no ordinary storm that any of them had ever seen before. No one could explain it but, they all knew something was different."

He went on to tell me how the winds picked up fast and blew fierce. The weather report stated that a serious storm cloud was headed toward our area and for everyone to seek shelter. Even wild animals were on the loose due to the storm. While they all listened to the weather report, it was just too hard to believe. Then everyone heard a commotion outside and ran to see Elsha staggering toward them before falling to the ground. Her dad and uncle rushed to her aid.

"She had been bleeding from her head, her clothes had been slightly torn, and she had some scratches. We were worried at first; but, when her dad examined her, he was very relieved to see that the marks had to come from her escaping the cave and not from a wild animal." He assured me. "Dr. Morgan picked her up and carried her into the house."

Tony also told me that she was whispering my name and Chief Spearhorn's. She had said that someone needed to find Chief Spearhorn right away to help me. Little did she know that he and others were already on the scene.

Chief Spearhorn was in one of the tents saying sacred prayers; you could hear drums all around the camp outside of the house and up in the hills. It was just about dawn when they saw a horse approaching, carrying me on its back. When I fell off everyone ran towards me. I was badly bleeding and my eyes were very dark.

"Dr. Morgan examined you and noticed claw marks on your back. It wasn't a pretty sight; your blood was dark, black almost." Tony's voice began to shake as he spoke. "Dr Morgan said that you were going to need a blood transfusion fast."

Doctor Morgan had asked my parents for my blood type and my mom said AB negative and something else.

"She didn't quite know how to explain it but, there was not time. She only said that it was very rare and no one around had that blood type," he tried to remember, but Chief Spearhorn knew someone.

Your parents were so scared they ordered the paramedics to get you to the nearest hospital right away."

He told me that, at the moment, Dr. Morgan gave my mother a long hard look and was about to speak. However, Chief Spearhorn intervened and said it would be better to bring you here to the reservation.

My dad argued with him and said that there was not enough time. You were dying and they had to act fast. Chief Spearhorn said to my father that when someone's blood runs black his life in already balanced between heaven and earth. My dad did not budge though. He said he had no time to hear about the Chiefs spiritual mumbo jumbo.

"He wanted the local medical teams work on you." He informed me as he explained.

Chief Spearhorn had begged my father to allow him to take me to the reservation to save my life. He said there was someone on the reservation with the same blood type as you. He urged them to move quickly, that time was not going to wait.

"Kyle." Tony said nervously as he continued.

"I didn't know what was happening that night. I had never seen Chief Spearhorn speak so calm but be stern at the same time. The look upon his face was so serious. His countenance began to change…your dad had no choice but to agree with him. It was as if Chief Spearhorn had cast a spell on him." He recalled. "His eyes sparkled and your dad calmed."

And, after a few seconds, the decision was made. Big John and the others took me away. Tony did not want to leave me, his best friend, so he jumped into Big John's truck. My parents followed close behind us while Police Chief Morgan led the way.

He said that when we arrived on the reservation, there was a team of doctors and nurses already waiting for us. They immediately took me to the Triage unit and started working on me. He told me that my pulse was steady but weak on the way to the hospital.

"Big John broke several laws getting you to the reservation," he laughed. "Chief Spearhorn spoke in his native language and placed his staff over your head while you were there."

He told me my eyes were rolling in the back of your head and my eye color was changing again. I moaned loud and then, I lost consciousness.

"I was so scared. Tony said. "I was watching my best friend die in front of me. Big John kept telling you to hold on, that they needed you. He said he would call upon the spirit world to help fight to keep you alive."

As Tony was talking, it dawned on me that perhaps that was what Big John meant a while ago when he was here.

Tony went on to say how Chief Spearhorn sent my parents to a waiting room and assured them that they would do whatever it took to save my life.

I felt a slight headache coming on as he talked. I felt faint and light headed. Tony's voice sounded muffled and I felt my body spiraling downward. I could see images flashing in my head of my accident. The faces on the walls of the cave seem to come alive in my head.

Then, almost instantly, I began to regain the rest of my memory. I was overwhelmed with emotions. My breathing increased and my pulse raced. I felt my face turning red and I felt even worse than before. Tony pressed the "call" button for help and a team of doctors and nurses rushed in.

Tony called my parents and, luckily, they were just arriving at the hospital. They gave me oxygen to help with my breathing, they told me to relax and to remain calm.

That was very hard to do; I thought I was dying again. The doctor ordered Tony outside as they checked my vital signs. The flashing images of men turning into giant beast plagued my mind terribly.

Tony said he would wait for my parents and explain to them what was happening. I nodded my head to him as a nurse gave me a shot to calm me down. The doctor checked my eyes.

"Your pupils are dilating,"

The doctor told me as my breathing became stable again.

"Just an anxiety attack; you will be fine," he assured me. "What were you doing before this all happened?"

I told him Tony was explaining everything that happened after I got out of the cave.

"It normally takes a person time to regain that much information," he thought out loud. "What did you see?"

So, I told him I saw everything, well not everything even though it was fresh in my memory now. Dr. Spears explained to me somehow my brain began functioning like an overloaded circuit breaker, triggered by recent events. In addition, since I could not remember all that had happened, once I did start to remember, it caused a chain reaction in my body. Like a satellite receiving data that was too much to handle all at once.

"It's like the past catching up to the present at lightning speed." He told me "Don't worry; take it each day at a time."

I agreed and he said he would let my parents know that I would be fine. Moment's later mom and dad entered my room with relief on their faces.

"I'm feeling better. It was just an anxiety attack." I explained. "Somehow, I regained my memory at once and it was too much for my brain to handle."

Tony was breathing a sigh of relief as well. Mom packed more clothes for me and dad had a gift. I could not wait to open it.

"It's something you can use to keep you entertained for a while." He hesitated to give me the gift. "But don't overwhelm yourself after what just happened."

"I'm all right, it's too late anyway."

He handed me the box and they both watched me open it. Mom even had the camera to capture my reaction. I wondered what it could be and, to my surprise, it was a brand new iPod touch. I was so happy I could not stop smiling.

"Stay calm; I don't want you to have another episode" my dad told me.

"After all that you've been through, we both thought we would give you something to help keep you entertained," mom smiled.

"Well it worked." Tony was surprised as well. "I wish my parents would do the same for me." Dad said turned to Tony.

"Son, we may not be your parents but, we did think of you as well. So, to say thank you for being a good friend to our son and helping us find him, we also got you a gift."

Tony was happier than a kid in a candy store. In addition, to his surprise he received an iPod touch as well.

"Now you two can be entertained even more," my dad added.

"How did you get your hands on such hot items?"

"I have a friend that gave me a two for one deal." He winked at me. "You two are not the only eBay shoppers around here."

We all laughed for a while then, sat and began to talk. I would be going home soon, not before Tony and I stayed for the Summer Bonfire though. Chief Spearhorn offered mom and dad a place to stay on the reservation until the doctors felt it was alright for me to leave. That way they would not have to keep driving back and forth; they accepted his offer.

Dad took some time off, since it was summer and school was out; one of the other coaches filled in for him. I had another therapy session in the morning. Since Tony had permission to stay on the reservation, he would be with my parents. I was happy to have a family regardless of my situation. I thought of Elsha often and could not wait to see her again. I really hoped and prayed she would be okay.

She is so stubborn; she should have never gone near that cave. Elsha does what Elsha wants and there is no stopping her once her mind is up. I can clearly understand why she did what she did though. She was just helping me understand my dreams more. The drawings on the cave walls were the same as the pictures I drew in my book. She was just trying to piece them all together.

I will never be able to get the images out of my mind. They are forever imbedded in my memory.

Perhaps I should call her and see how she was doing. I don't even have a number for her though. I could call Police Chief Morgan, but then again, he may be upset with me for the whole thing.

He is very protective over Elsha and I didn't know how he felt about me since all of this happened. I will just call her anyway and check on her. I called an information desk to get their number since I remembered her address; it was pretty easy. The operator asked me to hold while she connected the call. A couple of rings went by, and I had decided I would hang up, until I heard someone say hello.

I choked up for a second and then responded. It was Dr. Morgan on the phone.

"Can I speak with Elsha?" I asked.

"She is gone for a few days, spending time with her mother."

"Can you let her know that I called and wanted to see how she was doing?"

"She is doing better and should be coming home soon." He told me. "How are you doing?"

"I'm improving."

He went on to tell me how grateful he was that I helped Elsha get out of the cave. He also said he was happy that she and I were alive. He said he had seen too many cases where people are seriously injured or nearly killed doing cave explorations and some never even escape ones like the most recent event.

"What recent event?" I had to ask.

"No need to worry, I'm just glad that you and Elsha were not around."

"Could you tell me?"

"Since you've been back from Rocky Point, the murders have started again." I could tell he did not want to startle me.

"It was a good thing that you and Elsha are both safe. Police Chief Morgan has been flooded with phone calls for missing people." He told me again. "Can I have your number; I will have Elsha give you a call."

He let me know that he had to get to the hospital and get to work. He told me that I sounded stronger and he would see me when I returned home.

"More murders" I said to myself. I reached for my laptop to do some research.

I should have been home by now. Somehow, I had the feeling that I they were keeping me here a little longer than I needed to be. How many more tests do they need to run on me? I need to find out when I could go home. I knew they were planning a special bonfire for students but, I did not care. I needed to get some answers.

Once my laptop powered up, I immediately went to our local news station's website to catch up on what I had been missing. There was an article posted that more mutilated bodies were being discovered. The local authorities have been overwhelmed with phone calls about the most recent events.

The attacks seemed to happen at night. The town had been placed on high alert again too. Since this article had posted seven hunters had been reported missing up near Wolf Creek. They were last seen two nights ago and no one has heard from them since.

Chief Morgan has called in for reinforcements to help with the case. Some people are saying a curse has been placed over the town and would like spiritual leaders to come together and do a mass cleansing.

Others speculate that it's a serial killer and are ready to take matters into their own hands. With new some evidence and due to DNA testing, they have discovered some of the victims are related. The police have turned to experts to help them with the case.

It said that the murders had reached the borders of Arizona, New Mexico, and Texas too. Although it's been rumored that tribal leaders from far away states are planning a huge meeting to come together, no one knows when or where this meeting will take place. Some reporters have contacted local and long distance tribal leaders to confirm this but, they have been unsuccessful.

There were more articles about what had been going on. One even talked about me and Elsha. It read,

"No one seems to be talking about it but, everyone here in Patagonia is on high alert. Since two teenagers were rescued from a cave-it has been reported they both are recovering-the Tribal Union has sealed the cave off. There are other rumors stating that since the cave was disturbed we have brought great trouble.

Trespassers will face huge fines if they are caught on or near the property. Since the storm has passed, animal control has been busy setting traps and returning wild animals back into the forest. There were many phones calls of wolf sightings in the area and some local neighborhoods. Police Chief Morgan is cautioning everyone to be careful."

I kept reading more stories in other areas; it made me wonder if them keeping me here longer was to keep me safe from harm.

Texas has reported more bodies disappearing from the morgues along with Arizona. Local natives, along with other residence fear that this is an epidemic and some have turned to their spiritual leaders for help.

The more I read, I had an odd feeling come over me. If the Suhnoyee Wah is building his army, he is planning an attack but, when and where will he strike?

Chills ran up and down my back and I felt cold. I grabbed my blanket and kept reading more stories.

Liwanu swore he would get his revenge and that those in the bloodline would suffer. This all seemed so crazy but, it is very real. The world as we knew it was under attack by a supernatural being with a grudge.

I began to go over things in my mind about when this all started and why me. Then, it hit me. I got out of bed and grabbed the chart from my room door. As I looked over the chart, I didn't see Dr. Spears standing behind me.

Chapter Two

THE VISITOR

"Dr. Spears, I can explain this." I nervously said. "I just wanted to see what was wrong with my blood."

"Well son, all you had to do was ask."

"I know Dr. Spears but I'm going crazy in this place." I made sure he knew. "My mom says I have a rare blood type so, I got little curious."

"I don't blame you." Dr. Spears laughed at my comment.

I guess he had forgotten what it was like to be a teenager. I handed him the chart and he said once the results came in he would tell me. He said my blood type is unusual and he hoped the test would help him understand it better. He had stopped by to let me know my day was to be filled with more test unfortunately and therapy.

"How many rare blood types are there?" I asked.

"About 30 recognized types. Some inherited through family genes." He went on to explain, "People who normally have rare blood types could help local hospitals and blood banks by donating blood for transfusions. It can help save someone's life."

I had never thought about it that way. However, Dr. Spears did schedule me for a long day of tests so I needed to prepare myself.

He was very nice but, he never answered my question. Therefore, I asked him the question again.

"You have an AB blood type." I gave him a look.

"Dr. Spears, what else is in my blood? My mother said there is something else."

"Yes Kyle, there is something else but, we don't know what that is yet." I gave him a look again. "Look, let us worry about that right now; it's common to have a rare blood type. This is why we're doctors; let us do the research, okay."

"I guess you're right."

"Kyle, don't worry, you are in good hands. Our job is to see that you get better."

Dr. Spears patted me on my shoulder and told me that the nurse will be in shortly to pick me up. I sat there pondering in my head the mystery of my blood.

Dr. Spears was right; I should let them worry about doing the research. So far so good, after all, I am still alive.

After a day of therapy sessions and brain scans, I was exhausted. Dr. Spears encouraged me to try not to focus on my accident or anything else. He said my recovery and healing was most important. He gave me a couple of CDs so I could listen to them. He thought I might like them.

"This is the music of our people," he said. "We use them in many of our therapy sessions."

I told him I would listen to them. Since my parents bought me a new iPod touch, I decided I would download the music. The nurses brought me lunch and said if I needed anything just press the button. She smiled at me and walked out. Tony and my parents would be here a little later.

I connected the iPod touch to my laptop and started the download. Sixty-four gigabytes was not so bad. Oh, how I loved mom, and dad for this; it really came in handy.

After my downloads finished I was very tired and could barely keep my eyes open. I decided to take a nap and rest for a while.

I put my earphones on and let the music relax me. The music was so nice and soothing it took me into total relaxation mode. I found myself floating away in a dream. Only odd thing about this dream was that it was not relaxing at all, more like disturbing.

I am standing on a cliff in a high mountain ridge overlooking the valley. I can see a village below with people going about their day. Some gathered around to hear stories about their ancestors. Eagles are flying high soaring through the air scouting the land for food. Everyone seems to be at peace until the sky darkened and the clouds rolled in.

The winds picked up and lightening struck down on the village. The people scatter taking refuge in their teepee huts. I ran down the cliff toward the village, I had to get a closer look to see what was happening.

A young warrior walked along a huge black wolf. As the dark mist moved throughout the village, I could hear the people screaming. I stood and watched in horror as the dark images terrorized them. Then the young warrior stood face to face with the beast and then they merged becoming one.

The dark being commanded the others to bring those in the bloodline to him and he would devour their souls. He ordered the other night shifters to destroy everyone else and leave no one alive. I felt as if I were a ghost, walking in the mist of them. The wolves were shifting in and out of the darkness.

This must be Liwanu, the warrior.

He is one with the beast that walks in the night. I followed his every move; he was in search of those who were in the bloodline that could destroy him. The only way he could tell was to taste their blood. I stood and watched in horror as the young brave was brought before him.

Liwanu looked deep into his eyes sniffing his skin.

With his long sharp claws, he cut through his skin like a knife. Red blood began to run down the young braves arm. The beast, whose thirst for blood enraged him more, he licked the young braves arm with his long tongue.

Petrified with fear the young brave yelled out to the beast. Screaming as loud as he could he was helpless but, in spite of his fears, he tried to fight back. The shifter immediately grabbed him, as they disappeared into the darkness. I could hear him screaming as they did.

Then, a strange feeling came over me. My head felt dizzy and I ached with pain. I fell to my knees as if someone had dropped a ton of bricks on top of me. My back burned with fire, I screamed in agony. I clawed at the ground clutching dirt in my hands. I fell on my side and looked up at the dark sky.

The stars were sparkling very bright. As I stared, it appeared they were twinkling at me. These were not twinkling stars, they were eyes.

The sky seemed to move toward me, my breathing increased and I felt something oozing from my back. Was I dreaming inside a dream? I was back at the cave again where Elsha and I were trapped. I just laid there paralyzed and unable to move. Then a huge wolf approached me and growled I could feel something cold and wet on my back. The wolf, with its teeth showing, howled loudly and stared deep into my eyes.

With a loud voice, I yelled to the beast, telling it to go ahead and kill me. I yelled out again

"Kill me, kill me!"

The wolf just stared at me.

It howled as if to notify others to where we were. The blood ran beyond my body, the wolf came closer and sniffed me as if it were searching for something. It was after my blood for sure. Other wolves approached and stood around me in a circle, I could see glimpse of bright lights also approaching. They appear to startle the wolves; all they could do was move away from me.

My blood soaked the ground and my body felt empty. The bright lights grew brighter and I could feel my body lift from the ground. I did not know where I was going. Who knows where they were taking me.

I am now in a room, I can see a body lying still on a table.

Hovering over it, I could see it was my body only it did not appear to be my body. Suspended in the air like a ghost, I floated down toward the body and the eyes opened.

"Time draws near, the bloodline is strengthening." It said. "Wake up, my brother."

I awakened gasping for air, I was shaking, and my back hurt. I got out of bed and ran to the bathroom. I splashed cold water on my face; my pajamas were soaked with sweat. I took off my shirt and, for the first time, I saw the visible scars on back. They were bright red and looked awful; I felt so sick. I stared in the mirror at myself for a while.

"What is happening to me?" I said.

I must speak with Chief Spearhorn right away. I looked at the clock and it was later than I had expected. How long was I asleep? It was still daylight outside which was a good thing. I changed clothes, sat on my bed, and thought about my dream. I contacted the office of Chief Spearhorn and he was unavailable to take my call, so I left a message, an urgent one.

The bloodline is strengthening definitely another clue. I thought about everything that I could possibly think of; I was going back in my mind searching for more. The illegally adopted children, I wonder if they are also in the bloodline. Eric told me in my dream the bloodline is strengthening, perhaps the others know as well. I must find out.

Then it hit me, I was researching information about a reporter once who first broke the story about the illegal adoptions. I tried to remember her name. I paced the floors back and forth I felt a headache coming on. I really wanted to go home. So much is happening back at home I am starting to believe I should stay here.

I decided I would find the reporter that I had been searching for.

I reached for my laptop when my cell phone rang. It was Tony, letting me know he was on his way down to see me. He explained all the craziness that was going on in our town.

"You needed anything from your house," he asked after his explanation.

"No."

"Alright, I'll see you in a little while."

I hung up the phone and started to reach for my laptop again when there was a knock at my door. The nurse came in to check on me.

"How are you was doing?" She said as she came near. "I need to give you a couple of protein shots because your iron levels have dropped again."

"When will I be able to go home?"

"Soon as the doctor gives the order." I was getting a little irritated with all of this.

"Well, what if I just walked out of here and left?"

She looked at me funny. She just laughed and told me that I was not well enough to leave yet. They had to be sure my wounds have fully healed and make sure I did not have an infection.

"Lift your shirt," she told me as she started to examine my back. "You have some mild discoloration and the wound looks fresh."

"Fresh! What do you mean fresh?"

"Wait while I call for the doctor," she told me. Now I was worried. Dr. Spears came in, looked at me, and was puzzled.

"Do you feel any pain?" he asked.

"Yeah, my back feels like it's on fire."

"I need to take some blood from your back and some skin samples." I did not want him to touch me but, he said I had no choice; he wanted to be sure that I was not getting an infection.

He ordered the nurse to reattach the IV to my arm. I turned over and the nurse began to scrape my wounds. I had to lay still as I felt the needle go into my back. I held my breath as I felt the stinging increase. I yelled out in pain and the nurse hit the morphine button. After a few minutes, I could feel the liquid from the IV enter my arm; it was very cold.

All I could ask was what was happening to me.

The doctor turned to the nurse and ordered a rush placed on my blood and skin samples.

So many questions plagued my mind. I needed to get out of this hospital and off the reservation. I felt I was their prisoner here; for some reason, they did not want me to leave. The morphine was working and I felt tired all of a sudden but, morphine should not make me tired it should just take away the pain.

Then, I was out like a light. I do not know how long I was out but, by the time I had woke up, Tony had come and gone along with my parents. He left me a note with a few more newspaper clippings and mom had left some fresh baked cookies and a note that she would be back a little later to see me. I picked up the articles and noticed that inside one of them, Tony left me a note saying that he thought I would like to know what the doctors found up at Rocky Point.

One article was about Elsha's dad, Dr. John Morgan, who made a startling discovery up in the hills.

It was a gruesome site; one of the victim's chests had been ripped open and just a few yards away, next to the body, was another victim whose back was badly clawed. The victim must have been running away from something according to the report. However, they were puzzled when they saw that the victim was alive. One report stated that there were multiple deaths, which was not true. Somehow, they kept this information from the public just in case the perpetrator was to finish off what he or she had started.

Dr. Morgan and the other specialist were instructed to bring the victim to Rocky Point Medical Center for treatment right away. Once they reached the hospital, a team of Elders took the victim to an undisclosed area for protection.

Now any one can understand this but this area was away from the hospital and about a half an hour out of town.

Dr. Morgan was confused and did not know why this happened. Local authorities asked him to come down to Rocky Point to examine the bodies. In addition, wanted to know why he could not work on the survivor. Dr. Morgan was immediately told he did not have jurisdiction any longer and he should head back home because of the storm.

There had been several animal attacks in the area and some of the locals were scared.

I can always count on Tony to help me out.

I wondered what became of the person that survived the attack; I had to find out. I sure had a list of things I needed to add to my list of things to do. Therefore, I thought I should write them down before I forgot them.

I grabbed my notebook and made a list of people to contact. First, was the reporter whose name I could not remember, then, it was to research the victim who survived the animal attack.

I needed to find her she could tell me more I am sure of it. Then, it hit me like a ton of bricks. Her name was Veronica Banks. I picked up my laptop and began to search for people. There were several Veronica Banks listed in the Temple Cove area so I had to start at the top. Only one published number and the others were non-published.

I called the published number and, unfortunately, it was not her. Just an old woman with a shaky voice, I apologized and she said it was all right, it happens all the time. I asked her just out of curiosity if her number had ever been mistaken for the news reporter Veronica Banks. She said yes but, she does not know her personally. I thanked her for her time and hung up.

I hate dead ends; I just had to find her. Temple Cove was not that big so I started with the local newspaper there called the Sun Star

Times. It was a locally owned newspaper started by a retired attorney John Steel. I searched the newspaper company online for articles by local reporters to see if I could find her name and found nothing.

I even called to see if she worked for the company and, again, I had no luck.

I started to think that perhaps she changed her name, it could be possible since she quit right after the story of the illegal adoption aired on television. I wondered why she would quit; perhaps someone did not want this story to get out. All of the documents were sealed.

I paused for a moment.

I remembered that once the children returned the information was sealed on the reservation. I really needed to get into the archives but, how could I?

Tony, surely he would help me. I thought about the key pad on the door, we would have to get in somehow and find those sealed documents. Chief Spearhorn would never let us inside. I needed to come up with a plan.

Tony phoned and said he was running late; he remembered his mother had a given him a few things to do before he left home. I told him I was still in prison and that I was not going anywhere soon. I continued my research when there was a knock at my door. Thinking it was another nurse, I told whoever it was to come in. However, it was not the nurse but, a man. He was tall and muscular, long black hair.

He wore an acid wash denim jacket and his hat was rugged looking with a brown hawk's feather sticking out of the side. He walked in smiled at me and introduced himself. He looked at me long and hard first and asked if I remembered him. I told him no. He said probably not I was very young.

He opened his briefcase and pulled out some charms and necklaces; I stared at them with such amazement. He told me I had the same look on my face the night I ran into his tent. He looked at me tipped his hat and said.

"Allow me to introduce myself again, my name in Benjamin Wilson formally known as Tall Bull."

"How did you know I was here?"

"I've been watching you for a long time." He said. "Don't be alarmed, I'm not a stalker but, more like a guardian. I heard about the cave incident and decided to pay you a visit once I heard you were well enough."

"Can you tell me about the night I came into your tent?" I asked.

"You were a very frightened little boy; you kept looking over your shoulder," he reminded me, "how much of that night do you remember?"

"Not much."

He began to tell me it was the night of the Moon Festival and somehow I strayed away from my parents. He said the look upon my face was terrifying. I ran as if someone or something was chasing me. The more he talked, the more I felt calmness in the room.

However, before I let him continue, I had to ask what the reason behind his visit was.

"Ever since that night, I often wondered about you. Then when your parents found you, I felt an urgency to keep watch over you."

"So you have been watching me the whole time?" I said to him.

"Yes." He replied.

"Why?"

"It's my duty."

"Explain."

Benjamin took off his hat, opened his briefcase and pulled out a rare necklace with a silver stone in the center of it.

"Have you ever seen one of these?" He asked.

"Yes" I replied. "One of the teachers at my school has one or something like it."

Benjamin explained the guardian of the people in which he called "*QALETAQA*". He said we all have one, they are our spirit guides. He told me I was too young to understand at the time I came in to his tent that night. The more he talked the more I started to remember.

He also said he explained to my mother that I was a special child. However, I think she already knew that.

"That is also, why I am here." He said. "Your gifts are far beyond what you could ever imagine. You see the dark move when others think it stands still. Your eyes are not trained or fixed they just see what they see."

I sat back for a moment and folded my arms. It felt nice to know that there was someone else that believed in me and explained things exactly as I saw them. Benjamin told me a story of a couple that had a young child. One night the mother put the child to bed and left the room.

Moments later the child screamed and the mother came rushing in to his room. Only to discover that a dark shadow was hovering over the child staring down at him.

She screamed, and others in the house came running. The child's "*ududu*," meaning grandfather, was in the home at the time and knew something was wrong. He immediately said a sacred prayer to cover the house and everyone inside. The young couple was told that the evil had chosen the child and he had been marked.

News of this event spread throughout the community and parents with young children went to their spiritual leaders for help. Convinced that the same thing would happen to their children, they sent them away to hide them from the danger. This did not sit well with the leaders so each child received a stone for protection.

"How long ago was this?" I asked.

"A long time ago, when my father told me why he was sending me away, I could not believe it."

"You are a chosen one?"

"Yes." He said.

I was now speechless.

"Were the children illegally adopted sent away for safety," I said under my breath.

"It's a possibility," Benjamin told me.

"There was a reporter that did a story about the illegal adoptions from the reservation, could you help me find her?"

"What's the reporter's name?"

"Veronica Banks."

"I remember a reporter that did a story on the children; but, she was threatened for going public with her story."

"It's very important that I find her."

I gave him the only information I had on her to see if he could locate her for me.

In the mean time, the summer bonfire was in a few days and, after that, I would be going home. I also asked him why it took so long for him to come see me. He said he was waiting for the right time.

I told him everything about the dreams and the cave incident but, he had heard about it through the news and radio.

Benjamin went on to say that, on the night that I went missing, he, and other tribal leaders were sent to the cave. He stayed up in the high hills and offered up a sacred prayer for me. That night he said there were many strange things happening in the area. The storm was like no ordinary storm.

He said they could feel the evil in the air as they began singing their sacred prayer songs. Benjamin continued telling me that when the spirit leaders came together that night everyone cleared their minds and became one with the atmosphere.

They offered up prayers to protect the boundaries so the evil could not cross. While the other leaders said prayers to cover the living. However, on that particular night, no one could abandon their post. They had to make sure the boundary was kept safe.

I paced the floors back and forth rubbing my hands together. Benjamin asked if I had any nightmares lately, of course, the answer was yes.

"Do you feel like talking about it?" he asked me.

"No." He encouraged me to be strong but, I cut him off. "How can I be strong when my life is in danger? Whatever has been happening took place long before I was born. I have a twin brother who tells me in my dreams that time is drawing near the bloodline is strengthening."

By this time, I felt myself getting angry again. I did not want Benjamin to know that part of my dream but, it was too late.

"What else took place in my dreams?" he asked as he rose to his feet.

I spent another hour telling him about it. Then, he looked at my back and gasped.

"Your wounds are fresh." He said.

Then he spoke in his native language and pulled out a small brown pouch from his pocket.

"What is this?" I asked.

"Something you are going to need, you will know when to use it." He handed me the pouch. "Whatever you do Kyle, don't open this pouch, until the time is right, instinct will guide you."

"Why are you giving this to me?" The bag felt like marbles were inside.

"Because we all could use some protection," he made me promise him that I wouldn't use it, and, I did. Therefore, I placed the pouch in my bag.

With a grave look in his eyes, he said that he had to leave but he would see me in a little while.

"Remember." Benjamin said.

"I know, I know. Use the pouch when necessary."

Then, he was gone.

Darn these nightmares, I wanted to focus on something positive. The bonfire was going to be a big celebration. I have heard some of the nurses' staff talking about other natives from distant tribes traveling here just to they could be a part of the event. Great, I needed something to take my mind off things.

Somehow, I had a weird feeling come over me that I could not explain. Something was on the horizon but, what?

Chapter Three

WELCOME HOME

After my last therapy session and final brain scan, the doctor said it was all right for me to go home. I asked him about my test and he said that my protein levels somehow showed that I had a third blood type, which will require more tests. He said it could take months to figure out why but, he thought because I had improved so much, it was safe to send me home. He said it would be great if I came back before the big event for a follow up.

After spending nearly a month in the hospital, I was more than ready to go home. Dad had met with Chief Spearhorn and apologized for his actions. The Chief accepted his apology and said he understood that he was upset; they all wanted what was best for me. He told me he received my message and would meet with me soon.

Mom thanked the staff at the hospital and the nurses gave me a going away party. They said I was one of their best patients. Dr. Spears said I would be missed but, a doctor is always glad to send their patience home back in good health. I asked him if he was going to be at the bonfire driveand he said it depended on his schedule.

Mom and dad were anxious to get me home so they packed up the last of my belongings coming back perhaps, we would meet then.

"How are things were back at home?"

"The town is still on high alert. Police Chief Morgan is busier than ever with all of the press conferences he had scheduled," dad told me. "Son."

"Don't worry yourself about any of this; let the authorities handle it."

"Sure dad."

Finally, we arrived home. I could not wait to go to my room and sleep in my own bed. It seems the neighborhood was glad I was back at home.

Our house was decorated with flowers, balloons, and a huge welcome home sign.

"Did you have anything to do with this?" dad looked at mom as he asked.

"No, I'm just as surprised."

Then to my surprise, Tony arrived.

"Hey bro, welcome home."

"Thanks," I said.

"So Tony," mom said, "is this your idea of a welcome home party?"

"Yes ma'am," Tony said.

"Well good job, now would you mind giving us a hand?"

Tony helped my parents while I went to my room. There was a neat pile of cards on my desk. Mom must have organized them for me, just like she had organized my room.

I noticed a personal note left on my mirror from her. She must have spent hours in here worried about me. My room was so clean, pillows fluffed and my books in alphabetical order on the shelf.

Mom does things like this when she is worried about something. I sat on the bed and read the note. It was very touching, a mother never wants to lose a child but, this time she felt she had. She put a smiley face on it and told me that she was glad I was safe back at home.

Tony came into my room with my things and we talked for a while. He could not stay long which was fine; I needed to get some rest anyway. We would be going back to the reservation soon for the big bonfire and we both did not want to miss that. Mom and dad constantly asked if I needed anything but the answer was no, I would just rest a while.

After a very long nap, I decided to stay in my room and read some of my cards. Some were from friends at school and others from neighbors. However, there was one card from someone I had not heard from in a while, Ms. Creed.

She wrote to me stating that she had been away and heard the terrible news. She hoped and prayed for my safety and said that she would return before the next school term.

She was visiting her parents for the summer and she said she would keep in touch with me by email; so, she included her address in the letter.

"So it must be true." I said to myself.

Elsha said that Ms. Creed has a secret with all the crazy things happening I guess she had to go make sure everything was all right.

With my laptop close by, I decided to email Ms. Creed to let her know that I was back at home and doing well. I did not know where to begin so, I started with a simple hello and thanks for the card.

I told her that I was doing well and about how Dr. Spears felt it was time for me to come home. I asked if she was vacationing on a remote island somewhere, just to see what response I get.

Once I was finished I went downstairs to grab some food. Mom and dad left me a note that they went shopping for a while.

As I made lunch, I had an odd feeling come over me. I looked out the window to see a strange car parked across the street. It was the same car that I saw before, and old model sedan with dark windows. Perhaps they were visiting someone but, my gut told me different.

I peeked out the window to see if anyone moved inside the car but, nothing. I watched for a while, then the car drove slowly pass the house and was gone. I had no Idea who this mysterious person could be.

Why were they watching the house? Should I mention this to mom and dad or find out who this person is? I heard my cell phone ringing upstairs. I would just let it go to voicemail; whoever it was, they could call back. I wanted to be sure that no one else was watching the house.

I decided to take a walk outside and look around, a few neighbors saw me and waved; I wave back with a smile. The mail carrier greeted me as well.

"Welcome home, son."

"Thanks, it feels good to be back at home."

I went back inside to retrieve my phone; it was probably Tony. I really did not feel like hanging out that much today. I was feeling somewhat sluggish. I just wanted to relax. Therefore, I made myself some lunch, sorted the mail, and went up to my room.

More cards from well-wishers and a few brochures from colleges, there was a rather large manila envelope. I wondered who could have sent this to me. To my surprise, it was from Benjamin. I proceeded to open the envelope; it was full of newspaper clippings, articles on missing children.

To my surprise, again there was information about the reporter I was looking for. Benjamin had done well by finding this information; the envelope was quite full. I did not know where to begin. In the mist of all of this, a letter from Benjamin fell out.

I quickly picked it up and began to read. Benjamin stated he had to get special permission to enter the archive room. He enclosed some articles I had been searching for and urged me not to lose them.

Benjamin also said more and more people are starting to gather on the reservation. He feels this is going to be more than just a bonfire and he noted that there is additional information in the envelope that will interest me as well. He said he would keep in touch with me and would see me very soon.

I paused for a moment. I rechecked the envelope and, at the bottom, there was a small book called "Secret Legends." The book contained information about ancient warriors, one in particular, Running Bear.

I sat back on my bed and paused again, this time longer than the first. I started to organize each article; I wanted to take my time and read each piece. I started with the reporter who first broke the story about the illegal adoptions.

Clipped to the article about the illegal adoptions was a transcript of an interview by Veronica Banks. How did they get a copy of this? Must not be that hard since it is so easy to get public knowledge.

The interview was with Chief Spearhorn of the Tribal Union Reservation and other council members. The transcript states that she asked Chief Spearhorn if all of the children were accounted for and why was there such great fear among his people.

He stated that his people were afraid of their children being taken away. However, Veronica did not believe this at all. She told the Chief that there was something else going on. She said that she interviewed one of the mothers who told her, for fear of their children's' lives, some of them were voluntarily given up for protection.

Chief Spearhorn argued this allegation and assured her that this was not the case. Veronica went on to say how tribal legends stirred up the people because of strange happenings, close relatives missing, and rumors about the bloodline.

The more I read, I could feel something shift inside me. The very foundation of my soul had been shaken up. Veronica had uncovered a conspiracy and the Chief was trying to hide it. One part of the manuscript read how the tribal council urged her not to go public with her story. Some of the council members felt there would be wide spread panic. Veronica stated that she would only speak the facts by telling the truth. However, she did not want to upset the council members, despite wondering what would happen to the people.

She said leaders are to help guide the people and to encourage them, not to allow them to live in fear. Veronica told the council members that shielding the truth would cause rebellion among their people.

Chief Spearhorn disagreed with this. He stated that they encourage their people to embrace the spirits for guidance. They are protectors of their tribes, which is why they fought for centuries to keep their land so they could live in peace.

The manuscript also stated that Veronica asked the Chief if he felt there was someone out there with a vendetta against his people. Chief Spearhorn told her that his people have faced threats before but, not for reasons of this kind.

His people always received threats from outsiders to be kicked off their land by hunters, activist, and local protestors. He said there are even some who have speculated that the land did not belong to them and they were in this country illegally. Veronica asked the Chief why people would give up their own children and send them away from the reservation. She wanted to know what would scare the people that they would make such great sacrifices to give them up.

The Chief's response was not what she was expecting according to the transcript; he urged her again to be careful about her story and leave the rest for them to handle. Veronica's report also stated that she would continue her investigation as more information became available.

No wonder they wanted all this information concealed in the archives. I kept reading through more of the interview and skimmed through a few more pages it seemed Veronica was a very strong willed person. She was a reporter and they usually do not stop until they get their story. She felt the public needed to know, not that she would discredit the Chief, but it seemed more personal to her.

Did she have a relative involved somehow? Well I would just have to find that out as well.

After reading the report, I thought about Elsha and wondered if she was back. I wanted to call her but; I did not want to interrupt her visit with her mother. I decided to put the mail down for a while and give my brain a rest.

As I picked up the mail, an envelope fell on the floor.

I must have forgotten about this. When I picked it up, I noticed it was address to my mother. It was a letter from Doctor Frank D. Hill, a child specialist.

A dizzy spell hit me and I fell on my bed. I never thought I would ever hear this name again. My mind went back to that dreadful day when my session went horribly wrong. I wondered what Doctor Hill wanted.

I knew my mother would never approve of me doing this but, I just had to know. Therefore, I did a trick with the envelope by steaming the letter and carefully opening it from the seal. Something I learned in science class; paying attention does pays off.

With shaky hands, I unfolded the envelope. I do not know why I was so nervous; perhaps, it was just the shock of what I saw at such a young age.

As I read the letter, I calmed a little. It appears that the good doctor heard about my accident and wanted to know how I was doing. He wished me a speedy healing and wanted to know if I was still having nightmares. He still thinks he can help me and would like my mother to bring me in for a free consultation.

Sound more like a sales pitch. No thanks doc, my brain is not for sale to boost your medical career.

I resealed the envelope and placed it on the table. I thought to myself for a moment, remembering the events on that day. Doctor Hill said that he videotaped his sessions, I wonder how much of my session did he get on video. I would have never thought to go back to that place; however, it was just what I needed. I was going to pay Doctor Hill a visit.

I grabbed my bag and headed downstairs when my cell phone rang again. It was Tony and he wanted to hang out; I told him I had something important to do. Of course, Tony knew me all too well. I told him I would pick him up but, he insisted on driving me. He would pick me up in a few minutes since he was in my area. He said he was bringing me a surprise.

Now Tony is always full of surprises. Perhaps, now he has a girlfriend and wants to bring her by to introduce her. No way! He would tell me first; however, he is a good friend to offer to drive me, especially since he had no idea where we were going.

Most people would not even hang around me; some people think I am either too crazy or too dangerous to be around. No argument there, I did not want another dizzy spell especially while driving.

While I waited on Tony, I quickly wrote mom and dad a note telling them I had a few errands to run and would be home late. I ran upstairs to be sure I had everything I needed when I heard the doorbell ringing like crazy.

Yep, that is Tony. I ran downstairs, opened the door, and to my surprise, it was a beautiful surprise. My eyes gazing and mouth wide open.

"Well are you going to stand there or are you going to invite me in?"

It was Elsha.

Tony said he had run into her at the library and she insisted on seeing me.

"It's good to see you again," I said.

"You as well Kyle, my father told me that you called. While I was away I thought about you a lot."

My heart skipped a beat when she said that.

"Well, I will just excuse myself to the kitchen and give you two sometime to talk," Tony said.

He walked backwards out of the room as if he was going to miss something.

While Tony went into the kitchen to fix himself a snack for the road, Elsha and I sat down to talk.

I told Elsha I was happy to see her and I thought about her as well. She asked how my back was doing and I told her I was still healing. I explained that the doctors were afraid I would never heal, however, I improved. They felt it best to send me home then.

"I was afraid for you," she told me.

"Being in that cave, I was afraid for us both". She agreed and apologized for getting us in trouble.

"If I would've never gone into that cave, none of this would have ever happened," she said.

Placing my hand on her shoulder, I told her that I was glad we both got out alive. I did not know what I would do if I had lost her as a friend. She gently placed her hand on top of mine, smiled at me, and said the feeling was mutual. Then we stared at each other for a moment.

I was lost in her hazel eyes. She was so beautiful. I could feel my heart skip a beat and the palm of my hands began to sweat. I wanted to kiss her but, my father always taught me to be respectful. I did not want to do anything to ruin this moment. I could feel such a powerful force inside me that just wanted to explode.

"Careful Kyle, remember to be a gentleman," I mentally told myself.

As we stared at each other, I wondered what was going through her mind. Then I found myself leaning into her and drawing closer then, Tony came out from the kitchen.

"Hey Kyle, tell your mom thanks for the grub." Elsha and I both jumped. "Did I interrupt something?" Tony said.

"No, not at all," Elsha said with an embarrassing look on her face.

"So buddy, what adventure are we going on today?" Tony said while stuffing his face.

"Just some place a few hours out of town, I just need to get more answers."

"Kyle," Elsha brought my attention to her. "That's the reason I came by, I wanted to see you and return your book to you. I do apologize for keeping it so long. I feel responsible."

"No Elsha, somehow that cave holds clues to my dreams, I am glad you found it."

As I took the book from Elsha, I noticed that she had added photos to it. She matched my drawings with the pictures she took from the cave. This was remarkable; she did not have to go through all of this for me.

"Kyle, I hope you don't mind I want to help in any way I can so," she began to explain; "I took the liberty of matching the photos to better help you. In addition, I did some research on the symbols we saw inside the cave."

"Great, you can explain more on the way."

"By the way, where are we going?" Elsha asked.

"I must go and visit Dr. Frank D. Hill. I need him to answer a few questions for me."

"Kyle, are you sure you want to do this?" Tony asked with a concerned look on his face.

"Yes, I must do this, and forgive me, I shouldn't ask you two to come along. It's very selfish of me; I don't want anyone else getting hurt. Besides, I almost lost a good friend and I do not want to do anything to jeopardize our friendship."

Elsha and Tony both had looks upon their faces as if they wanted to crucify me.

"We are in this together." Tony said; moreover, Elsha agreed. "So let's get going. We have a long drive and it's starting to rain. Don't worry Kyle; I will have you home before dinner." Tony said.

Therefore, we set out to visit the hospital. Elsha took the time to explain to me what the strange symbols meant that we saw in the cave. One symbol had a triangle head and a circular base. Aligned in the middle of it were stars that looked like eyes.

Another symbol looked like an animal of some sort inside a circle with strange writings around it. Each meaning was at the bottom, which gave an explanation. Elsha told me while she visited her mother on the yacht; it gave her time to research.

She got tired of hearing about her mother's stories of sailing around the world. She got tired of hearing about the life of the rich and famous.

Elsha really detailed my book. As I read, I learned that these were more than just symbols they were spells. I remembered the wall like stone we came across in the cave.

Elsha stated, from what she could remember, it looked like a chamber of some kind. I remembered as well. Elsha stated, in her research, she learned that the property where her dad had their home built could be part of the forbidden land.

"What is the forbidden land?" Tony asked.

"There is a book written by Jeremiah Flynn, a scientist who told stories about an ancient burial ground where warriors are buried. The land was to be kept and undisturbed. I believe the chamber we found was a tomb, but for who?" Elsha explained.

She said she needed to do more research and find out what the symbols meant. From what I could remember, the wall painting showed a priest on the opposite side of the chamber wall with seven glowing stones around the rock.

My gut told me I already know what the symbols meant. The prayers were to keep something in, not out. Whatever was behind that wall must be there for a reason.

As Tony drove I kept pondering in my head all of the dreams I had. The drawings kept everything fresh in my memory. The dark man I saw with the crystal blue eyes that stood on the cliff in my dream. I remembered, he placed his thumb on my forehead and blew a strange smoke in my face. It is as if he pushed me out of the dream. I wondered who this man was; could he be my spiritual guide?

We were almost at the hospital when I noticed something. The car that I saw parked in front of my house was behind us. Tony said he had noticed the car had been following us for a while. Elsha said she wondered whom it was she was starting to worry. I told them I did not know and when I had first spotted the car in my neighbor.

"Perhaps they are just going the same direction we are." Tony said.

The car veered to the left and proceeded to pass us. I tried to get the license plate number but it was raining too hard to see.

"Whoever they are, they seem to be in a hurry." Elsha said.

After that ordeal, we finally reached the hospital. It was just as I remembered, the long driveway, the tall trees that met at the top. I forgot how much this place looked like an asylum.

As I stared at the trees and looked at the woods near the hospital, it dawned on me; I had seen this place in my dreams.

A cold odd feeling came over me and I shivered a little. Tony asked what I was hoping to find at this place. I never thought I would repeat this story to anyone but, I did.

I explained to Tony and Elsha the events that took place here during my session when I was younger. They were my friends and they understood me.

After I explained things, Tony parked the car and I asked both to stay put while I went in to speak with Doctor Hill. They both agreed.

As nervous as I was I looked across the courtyard into the woods. Fear started to grip me but I had to continue. I ran in quickly to get out of the rain and once inside I inquired about Dr. Hill.

"Do you have an appointment young man?" A nurse said to me.

"No, I don't. I am here to see Dr. Hill, is he available?"

"Well I'm afraid the doctor is busy seeing patients and without an appointment that would be impossible."

I just had to see him so I told her who I was and how my parents brought me to see him when I was little. I figured if I tell the nurse how the good doctor cured me she would be happy squeeze me in. Well after explaining it to her, it worked. She sent me to the waiting room.

As I sat there, I could remember what it was like as a child and how scared I was. I did not want to keep my friends waiting too long.

Finally, the nurse came in to the waiting room and said.

"The doctor will see you now."

She escorted me to Dr. Hill's office; she said he would be with me in a moment and that his appointment was running longer than usual. I just sat in his office looking around.

I noticed he had newspaper articles about his success stories in curing children of their nightmares and other things. I did notice a newspaper clipping on his desk about two teenagers trapped in a cave. Therefore, that is how he knew about me. I did know that the good doctor kept videos of his patients but, where?

I scanned the room and saw a cabinet that was slightly open. I looked around to see if anyone was coming and quickly opened it. I highly doubted that the doctor would freely give me a copy but, I would check just in case.

Inside the cabinets were the names of his patients and he had copies of all of their sessions. There were volumes of discs so I had to act quickly to locate my own. I searched each cabinet and file until I came across a file marked private, for doctor viewing only. I found it, somewhat odd that none of the others were marked like this one but, it had to be mine.

I picked up the file and looked through it skimming over the doctors notes. I then noticed that the doctor referred to me as one of his subjects, as if I was some scientific experiment. I looked around to see if anyone was approaching and quickly started copying my file. I even got lucky, used the good doctor's blank disc, and burned a copy from his computer.

You would think he would password protect his computer. I know I am wrong for this however; what other choice do I have. Dr. Hill's computer was very slow, I could hear talking coming from down the hall. I peeked out to see and, of course, it was Dr. Hill. He was speaking with one of the parents. I just needed a few more minutes.

"Come on computer, hurry up." I whispered.

Seventy-five percent left.

I looked out again and he had his backed turned escorting the lovely couple around the corner. I breathed for a moment. Finally, I removed the disc, replaced it in the file, and left the cabinet just as I found it, slightly open. I folded the papers, tucked the disc inside, and placed them inside my jacket pocket.

I leaned over the doctor's desk and made sure everything was back in place. Just as I set the newspapers in place, the good doctor walked in.

"Did you find what you are looking for?"

Oh, no, I am so busted.

"The papers on my desk, did you find what you were looking for?"

"I do apologize sir, I just happened to notice the article when I was trapped in the cave and-"He stopped me in mid sentence.

"No need to worry young man, I should apologize for keeping you waiting so long. Please sit down."

Dr. Hill was an odd-looking man. He was not that tall at all. He wore a long white coat with suspenders, his hair was short, and he had a slight bald spot. His square glasses could barely fit on his face. His voice was very raspy when he spoke and he walked with a limp.

When you are a child and someone appears scary to you, you can pretty much remember them in detail, especially, when they are "Dr. Hill" creepy.

"So young man, what do I owe you for this visit?" He said adjusting his glasses.

"Well, I wanted to talk to you about my session I had with you years ago."

"Oh yes, I remember. You were one scared little boy; tell me, do you still have the nightmares? Your parents were very worried about you. I wanted to continue my research but, your mother didn't want to continue," he told me. "Never seen anything like it before," he mumbled.

"Excuse me," I said as if I did not hear what he said.

"Well young man, I normally do not discuss these things without a parent present. Tell me son, are you 18 yet?"

"No sir, I'm not 18 yet." I proudly said.

"Well you seem mature enough, what do you want to know?"

"Dr. Hill, when my parents brought me here, did you notice anything unusual or out of the ordinary on that day?"

He leaned back in his chair scratching the back of his head. He took a long look at me and said that he found that there was nothing wrong with me. I was just dealing with nightmares that triggered by an epileptic episode or something in my early childhood.

He explained that before he could start his procedure, I started yelling or screaming at the ceiling. Apparently, the good doctor thought I was faking. However, if that were the case, why tell my mom that he wanted to continue his research?

Chapter Four

COVENANT BROTHERS

Moreover, what about the letter he sent my mother?

Surely, this doctor was hiding something. He said he was concerned about me and suggested that I come see him again.

His nurse knocked on the door and told him his patient was ready. He wanted me to consider setting up an appointment if my nightmares increased again. Since he claims nothing is wrong, I know he is lying. His notes stated otherwise. I told him I would see myself out. I hurried out of his office and ran to the car.

When I arrived, Tony and Elsha were not there. It was getting late and I wondered where they could have gone. I did not have any reception inside the building so there were no missed calls or messages. I called Tony on his cell and it went to voicemail. Where could they be?

The rain had let up a little so I just decided to wait in the car.

As I waited, I took the paper work out of my pocket to look at it. Dr. Hill's handwriting was very bad. Good thing I copied the nurses notes.

In his report, he stated that I was a young child who suffered from delusions, which caused me to have nightmares. He stated how my body responded when he dimmed the lights. He said I responded out of fear, as if I were seeing something horrific.

According to my vital signs, my heartbeat was three times as fast and my pulse raced. The signs were as a patient having a heart attack. His notes also state that for a few seconds, the room appeared to grow darker. He noted it had to have been a power surge.

I kept reading as I waited for Elsha and Tony. In his notes, he also stated how my symptoms were like other children he had examined. He noticed my eyes fixed on the ceiling; the sensors indicated a rapid increase in breathing. Although he was somewhat convinced, I was experiencing something he just could not figure out what.

This just plagued my mind all over again. I could not help but to wonder how many others like me he had seen. I also wondered what was taking my friends so long; the storm was starting to pick up again.

As I kept reading, I could feel a dark shadow come over the car. My pulse raced, and my heartbeat started to pick up. I quickly turned to my right and saw a shadow, I could not move. It was hard to make out then, it hit against the window. I jumped, only to see it was Tony. He quickly jumped in the back seat of the car-soaking wet.

"What the heck! You scared me half to death man!" I yelled at Tony.

"Sorry dude, I did not mean to scare you but, I wanted to be sure it was you in the car."

"Well who else could it be?" I was trying to calm my nerves but, Tony had ticked me off. Elsha got in the car before I could ask about her.

"Where have you two been? I have been waiting out here for more than a half an hour."

"Sorry we kept you waiting. I will tell you once we get on the main road." Elsha explained.

Elsha drove out of there as if she was a speedway driver.

"Why are you driving so fast?" I asked.

She did not say anything; she kept driving, looking in the rearview mirror constantly. I could not tell if the expression on her face was for Tony not to say anything or she was afraid of something. It was like she was making sure, no one was following us.

Once we got on the main road, I asked her again where they were and what took them so long. Elsha began to slow down the car back to the regular speed limit.

"There is something weird about that hospital," Tony said.

What do you mean?" I asked but, Elsha quickly interrupted.

"Will somebody please tell me what is going on?" I asked again as my voice escalated.

By this time, my friends could tell I was getting agitated. Elsha went on to explain that by the time I went in to see Dr. Hill, she saw the strange car pull in and drive around to the back of the hospital. She said she was curious and wanted to see who the driver was. Tony objected to her being nosy. He insisted she stay in the car since we know nothing about the person or people.

Nevertheless, of course Elsha does what Elsha wants. She went onto to explain that when your uncle is the Chief of Police, there are many things you learn, like how to be undercover.

Elsha said in the back of the hospital, near the delivery area, it leads to a long brick driveway. She saw the car drive in the back and park by a huge door. The driver flashed the headlights as if to signal Morse code then, the huge doors opened. The car proceeded to drive inside. She just had to see who it was.

"Where were you Tony?" I asked him.

"Standing guard," he replied.

"What do you mean standing guard?"

"Well somebody had to watch out for Ms. Detective over here." He said leaning towards Elsha.

"Well anyway, what happened?" I asked again this time sounding irritated.

Elsha continued the story. She snuck inside the big door before it could close, climbed up on some type of ledge to look down and see if she could identify the mystery driver. Tony stood watch outside; they both decided to turn off their phones just in case.

The driver got out with two other people; she could not make out who they were because the place was dark. She said she could hear someone approaching so, she moved in to get a closer look. It was a man in a white coat and he walked with a limp.

"Dr. Hill." I said.

She went on to explain how he ushered them to a room and asked them to wait because he had a visitor waiting to see him. The person told him not to be long their time is very important. Dr. Hill agreed and walked back into the hospital.

From what Elsha could see, the strange people wore long dark coats and big hats; therefore, she could not see their faces.

One of the voices was female and according to Elsha, she walked to the window and looked out saying.

"The moon will be full soon, we have to act fast."

Elsha tried to get as much information as possible. Later, the doctor returned with a folder and handed it to the woman. She carefully reviewed the file and said.

"Ahh, we've been watching this one. Thank you doctor, you've been very helpful to me in my research."

Dr. Hill agreed and stated to her that he was afraid this was the only one left and he had not encountered anymore. She did not know what he meant by "encountered" but, I did.

According to the good doctor's notes, it appears that he encountered other children just like me. Elsha said she feels the good doctor has been disobeying H.I.P.P.A. laws. Giving away patient files was against the law.

She also said she believes these mystery people must be watching me. I asked her if she was able to get more information from the car and she said no. The license plate appeared shielded somehow; she needed to move in to get a closer look.

As she moved in closer she accidentally kicked loose a brick from the wall and it fell to the ground and broke. Elsha laid still and did not move, as one of the men moved closer, she still didn't move.

Luckily for her, a few rats made noises to distract the man. She covered her mouth to keep from screaming as they started to crawl on her feet.

Imagine that, Ms. bold and beautiful, afraid of a few measly rats, go figure. Well at least she found out what the good doctor was up to; now to find out what these strangers want.

Elsha went on to say that she waited for them to leave so she could get another look at the license plate. She took out her phone to snap a photo, of course remembering to turn off the flash; she did not want to draw any more attention to herself. As she drove I looked, she said she would get someone in her dads office to look up the number. She said they owed her a favor.

"Well now I see why it took you two so long. Did you hear anything else?"

"Just a lot of talk about the moon and getting prepared, they spoke among themselves while they waited on the doctor." She explained.

As we approached Patagonia, I read some of the notes from my file. I know it is wrong to steal; perhaps, God will grant me forgiveness and have mercy on me. I just had to know. I told them I was able to get my hands on the taped session and how the doctor almost caught me.

We all decided to watch the video together at Tony's house. I called home and my parents were worried about me. I told them I was on my way home and needed to grab some clothes. Mom asked if I was all right and I told her yes. I just wanted to spend time with Tony and play catch up. I told her I would be home first thing. She agreed. We dropped Elsha off at home and decided a time to meet up.

After I arrived home, I gathered my books and papers, stuffed them in my bag while Tony loaded my bike in his car. Mom told me not to be late. She reminded us of the bonfire on the reservation that was vastly approaching. She told Tony she would pack some food for the trip. Tony smiled and said he would like that.

We set off to Tony's house and I had so much on my mind. I needed to put all of these pieces together. Tony thought I should relax a while so we played a few video games, laughed awhile, talking about school.

Then, Tony shared with me about how scared he was for Elsha and me. He said he would stop at nothing to find us. He could not bare the thought of him losing his best friend. I told Tony how much I appreciated him believing in me. He said it was no problem at all that is what best friends do for each other. I asked Tony if he ever had any experiences that he could not share with anyone he knew because people would it unbelievable. He said yes. He said it was the oddest thing he had ever seen.

When he was camping with his father once, he was about ten years old. His father told him to stay near the fire while he went to go gather more firewood. His father was gone for a while so he did what he asked. The fire was starting to die down and there was not much firewood left. Then he said he heard a noise as if someone was approaching. He thought it was his father so he turned around to greet him, only he was not there. However, he could feel something as though someone were there. He did not know how to explain it.

Later that night, he heard a strange noise. He was too frightened to look outside and he was too scared to move. He said he saw a shadow slowly move over the tent, he could not make out what it was, but it made a terrifying sound. He laid there in fear waiting on it to strike but, it never did. It just hovered over them like a giant bird. Then it was gone.

Tony said he never told his father because he felt his father would never believe him. Tony said he would never forget the image he saw. We sat and talked about how as children, when we see things that terrify us, adults do not quite believe us. They tell us we are watching too much television, or it is our imagination.

Tony went on to tell me that he understands how I feel. He considers me a brother since he is an only child; it is nice to have someone that he can call friend or brother. He said we all go through life experiencing some kind of an encounter. That is why he wants to continue helping me. I thanked Tony and told him I had no idea he had experienced something so terrifying.

I told him I believed his story; he chuckled a little. I asked him if he ever had any nightmares about it and he said no. He never wanted to see that again. He understands what it is like when you see something that horrible and want to tell someone. When he first heard the students at school talking about me, he felt that no one should have to face it alone. On the other hand, worry about whose calling you crazy. Then come to school only to listen to the whispers by people who do not understand you. He was glad that we are friends. I am to.

Tony says if circumstances were reversed, he would be glad to have someone with him rather than face his problems alone. That way he would not go through it by himself.

Then Tony had an idea, since I had native blood running through my veins, he said when the natives found a true friend they became blood brothers. He wanted to have a ritual binding us as blood brothers just as my ancestors did. Tony pulled out his pocketknife and I explained that when our blood connects, then it would be official. I did not have a speech or anything so I said what was on my heart.

"As my blood runs, I share it with you. Let this ritual link us together as blood brothers forever." I took the knife; slit my palm then Tony's. "Together we lock hands," I said as he took my hand. "Now we are blood brothers for life."

Tony's hand began to shake; the look on his face was as if he was in pain. He yanked his hand away from me quickly.

"What's wrong?" I said.

"Your blood burns like fire."

Tony ran into the bathroom to wash his hands.

"Sorry dude, I had no idea. Are you all right?"

"Yes I will be fine." Tony said, wiping his hands.

"Whatever is in your blood, it's not normal."

"This is so strange. What could cause my blood to be like this?"

When I was in the hospital, they said my blood had something else in it and they did not know what that was. I asked Tony again if he was all right. He showed me his hand; it looked okay.

"Well now that we are blood brothers, it was time to get some rest," I told him.

Elsha was coming over tomorrow so, we could piece more of the puzzles together.

That night I kept thinking about Tony and how the touch of my blood burned him. Was I turning into some kind of freak? I tried not to think about it, as long as Tony was okay. Apparently, my blood temperature is much higher. I did not feel feverish or anything. I felt normal. I even took my temperature and it was regular. Weird things have happened to me before but, never like this.

Well, after that ordeal, Tony and I sat and watched television when breaking news flashed across the screen.

The news reporter stated that hunters in South Dakota discovered mutilated bodies. Chills ran up and down my spine. More reports came in from around the globe as bodies of missing people were found. The local police are urging local townspeople to take precaution.

As for the hunters, they were advised to set animal traps and curfews were put in place. I closed my eyes and tried to put it out of my mind. I could not stand to watch anymore. I felt sick because I knew the truth. People are dying and the police are baffled. They do not know if this is some serial killer, copycat killer, or what. Something had to be done to stop this. I knew of a way, and it could not be handled alone. It was going to take some strong forces to come together to defeat them.

Tony was in serious shock and went downstairs to calm himself by grabbing a snack. Apparently, nothing ever stops his appetite. I needed to clear my head so, I put my headphones on to relax my mind. I forgot about the music Dr. Spears gave me. I let it just take me away.

I grabbed my laptop to check my emails. I noticed I had one at from Ms. Creed she marked the email as urgent. I opened it up to read that she was back in town and needed to meet with me right away. She wanted to meet at the library; she had permission to use it after hours. She needed me to be there by five o'clock.

I wondered what the urgency was. She did not disclose much in her emails except that it was of great importance that I attend. She did not say to come alone I wondered if she would mind if my friends tagged along. I thought to myself for a moment I had better go alone.

I told my parents I would be home first thing in the morning. Well that is going to have to change. I called mom and explained that I needed to stop at the library first before coming home. She was not too happy about it but, she said it was okay. I decided to go alone just incase.

After Tony and I chatted for a while, I drifted off to sleep. I found myself having another nightmare. I'm standing in the middle of a village, watching it burn to the ground. I see a warrior in the middle, tied to a stake. Others are with him.

One of the leaders approached him with a torch. He was an older man and walked with a limp. He spoke to the warrior and told him his days of killing were over. There would be no more bloodshed. The warrior laughed and said he would have his revenge upon him and everyone and the generations to come.

The Elder Chief called for his brethren to assist him. They each placed torches at the base of the stakes and the wood caught fire. The man vowed he would seek his revenge and screamed out in pain.

The sky blackened with smoke and the smell of death filled the air. The sound of wolves drew close in the distance. As the men burned, he spoke and a cloud of smoke circled him. He yelled aloud in his native language.

"Atleisdi, Atleisdi, Atleisdi!"

The thick black smoke encircled him and covered his body. The Elders stood around and watched. The fire grew intensely the screams were gut wrenching. I stood there, watched the black smoke swirl around, and almost transform.

The wind picked up and the sky was in total blackness. The smell of burning flesh was all in the air. I stood there watching in horror. The crackling sound coming from the fire sounded like breaking bones. I could feel an evil presence around me. Whatever it was, it was very close. My skin began to crawl.

I stepped backwards from the terrifying scene to walk away. As I walked, I felt as though something was following me. Slightly turning my head, I looked out of the corner of my eye and no one was there. Every step I took I could feel movement behind me. The wind sounded like whispers of deep voices. The smell of burnt flesh gripped my nose.

I looked back again at the charred bodies and saw odd black smoke. The black smoke swarmed as if ghost were flying. Something told me to run but, I could not move.

The black image moved quickly towards me, transforming into a ghastly image. Its eyes were gaping wide and it let out a loud scream. It passed through me light a bolt of lightening I hit the ground hard. I could feel the ground sinking beneath me as if gravity was pulling me deep within the earth. I tried to pull myself up, but I was sinking too fast.

Creature like hands came up from beneath me and pulled me down further. I tried hard to fight against them, trying to pull away. They were overpowering me. I was sinking deeper into the ground. As I screamed and yelled for help, the dirt covered my nose and mouth. The darkness was suffocating me as I was falling into the dark abyss.

Chapter Five

CHANGELING

I do not know how long or how loud I was screaming. Tony was leaning over me shaking me and calling my name, telling me to wake up.

I jumped once my eyes opened. I was drenched in sweat, and my shirt was torn to shreds. Tony's parents knocked on the door, with great concern; they asked if everything was all right.

Tony told them everything was fine, that I had fallen off the bed and hit my head. Tony said I had started moaning in my sleep and breathing heavy, he knew I must have been having a nightmare so he tried to awaken me. He said I was screaming native words. I asked him what it was I was yelling. He said I yelled out,

"**Adanádoa Adasehedi Alisdeládi Ayá.**"

He struggled to say the words.

He asked me if I knew what the words meant but I didn't. I got up and went to the bathroom, splashed cold water on my face and sat down for a moment. I needed to collect my thoughts. I put my hands on top of my head.

"What is happening to me?" I whispered.

Flashes of the burning men plagued my mind. I now know how Liwanu died; he was burned at the stake. Tony knocked on the door.

"Hey are you okay?"

"Yeah, I will be out in a minute."

I stared into the mirror for a moment looking at my reflection. I asked Tony what time was Elsha coming over and he said she would be over soon.

I walked out of the bathroom and thanked Tony for waking me up. He asked if I wanted to talk about it and I told him I did not feel like discussing it at all.

"Well whatever it was you were dreaming about must have been a bad one." Tony said. "Look Kyle, there are a lot of weird things going on here. My parents are so worried they are ready to ship me back east to my Aunt's house in Florida." He said with his voice shaking.

"What more can I do to help you?" I looked at him long and hard for a moment staring at him.

"Stay alive, you just stay alive."

My look must have startled him; he said something in my eyes moved. He asked me how I felt again and I told him fine. I was feeling angry again, Chiefs Spearhorns words were ringing in my head.

"Patience, young man, have patience."

I apologized to Tony for my attitude. If I could run away from all of this, I would. Running away is not going to solve anything at all.

I grabbed by bag to retrieve my envelope. I decided to read the information on Running Bear. After the death of his father, everything about him seemed to change. Perhaps if I can get more of an understanding about him before he changed. According to the book of ancient warriors, Liwanu, aka Running Bear, was amongst the fiercest of his time. After he rebelled against his people, his army grew by the thousands. He was so full of hatred and anger that he vowed to get his revenge on the Elders.

From what I have read about him so far, he did not have much patience. The horrible things he did were unforgivable. The Elders tried to teach him but, he allowed anger to overtake him. I thought about what Chief Spearhorn once told me about anger poisoning your soul. In some ways, I guess I am like Running Bear, very impatient.

Tony and I started out our day with a huge breakfast that his mom had prepared for us. While sitting at the breakfast table, the doorbell rang. As his mother entered, she placed more pancakes on the table for us to scarf down, she headed toward the door.

"Hi, my name is Elsha. Is Tony and Kyle here?" When I heard her voice, my thoughts went back to the cave. I shivered a little in my seat. Tony's mother entered the kitchen with Elsha following behind her.

"Well it seems you two have company. Elsha, would you care to join us for breakfast?" Elsha smiled at everyone.

"Sure, why not."

"So what do you kids have planned for the today?" Tony's dad, who sat at the other end of table, pulled a chair for Elsha to sit down. We all just looked at each other for a moment. Tony started to speak when Elsha quickly responded.

"I came over to show them the pictures that I took when Chief Spearhorn was here."

"Elsha is a great photographer, dad." Tony said.

"Yeah she is good." I decided to echo that as well. Tony's dad smiled as he looked at Elsha and spoke.

"Well perhaps you can show them to me sometime. Right now though, I must get to work. These houses are not going to build themselves you know." He said while excusing himself from the table. Tony responded.

"Okay, dad. See you later."

Tony's father, Brad, is a local contractor; he owns a company called Strattford Construction. His mother, Sophie, works with autistic children and at the community center. His parents are really nice; I hoped I didn't scare them too bad last night.

After breakfast, Tony said that we could use his father's office to talk since Elsha had something very important to tell us. Tony closed the door and Elsha dug through her bag as we settled in.

"So what is so important?" I asked.

She pulled out a book that I was familiar with, *The Forbidden Lands*. Elsha had gone to the library and did some research. She also pulled out some geographical maps and old photos.

"What is the meaning behind all of this?" Tony asked as he approached her.

"I will explain that in a moment," She said while spreading maps across the desk. "I discovered something about the property where my dad had our house built. According to the map, the property was once a dwelling place for Native American Indians, perhaps around the sixteenth or seventh century. I discovered it when she was reading Jeremiah Flynn's book."

"Who is Jeremiah Flynn?" Tony asked.

"It's a book I was reading to learn more about the sacred boundaries." I told him. Tony only answered with a look of confusion. Elsha turned to both of us and instructed us to look at the map. She pointed to the location of her property line.

"See, here is Hunter Valley. According to the book, sacred burial grounds are all over this plain. Ancient warriors were once buried there. Only certain people were allowed to walk the land. They protected it so the warriors would remain undisturbed."

"I remember reading about that. Some thought it to be a myth because the caves were actually diamond mines." Tony's confusion turned to surprised.

"You mean to tell me that your neighborhood is one big diamond mine?" He begins to pace the floor.

"Yes!"

Elsha confirmed.

"I believe the stories are true too. When I think about what's been happening in our town, it brings me to my next point."

Elsha pulled out a notebook identical to the one I have. She had created her own version of my book. She opened it and showed Tony and I the pictures from inside the cave. Even looking at them again made me shiver inside.

"Kyle, I'm sorry I should have asked if you were ready for this." Elsha said with a sorrowful look.

"No, it's okay. Some things I don't think I will ever get over."

"We don't have to do this if you don't want to, Kyle."

"Continue, I need to see what you discovered."

"Alright," she stated. "When we were in the cave, there was a stone wall with symbols all around it. Look here on page seventeen in the book."

She directed our attention to the book.

"It's the same symbol, Jeremiah Flynn discovered and ancient secret of the Shahwanee Tribe." She pointed to a symbol of a wolf inside a bright circle.

"Now compare the two together."

Elsha's photos were identical to the book. According to her research, the symbol marks the whereabouts of an ancient warrior. The diamond shaped stones around the all represents the guardians. Each of the other symbols had shapes of spirals, triangles and animal like shapes. Each animal was incased inside a circle with a stone over it. This must represent a spell to bind the spirit for all eternity.

"Isn't there a law against building on native land?" Tony examined the map further. "I have been on a few building sites with my dad and, from what I've heard, if anything unusual is found, it is supposed to be reported or the contractor can get into trouble.

Tony turned to Elsha.

"Do you know if surveyors came out to inspect the property before your home was built?" Elsha scratched her head for a moment.

"I don't know; my dad handled everything." Tony seemed to be getting upset so I stepped up to him telling him to calm down.

"What are you getting at Tony?" Tony sighed for a moment.

"How long have you known the cave was there?" Elsha gets defensive with Tony.

"Long enough. It was so no one would bother it! Why the questions all of a sudden, Tony? Come on." It wasn't long before Elsha and Tony started arguing back and forth. Tony's mother entered the office.

"Is everything alright in here?"

"Sure mom; we just disagreed on something, that's all." Tony responded. She noticed maps and books on the desks and walked over to take a look.

"What are you guys doing research on our town for?" She turned to Elsha. "Are these yours?" Elsha nervously responds.

"Yes ma'am, I took them awhile ago."

"Well you do very good work," she leaned into her and said.

"Don't you let these boys get to you, stick to what you know." His mother smiled and told Tony she would be out for a while. As she left, Tony paused for a moment.

"That was close. Look Elsha, I'm sorry. It's just that I don't want my dad to get into trouble if an investigation is launched. Since the cave has been sealed, I guess everything is okay. Again, I'm sorry." Elsha twisted her lips to reply.

"It's okay; I guess we all have been dealing with a lot lately." I agreed with both of them. "Now, shall we get back to work here?" Elsha went on to explain that there are more caves in Hunter Valley; she narrowed them down to certain areas. She is almost certain and convinced that Jeremiah Flynn explored the area before.

"No one knows what happened to the people that dwelled here. According to legend, they all disappeared." Elsha stated "Dr. Hill is hiding something." She turned to face me. "Kyle, after examining your book and drawings, I noticed how you mentioned a clearing where the trees meet at the top."

"Yes, I see it in my dreams a lot. What about it?" Elsha sat down and pulled out another map from her bag. She laid it on top of the other maps and she explained what she found as she pointed our areas on it.

"According to this area here, this used to be the dwelling place of many tribes. While I was researching, I found out that the land was part of a treaty. Each leader of every tribe came together and decided that they would live in peace. Per every tribe a boundary was set up, splitting the land by tribes settling in the north, south, east, and west."

"You mean to say where the hospital sits now belonged to the tribal union?" I had to interject for a moment. It all started to make sense now. Elsha continued.

"Yes, the only way for the tribes to survive was to stay together." She pointed to the map again. "See here, all this used to be the boundary, which divided the land amongst the people. They stayed together so their land would not by dispersed by wars. But something must have happened."

My mind reverted back to my dreams. Suddenly, I felt weak and hit the floor. I lifted my head to find the room was spinning. Elsha and Tony came near talking but their voices were muffled. I had to get some air.

"I must go; I've got to get out of here." I grabbed my bag and headed for the door. Tony and Elsha were right behind me. I told them to leave me alone for a while. Tony spoke as he put his hand on the door.

"He's overwhelmed again, let's give him time." Elsha agreed.

I got on my bike and just peddled. The hospital was always the key. It must hold more secrets than I thought.

I found myself at the library. Somehow, while I was thinking about everything, my brain must have remembered to meet Ms. Creed at the library. I wondered what she wanted to discuss that was so important. Everything was happening so fast; there must be something else I was missing.

While I waited for Ms. Creed, I sat down on the bench, took out my book, and read my notes. I looked at the pictures of the trees and had an awakening nightmare.

In my dream, I am running away but headed to the clearing. The Shifters are moving fast, there is a white mist that is leading me to safety. Once I reached the boundary line, they could not cross it.

Just beyond the clearing was a cave. On the outside, at the top, was a drawing of a man holding some kind of symbol. In my dreams, I had never seen this part before because I wake up somehow. The other thing is the hospital must have been built on sacred grounds. This is the connection; this must have been where it all began.

I was so deep in thought I couldn't hear Ms. Creed calling my name.

"Kyle...Kyle, are you alright?" She touched my shoulder and I jumped. "Sorry to startle you, what's wrong?" She was looking very concerned about me.

"I'm just putting more pieces to the puzzle of my life together." She took out the keys to the library and opened the door.

"Come on in, I won't keep you long." As soon as we started to enter the library, we heard a horn beeping. We turned to see Tony and Elsha arriving at the library. Ms. Creed turned to me.

"Hey, don't look at me. I told no one about this meeting." I explained trying to sound convincing. As they approached Tony had my laptop.

"Kyle, sorry but your laptop was open and..." Elsha interrupted. "We couldn't help but notice your email from Ms. Creed. We didn't mean to invade your privacy." Elsha seemed sympathetic enough. I didn't know whether to glad or angry at them. I really didn't know what to feel; I was numb all over.

Ms. Creed said there was no time since we all were gathered together under unusual circumstances she ushered us inside the library. I just had to know what the emergency was.

"Why'd you want me to meet you here? What's going on?" She began to set up her computer.

"Please sit down, I will explain momentarily. Since your friends are here I have no choice. However, Elsha, I am glad you are here as well. You need to hear this." Elsha gave Ms. Creed a surprising look.

"What does this have to do with me?" Ms. Creed turned to face Elsha.

"Not you, your father."

"My father!" She said surprisingly.

"Yes, your father. I was in Rocky Point when your father was called to help with an investigation. By the way, I'm glad to see you two are alive and well."

"Thanks," we both said. Ms. Creed proceeded to tell us what was going on.

"While I was visiting my parents, there had been some mysterious deaths. Dr. Morgan and a team of others went up into the foothills, not far from her parent's home. Some of the local students there were out exploring during the same time."

She started to explain.

"Just as the local authorities were sealing off the area. They discovered a cave and decided to go inside to look around. Once inside they noticed strange markings and an ancient language on the cave walls."

Tony was so eager to find out more he just had to ask.

"What does this have to do with Kyle?" Ms. Creed looked in Tony's direction and responded.

"It has everything to do with Kyle. Now may I continue?"

"Yes, sorry." Tony said.

"The students quickly took pictures before they were discovered by the police. What they found was an ancient language of a tribe, thought to have been extinct."

As Ms. Creed spoke, I had that odd feeling again. I was afraid that she was going to tell me something I did not want to hear. Ms. Creed said she wanted to help me understand my dreams more; she wanted to know if I could remember anything about my dreams starting with languages.

I told her I could vaguely remember however, pronouncing them is the tricky part. Then Tony interrupted.

"Tell her about your most recent dream, Kyle?" I gave him a hard stare.

"What was your dream about?" I told her only a little part of it but, this time the language stuck with me. I struggled to say the words.

"In my dream, I heard something like "**adanádoa adasehedi alisdeládi ayá**". What does it mean?" Ms. Creed turned her laptop around so we all could see.

"I had the students email me the photos of the cave so I could do further research." She pointed to each symbol and told us what each one meant.

"See here, according the drawings, they were keepers or guardians of the cave. Each of these symbols represents prayers to the great spirits. The meaning to the words in your dream means a cry for help. Whoever or whatever was after you, the great spirits protected you from them."

Elsha was pleased to hear this; she took out her book and showed Ms. Creed. We both explained while we were both inside the cave we also discovered drawings. As they viewed the photos, Ms. Creed compared them to what she had on her computer. She was very surprised to see the similarities.

"Can I borrow this book to do more research?" Elsha agreed but she did question Ms. Creed about her father.

"So how is my father involved with this?" She asked. Ms. Creed pulled her hair back and sighed.

"Well, when the victims were discovered one of them was alive. Your father and his team brought the individual to Rocky Point Medical Center to examine him. Once they were there, the survivor was taken away. Your father no longer had jurisdiction and was told to leave."

Elsha was not at all surprised because we already knew this. Ms. Creed continued to tell her story though. "While in route to the hospital, the victim was mumbling words that Dr. Morgan couldn't understand. Since I volunteer my services there during the summer, it was not hard for your father to find me."

Everyone was now very eager to know what Ms. Creed was going to say. My stomach was twisting in knots so I slowed my breathing. Ms. Creed went on.

"Dr. Morgan paid me a visit because he wanted to know and understand the language the victim was mumbling. The victim mumbled "sánoyi di-ga-do-li" which means "night eyes". The victim saw something terrifying come out of the night, all he saw was its eyes." I shuttered in my seat as she talked. I could not move.

"The people that took him away, why keep it from the public?" Tony asked Ms. Creed with a scared look on his face.

"That I don't know however, we must be careful. When you go out, make sure you stay together. I have a feeling that more people are involved in this than we know."

"What do you mean more people?" I nervously asked.

"Someone in a dark colored sedan has been in the area. The car has dark colored windows so I couldn't tell who was driving." Ms. Creed explained. Elsha, Tony and I just stared at each other.

"I saw a car just like that in my neighborhood."

"I feel that whoever it is, they must be interested in what has been happening."

Still concerned about her father's involvement, Elsha asked Ms. Creed if there was anything else she wanted to tell her or thought she should know.

"You're just like father...very persistent," Ms. Creed told her. "Your father continued to investigate the situation on his own. That's when he asked for her help. I spent time with her father explaining ancient legends. He is very determined to learn more and it would help him get a better understanding. Since the cave incident, he has come across more information, he is on to something. I asked him about it but, he would not say. Although, he does have an interest in me," she finished. I looked at her kind of odd.

"What do mean he has an interest in me?" I could tell that Elsha also wondered why.

"I do not know. Have you spoken with him yet?"

"No," I answered her.

"Whatever he has discovered, it has something to do with that night."

I felt there was more she wanted to say to me that was of great importance. However, I couldn't help but notice something on her computer. Therefore, I asked her what it was.

"It's my last piece of information. Take a closer look at the screen..." she asked us.

As we moved in closer, I could see the image of people gathered together under a big silver moon. The stars were aligned and the night was even darker.

"I have to study it further," Ms. Creed said. "I want to help you out as much as possible…" she told me.

"I don't know what good it would do. I just wish people would stop dying."

I couldn't take any more information, I was getting overwhelmed again. Tony had to get going and Elsha did as well. Though the hour grew late, I had to know more but, I did not want to push myself. Ms. Creed would not go through all this trouble to explain things so we all agreed to meet up again.

Tony gave me a ride home. When I arrived, I realized mom and dad left a note; they would be home late. I didn't feel like doing much of anything so, I decided to go to bed. I thought I would turn off my cell phone. That way I wouldn't be disturbed by anyone. However, as I hit the power button, "ring ring" goes my phone. I hesitated to answer it since I didn't even recognize the number. I answered it anyway though.

"Hello?" Silence was on the other end. "Hello…hello."

I heard a clicking noise then silence again. Perhaps it was someone with the wrong number or their reception was just bad. However, I did not want to think about anything but sleep right now. Yeah sleep, most people do. Me, on the other hand, I wished could stay awake and never sleep.

As I put my hand to my mouth and yawned, I made my way to the bed to let sleep come for me. There was no use fighting it; I could feel my body drifting away into total darkness and silence.

The next morning, my alarm goes off awakening me. I could hear dad outside mowing the lawn. The smell of breakfast hit my nose and my stomach growled loudly. As I made my way down stairs, my hunger increased like crazy. The smell of bacon and eggs drove me like a wild animal.

I sat down and didn't even bother to wait for mom; I just dug right in. She looked at me laughing.

"Wow, someone has a hearty appetite this morning." Dad walked in and saw me eating like a mad man.

"Son, are you alright? You're eating like your mother and I don't feed you enough." I looked up a little at them both with a mouth full of food.

"Just woke up a little hungry, that's all." Mom frowned at me a little.

"Well save some for your father, will ya?"

"Sure mom." I said a little embarrassed for my actions.

After breakfast, dad asked me to help him finish the lawn and to grab some garbage bags from the garage. Still a little hungry, I grabbed more food before heading out to the garage. I thought about my appetite, I usually don't eat much and never like this. I felt as if I just couldn't get enough to eat; my hunger for meat seemed to increase. What was happening to me? Perhaps all of these events have just affected my eating habits somehow.

I'm not that big of a guy anyway; my build is kind of on the medium scrawny side.

While I was busy trying figure out my sudden eating habits, dad and I finished the yard. I helped mom around the house for a while then went to my room. I had so much on my agenda; I thought I would get back to my things to do list.

I reached in my bag to get my laptop and a disc fell out of my bag.

"Oh…I forgot about this."

It was the DVD of my taped session with Dr. Hill. Do I dare watch it or forget about?

My curiosity got the best of me. One would think after experiencing something so horrible you would put it behind you. But I just couldn't.

I placed the disc in the disc drive and watched it unfold before me. When it started, I discovered a prerecorded message from Dr. Hill. He explained how he's about to see a patient with severe nightmares. He gave details about how he hopes to discover what triggers them and why the patient suffers from them. My mind went into a backwards spiral. I was about to relive the events of that day. He lastly stated that he had seen this before in past patients and hopes from to learn more from my session.

I sat back and watched myself, so young, so afraid. I watched as I saw myself shaking, hyperventilating, and my eyes bulging. Dr. Hill questioned me about what is it was that I was seeing. I didn't want to watch it anymore but, something inside me forced me to. During my session, the lights were dimmed in the back of the room I swore there was an image. I pressed paused on the video screen to take a closer look.

Chills ran through me, deeper than they ever did. My eyes looked upon a grizzly image in the background, its eyes peeking through the darkness. No one could see this but me. Not wanting to view the video any longer, I fast forward it to see if there was anything to see. Dr. Hill had closing remarks about my session.

He talked about how he viewed the video countless times. He said he knew I was seeing something but, it was hard to tell. He couldn't see it himself. Then he compared my tape to another patient. He said an earlier patient, with the same resemblance as me, suffered the same episode except his grandfather interrupted his session. Dr. Hill was shocked when he saw me at first because I resembled his former patient so much. I thought to myself that it must have been Eric. I had to know more so I kept watching.

According to Dr. Hill, well into the session, he was interrupted by the grandfather who was a tribal chief. He said that there would be no more of it. The mother argued with the grandfather and told him that it would help him. She wondered how he knew they were there.

Dr. Hill said that something in the eyes of the grandfather made the mother calm down and sent chills through him. Dr. Hill also stated that the child was screaming an ancient language; he repeated the familiar words that I even remembered.

"Adanádoa adasehedi alisdeládi ayá"

Eric cried out to the great spirits to help him. A very confused Dr. Hill said he needed to research the meaning much further to get more of an understanding. He mentioned that after that day he never saw the patient again, nor did he hear from his mother. He made several attempts to locate them for another session but, he was unsuccessful.

However; when I came on the scene, he wanted to know how I was doing by keeping in touch with my mother. I could not believe this guy, what a jerk.

After watching the video, nothing seemed to surprise me about the doctor. That was until he stated that there were others interested in this type of behavior. Apparently, there have been other cases in different states and even in Rocky Point. I wondered why Dr. Hill was disclosing so much; the way he talked was as if he made this video for someone else.

I sat back in my chair for a moment. Elsha said that she saw Dr. Hill give something to people who drove the strange black car. My anger began to refuel. Now it all made sense; that's why they are watching me. But I wonder what do they want with me? I wonder if Elsha found anything on the car. Maybe I should call her.

Then I remembered, I never turned my cell phone on after I powered it off last night. I just knew I'd have tons of messages. I turned it back on only to discover a few missed calls from an unknown number and from Elsha and Tony. I needed to speak with Elsha first so, Tony would just have to wait.

I called Elsha and she was in a panic almost. She said she needed to talk to me right away and wanted to know if I could meet her at the library.

"No problem, I will be there soon," I told her.

"I already called Tony."

"What is so urgent?"

"Not over the phone. Just get here as soon as you can." She sounded very serious.

There were just a few more things I needed to do before heading out. I needed to check my emails; I was still doing research on Veronica Banks. Since Benjamin was nice enough to help me out, I was glad to see that I had received a very important email from him.

He said he did some investigating and found that, after Veronica left the newspaper, she disappeared for a while. She continued her research on the missing children on her own. Benjamin said his sources told him that someone else is also investigating the murders around town and in other places as far as Rocky Point.

He felt that Veronica must be keeping a very low profile; due to the attempts on her life he felt that she may be scared. However; he stated he doesn't believe it. Benjamin feels the low profile may be a front to cover up her ongoing work. Someone has been asking questions about the victims and their untimely deaths.

Benjamin went on to say that, if Veronica is around, she might have changed her appearance or she may have others working for her. No one seems to know what happened to the missing. Although, Benjamin says he has a strange feeling about an unknown watcher.

One of his sources told him that someone disguising themselves as paranormal researcher visited a local hospital. They discovered that one of the doctors had a special interest in children with nightmares about dark beings.

He knows this to be true because the doctor is a very good friend of his. He said the woman was well dressed and had only a special interest in children that shared the same dreams. The individual stated they were doing research and wanted to conduct an interview to learn more. Benjamin's email stated this was a way for them to find out about the children and their ages.

The more I read I thought about Dr. Hill; they visited him as well but he turned over information about me. The more I pieced things together it all made sense. I grabbed my notebook and began to write out my thoughts. The disappearing bodies, the strange car, other children with the same nightmares, the blood line. I kept repeating it over and over again.

Then it hit me.

Why was Dr. Morgan interested in me?

I remembered when Tony and I became covenant brothers; he said my blood burned like fire. I had a strange feeling come over me, an overwhelming sensation of strength.

I left the house to meet Elsha at the library. As I did, I felt something inside me was changing, first hunger and now strength. I remembered parts of my dream when Eric told me the blood line was strengthening. It all made sense now; my blood was not like any others but a rare type. Is it possible that the victims that shared the same DNA could be linked to Liwanu? Perhaps Chief Spearhorn could enlighten me at the bonfire.

Chapter Six

NIGHT OF THE SILVER MOON

I could still feel the overwhelming sensation of strength, so much I could hear my heart beat. It was louder than usual.

I wasn't sweating, nor had I even been running. Maybe it's stress from all of these changes; who knows. I really don't have time to think about this right now. I had to meet Elsha at the library.

When I got there, she had a worried look on her face.

"How are you doing?" She asked me.

"I'm fine."

I didn't feel so good though.

"Have you been experiencing any changes lately?"

I couldn't help but give her an odd look.

"What do you mean changes?"

She shook her head at me, grabbed me by my arm and pulled me to table in the back of the library. Her hands were shaking as she pulled a folder from her bag, her voice was even shakier.

"If my father finds out about this he's going to kill me." She told me.

"What is wrong?"

"My father discovered something; that's where the sudden interest in you came from." She looked at me with a scared look in her eyes. I just had to know what was wrong.

"Elsha what is going on? What is wrong with you?"

Nothing could have prepared me for what she had to say next.

"Have you noticed anything different since the wolf attack?"

She wanted to know if I have been experiencing any abnormalities. She sounded like a true to doctor.

"Why do you want to know?"

"Read this."

She slid the folder across the table. It was a report on the victims in Rocky Point. I had no choice but to read the documents; Elsha was very persistent.

According to the notes each victim shared a rare blood type, the investigators believed they were targeted for ritual purposes.

Blood samples taken from the survivor showed he also had a rare blood type; and, after doctors monitored him they noticed low levels of protein in his blood. The wounds on his back showed that the victim was running away at the time of the attack. When asked by the doctors if he was feeling any symptoms the patient said that his appetite increased tremendously; all he wanted to eat was meat.

The doctors continued to monitor him only to discover that he was taken away by a group of people. All studies were immediately stopped. I was in shock; I did not know what to say.

I looked up at Elsha to see that she was staring at me.

"Elsha, where did your father get this information? I thought they took the victim away when they arrived at the hospital with him."

"They did." She said. "My father took a sample of his blood before they got there. He analyzed it in his lab."

She pointed out to me that her father had been investigating these strange events for a while. The information he received on the first victim was almost the exact same as the second one. They shared the same blood type which was very rare. Doctor Morgan was able to make a connection.

"Have you spoken to anyone else about this?" I asked her.

"No."

I knew her; she would not dare say anything to anyone.

"Thank you," I told her. "Be careful."

I could feel something deep inside me telling me danger was coming. I shivered as I tried to piece things together in my mind.

Elsha had such a worried look on her face; I did not know what to say to her. So I just buried my head in my hands and tried to think. Elsha's hand reached out to me but, I reverted backwards. I did not mean to be rude to she was just trying to comfort me. I sighed a moment then looked at her and spoke calmly.

"Look, Elsha I don't want you to worry about me, let me figure this out okay. From this moment on no more research, snooping, or anything you leave all of this to me alright?"

She backed away from me and just stared for a moment.

"Fine, just fine, I will back off and leave you alone! I was just trying to help."

I looked at her and apologized, she turned to walk away.

"Elsha wait."

She stopped and turned to face me.

"Look, just give me some time to absorb all of this."

I took her by the hand and we sat down. I explained to her that there are just too many coincidences and somehow I felt that I was linked to some of the victims. Elsha explained that something in the blood of the victims attracts the shifters. According to her father's research each surviving victim was taken away by an unknown group of people.

Elsha said her father noted he felt there must be a connection between the tribes and these people. I looked at her and asked her why. She took a deep breath, crossed her arms and said.

"My father hired a private investigator to find our more information, whomever he or she was to keep a low profile."

I was shocked but I just had to ask.

"Does your uncle Chief Morgan know about this?"

Elsha replied slowly.

"No, no one is supposed to know about this."

I told Elsha that this is getting too dangerous; perhaps we all should keep a low profile until we find out who these mystery people are. Elsha responded.

"That's why I feel I must continue to help you, Kyle our whole town is in danger, between Ms. Creed, Tony and me you are the key! Remember the map I showed you and Tony a while ago?"

I nodded my head.

"Well according to the scientist Jeremiah Flynn my house was built near an ancient burial ground." Elsha seemed very convinced of this; she continued to show me the geographical map dated around the early 1700's indicating the dwelling place where ancient villages used to be. According Mr. Flynn there was an ancient tribe that dwelled in this area long ago.

I looked at her for a moment replying to her statement.

"I remember reading about this, according to legend the people disappeared a long time ago, no one knew what happened to them. They just disappeared."

Elsha continued pointed to the map.

"See here the map gives a geographical breakdown of the area of long ago and today's time. I am convinced that Jeremiah Flynn knew the land was a sacred land and vowed to discover more of its secrets."

I shook my head and then I had a thought from something I remembered reading. I checked my bag to see if perhaps I had the book by Jeremiah and to my surprise there it was buried in the bottom. I quickly turned to the page where it talked about only certain people could walk the grounds.

Someone knew what was happening and Jeremiah was trying to find out. Elsha and I kept reading the book and came upon a section of about the ancient warriors. It appeared that some of the local people told him about the guardians and explained how there once was evil upon the land, an evil so great that tribal Elders consecrated the grounds constantly to keep the evil spirits out.

According to the Elders there was an ancient warrior from the Shawanee tribe who cloaked the land in darkness.

He killed so many innocent people that after his death they had to purge the land of his spirit by cleansing the atmosphere. I could feel the chills up my spine as I read this I slowed my breathing as much as I could. Elsha asked me if I was alright I told her yes, but I did not feel well at all.

I started thinking about the time we were inside the cave when Elsha and I found a stone wall with the strange symbols. I remembered the paintings that showed a priest opposite side of the chamber with seven glowing stones around the rock. My knees buckled a little. I turned to Elsha with such haste I startled her.

"Elsha, remember when we were inside the cave and we found the huge round stone?"

"Yes."

She replied.

"Did you find out anything about the symbols and what they meant?"

"No, not yet I'm still researching that. Why do you ask?"

I took a deep breath trying to keep calm. Elsha I believe the stone wall was a tomb of one of the ancient warriors that Jeremiah Flynn was searching for.

"Kyle are you sure, are you absolutely sure?"

"Positive." I said quickly.

Elsha and I started making notes from the book and other things we remembered from the cave. She wondered since only chosen people were aloud on the land during that time, how many were chosen to be guardians over the dead.

She also wondered how many tribes live here long ago. Well somehow I could answer that question for her. I believed in Jeremiah's research, I believed in the stories that were told about this place.

I asked Elsha if she had any photos from the cave with her she said she wasn't sure if I was ready to see them, but she figured I have see more than enough she handed them to me in book form. Elsha was so organized I could kiss her, but not now I must stay focused. I told her I needed to get going and that I would call her later.

As I stood up I felt light headed and staggered a little put my hand on my head, Elsha rushed to my side.

"Kyle, are you alright? What's wrong?"

I did not want to worry her anymore than I already had so I just put on my macho face and shook it off.

"Nothing, I just felt a little light headed that's all, perhaps I'm just overdoing it with all of this research."

Looking at me strange she responded by saying.

"Perhaps I have been doing the same thing as well, however I don't look as bad as you do."

I took it has a joke, only she was serious. So I laughed anyway. Only she was serious.

"Kyle, I'm not joking, you look different, really. I gave her an odd look. "What do you mean?"

"I don't know, you just look different, I can't explain it. Are you sure you are feeling okay?"

She stepped closer to me touching my forehead.

"Oh my gosh! Kyle! You're burning up!"

I stepped away from her. "But I feel just fine Elsha really; I don't feel feverish at all."

I did not want to lie to her; however I could not explain what was happening to me. I did not understand why I was going through these changes.

"Wait here and don't move!"

She spoke to me like I was a child or something. Elsha ran to the bathroom and came back with a hand full of paper towels.

She put them under the water fountain and gently placed them on my forehead.

"Here, does this help?"

I looked at her and said.

"I think so."

But I could not fight it whatever it was. My head felt weird and my back started to burn. Just then Elsha's dad came into the back of the library and found us.

"Elsha I have been looking for you, more packages arrived at the house today and I'm afraid I have to leave town again soon."

He looked at me with great concern. "Kyle, are you okay son?" Elsha intervened quickly.

"Dad he doesn't look so good."

Dr. Morgan placed his hand on my forehead and quickly removed his hand.

"Don't move I'll be right back."

He ran out to his car and came back with his medical bag. He began to question me asking me how long I have been having these symptoms. I told him since early this morning.

He shined a light in my eyes and noticed my pupils changing sizes. Then he ran the thermometer across my forehead and that's when all hell broke loose.

"104.5 and steady rising. Dr Morgan said. "Alright young man you are out of here up on your feet."

Dr. Morgan was serious; I went to stand and staggered a little, he caught me by my arm and helped me. All I could think of was what was happening to me. By the time, Elsha and her dad helped me into the car I must have passed out.

When they had reached the hospital with me, waiting for us were my parents, Tony, and Ms. Creed. It turns out Ms. Creed was headed to the library to meet with Dr. Morgan. Elsha overheard them talking.

As everyone waited for an update on my condition, my insides felt like they were on fire. My breathing was very heavy and I could not control it, I felt such a great pain in my back I cringed. My hands gripped the sides of the bed nearly tearing the sheets.

"Aaaagh, what's happening to me?" I yelled out loud.

I could see a figure walking towards me, my vision was blurry and I couldn't make out who or what it was. It spoke in an ancient language that I understood, but did not know how.

"Ekua didanádo, gutládi ale askuanigododi akuatseli tsulitsyasdi sakuu, were the words I could hear being spoken over me which meant,

"*Great spirits cover and keep our young brave.*"

Whoever this way they were serious, I could hear the sound of something rattling over my head.

I fought to see who it was; as my body shook I was determined to fight off whatever sickness that was attacking me. I opened my eyes to see Dr. Spears standing, shining a light in my eyes. Dr Spears treated me at the hospital on the reservation I was very surprised to see him.

"So again you man, I see you are in the job of scaring people." He laughed a little. I was still kind of out of it; I struggled to sit up on the bed.

"So, doc give it to me straight, what's wrong with me?"

"We are waiting on your test results to come in, however; you were showing signs of a small infection which caused symptoms of fever and chills sort of like the flu. We gave you plenty of fluids, I'm afraid if Dr. Morgan and his daughter didn't get you here sooner your situation would have been far more serious."

I just nodded my head with relief. "Well thanks again, good seeing ya."

Dr. Spears smiled.

"You too kid. Good seeing you too."

He walked out and in walks everyone to see how I was doing. I did feel better but I wondered for how long though. As everyone entered the room I sat up slowly on the bed. My mother came to my side worried as ever and full of questions.

"Kyle, honey how are you feeling, How long have you been feeling sick?"

I turned to her. "Not long mom, just a few odd feelings off and on."

"I thought you guys were out of town?"

Dad placed his hand on my shoulder. "We were I had left something important behind and got a messaged from the Dr. that you were ill.

"Well son we are glad that you are feeling better."

Dad turned to Elsha and her Dr. Morgan. "Thank you, Dr. Morgan so much for bringing Kyle here."

Dr. Morgan raised his hand to my dad.

"No problem, just glad I was there at the time."

It was nice to have my family and friends with me; it was even good to see Ms. Creed. After talking for a while Dr. Spears came back to let me know I could return home. Tony and Elsha said they would stop by later.

I wanted to speak with Dr. Spears about my results; my parents went to the nurse's station to sign paperwork.

I couldn't help but think about the interest in my blood. Someone was going to give me answers so I decided to take advantage while I had the chance to. I asked Dr. Spears if he had heard any strange stories about a victim that was found alive after being attack by a wild animal.

I knew it was crazy to ask that question but I just had start somewhere. Dr Spears entered the room and asked where my parents were. I told him at the nurse's station, he gave me a prescription for an antibiotic to take for the next two weeks.

I asked him about my blood and if he noticed anything unusual. He said being that I had a rare blood type it can offset some of the test;

however he did tell me that I inherited a genetic gene that had him puzzled. I look at him strangely.

"What do you mean, you already knew about my blood before has anything changed?" Dr. Spears sighed for a moment.

"Your blood cells are abnormal." I looked at him a little odd.

"So what does that mean?"

Dr. Spears sat down to explain.

"Your blood count was a little low, so were your red blood cells. What's puzzling is your platelet count is extremely high."

I had a confused look on my face; I did not know what this meant at all Dr. Spears went on.

"Normally when white blood cells are low there is an increased risk of infection, yours is the total opposite."

I sat back on the bed and looked up at the ceiling. So that's why I have been feeling so strange lately. I asked Dr. Spears if he had other risk that could affect my health. Just as he was about to speak my parents walked in the room. He explained the results again to them, they were a little relieved but still concerned.

Dr. Spears told them how important it was for me to take the medicine for a couple of weeks. However; if for any reason the symptoms return again I was to come back to the hospital.

I felt I needed to get away for a while; I needed to go to a place where I could clear my head and think. Mom suggested when I get home to rest a while, but I just couldn't. I didn't want to disappoint her or dad so once we got home I headed straight to my room.

I overheard them talking about going back up to the cabin to check on it, and make sure the cabinets are stocked with canned food.

There had been reports of bears breaking in to cabins and dad wanted to be sure our cabin was alright.

Mom was hesitant on leaving me but dad said with doctors as friends I would be safe and in good hands.

After a restful nap I called Elsha and Tony and asked them to meet me later, Elsha decided her place would be best. I agreed since I needed to get a way to gather my thoughts.

Tony said he would pick me up, while I waited dad suggested I eat something, but I had no appetite. That was really odd, the other day I was eating like crazy and now nothing. Not even a craving. It is very strange how your body goes through changes, even when you don't know your body is changing.

I could hear the television in the other room, I had a very disturbing feeling come over me. I couldn't help it so I walked down the hall to listen closer.

What I heard so shocking it sent me to my knees. Two children are missing from a campsite in the foothills of Montana.

The police are searching desperately trying to find them. According to the police the children were last seen playing near cobble creek, which was downstream from their campsite. Volunteers are arriving on the scene to join in on the search.

The park rangers remember seeing the children just moments before they disappeared, there had been no flash flood warnings so the children cannot be far. The media will follow this story and update the public as more information comes in.

I was frozen and felt sick. I hoped and prayed they find those children.

I could hear a car pulling up in the drive way, it was Tony honking his horn as usual.

I called out to my parents letting them know that I would return home soon.

I didn't talk much on the way to Elsha's; I couldn't help but think about those missing children. So innocent I really hoped they find them soon. I must have been in deep thought about it Tony had been calling my name for a few minutes.

"Dude, you okay?" I answered slowly. "Yes, yes just fine, I just have a few things on my mind that's all."

"Oh alright then, you just had this worried look upon your face that's all."

I needed to reassure him a little. "No I'm okay, trust me."

We were almost at Elsha's house there was so much to talk about. I could see her horses running around the corrals, and her dogs ran up to us in the driveway. Elsha met Tony and I at the door, quickly rushing us inside she shoved both of kind of hard to quickly get inside the house.

"Hurry up we don't have much time!"

"What's the hurry?" Tony said.

"Yeah what is the rush?" I replied.

Elsha walked us over to the window and drew back the curtain a little.

"Watch carefully." She said.

Just then a strange car slowly drove passed her house. It was the same car we saw at the hospital when I paid Dr. Frank Hill a visit.

I couldn't help but wonder who or what they wanted. Elsha was a little nervous as she peeked through the curtain again.

"That's the third time that car has slowed down in front of my house."

Tony thought maybe we should find out who they are. I suggested we just lay low for a while and watch our backs. Now we know why she rushed us inside so fast, Elsha did not want whoever it was in the strange car to know we were there.

Tony said he would go out and take a look around, I said I would join him.

"No!" Elsha shouted at us. "Don't go outside!"

I turned to her quickly.

"Why the heck not? Elsha what is wrong with you today?" Tony joined in.

"Yeah what gives, you are acting paranoid."

She sighed and had a frightened look upon her face. "Kyle, I have something to tell you and it is not good."

"What do you mean?" I asked curiously.

Elsha was hesitant to tell me. Come into the kitchen and I will tell you. Tony and I followed her into the kitchen where she had photos and papers scattered everywhere.

"What's all this?" Tony said.

"More research." Elsha replied.

She started to explain that she had sent the photos to a research lab in Oklahoma about the symbols we found in the cave. Only to inform us that someone else is also interested in knowing about these symbols. Startled by this I had to ask.

"Who else is interested and why?"

"I don't know that yet?" Elsha replied.

Tony interjected.

"Wait a minute you mean to tell me that you sent away photos for research to get answers to get told that someone else is also interested and that's it case closed!" Bull!

Tony was not happy at all with Elsha; he felt there was more than what she was telling us. Tony and I both know Elsha very well; she is very persistent and usually gets what she wants. They both started to argue and I had to do something. I know how they both felt about me but I couldn't take this any longer.

I stepped in between both of them and asked them to stop. I asked Tony to give Elsha and me a few minutes to talk. As we head into the living room to talk, Elsha was still upset. She told Tony to help himself to the fridge, at least with his mouth stuffed with food she didn't have to hear him talk.

He turned slowly to say something to her so I put my hand on his shoulder pushing him away telling him to let it go and to give us a few minutes.

Tony agreed and said. "No problem, I need a little break anyway."

"So Elsha tell me what is really going on here."

She was a little reluctant but went on anyway. Elsha explained that there was a professor at the Archeological Institute in Oklahoma who was very interested in my photos of the cave. Apparently there had been some connection between the drawings and some ancient prophesies. They were very amazed and wanted to know where I found them. My mind burned with curiosity so I just had to ask.

"Elsha, who is this professor and what's the big secret, I mean why are you so hesitant?" Elsha took a deep breath and told me that the drawings on the cave walls are indeed prophesies, but there is more. The professor that contacted me was Professor Faye Lynn Jones; she is the one of the top professors amongst the archeological scientist at the institute. By this time Tony walked in to apologize to Elsha.

"Hey I don't mean to interrupt but I just wanted to say that I'm sorry."

Elsha rolled her eyes and said. "No problem, apology accepted."

Tony waved a sandwich in the air and thanked her. I had to ask her more about this professor.

She went on to say that Professor Jones had been studying the drawings for a while and the reason why she was interest was because her great, great, great, Grandfather Jeremiah Flynn was interested in it too.

"No way, are you serious!"

"Yes, I am." she said. Tony asked her how she knew this to be true, Elsha said because she looked up the ancestry information on Jeremiah Flynn on the internet, and found his family photos. She even researched the ancestry of Faye Lynn Jones. Tony interjected again.

"Wait a minute; you know nothing about this woman how could you possibly know she is a direct descendant of Jeremiah Flynn?"

Elsha pulls a book out from under a stack of papers.

"Because you idiot she sent it to me. I took the book from Elsha and read the title.

"Family Tree, How To Find Your Missing Link" I was surprised.

"Well that explains it then."

Elsha went on to explain that she was shocked as well. Tony wanted to know why she was so hesitant in telling us about her discovery. He could understand why she was paranoid about the strange car driving past her house. Elsha told Tony and me that she was nervous about the car and said that she has a strong suspicion that whoever is driving the car is watching those in the blood line of an ancient warrior of a certain tribe.

She also said that while her father was in Mexico a strange car was reported at the scene when the victim was taken away. She feels that when a person is attacked there must be others watching their every move. That's why she was hesitant in telling me because she feels since my attack they could be watching me as well.

Elsha showed us more of her discovery and we all sat talking for a while, After hours of information we discovered that the ancient symbols on the cave wall around the big stone was a spell to keep whatever was on the other side in so it would never get out. I asked Elsha if I could look at the professor's book for a moment. She passed me the book and a paper fell out from the back cover, it was a note.

I asked Elsha if she knew the note was in the back of the book and she said no she only looked at the first few pages of pictures.

I unfolded the note and was startled by it. According to Professor Jones, she warned Elsha to be careful who she sends information to about the ancient drawings. Not everyone is who they say they are.

She explained what we are dealing with is beyond our world and we should use caution. She is planning a trip to our town and she would love to meet up with us. However she has discovered more about her great ancestor's research and would like to know what happened to him.

She did however state she was grateful we survived the cave ordeal; all I could think about was how news travels. I told Elsha and Tony that she seemed friendly however I was deeply puzzled. I know we are dealing with something strange and weird buy why would she go through so much trouble.

Then I noticed something else, she sent a photo of Jeremiah it appears he is in a village with some of the natives. I asked Elsha is this all that she sent to her, she said no. Then Elsha had a grey look on her face.

"What's wrong now?" Tony said.

"Well I did not want to tell you this but it appears that the professor has found another link in our case."

I gave her a look and a serious one. "What else did she discover?" there appear to be some photos taken of an ancient tribe and some warriors of the late 1700's she says it could be part of a tribe that dwelled here years ago but she is checking the archives of her great grandfather's research.

She says it could be the face of a fierce warrior that was banned centuries ago. I swallowed hard and shut my eyes for a second; I stretched out my hand to her.

"Let me see the photo." Elsha was very hesitant again.

"Kyle I don't think you should look at this photo the quality is not very good. I told her I did not care just let me see it. Elsha handed me the photo and it was a picture of a drawing of an ancient warrior, who bore a striking resemblance to me.

I could feel my knees buckle but I stayed strong.

"How did she get this photo?"

Elsha spoke slowly. "From me Kyle I sent it to her." Tony did not like this at all.

"From you…, you?" "Yes, Tony from me, I just had to know."

I was so speechless. "But how did you find this?"

Elsha said she was looking through some of her photos and noticed some stone carve outs, she then did a data records search on ancient warriors that were banned and came across several photos. She said the one that bore a close resemblance to me she sent it off with her other photos to ask who the warrior was.

And it came back the warrior is in fact Liwanu of the Shahwanee tribe. I could feel the blood leave my body, I grew pale and cold. The room began to spin and I could hear the dogs barking outside.

Elsha was talking to me but I couldn't hear her, Tony walked toward me and the room began to spin. I was paralyzed and I couldn't move.

"Snap out of it!" Kyle, Kyle, are you okay?"

Elsha was trying to get me to respond. The sound of the dogs barking grew louder and louder. I could hear whispers in the air as the wind blew outside. Suddenly I snapped out of it. Tony and Elsha stared at me strange.

"Dude, you spaced out for a moment, are you alright?" I tried to shake it off.

"Yeah I just need to get some air".

Elsha suggested I lay down on the couch but I declined. Actually I need to get going, there is something I need to do.

I told Elsha I would call her later. When we left Elsha's house Tony tried to find out more about my spacing out. I told him I needed to think and get my head clear. I asked him to drop me off at the library and I would walk home from there.

We arrived at the library and Tony was still asking questions, I told him not to worry I just needed to be alone for a while. I went inside the library to find my usual spot way in the back; no one was there which made things better.

All I could think see was the face of the warrior, I tried to relax my mind then I started to feel strange again. I put my head down on the table; my body felt like it was being pulled into another dimension, I was traveling in time, yet awake. Flash points from my haunting dreams were coming back to me. The visions, the faces of the man burned at the stake.

I could see something else. It was another open vision. The moon was full and bright like a silver dollar. Beneath the moon there are people gathered around huge bonfire dancing and singing. There are men sitting in a circle each with a head piece to represent their tribe. I had no idea where I was, only that I knew I have left my body.

As the vision grew stronger I could see more people gathering under this huge moon, they were having a festival of some kind. Each dressed in tribal colors.

Their faces were painted and some had the silver stones around their necks. The moon was the brightest ever; it was so close I felt I could reach out and touch it. I could see and hear wolves howling in the distance, and others joined in. The sound of music in the background was of drums, flutes, and other musical instruments.

I walked through the crowd and saw a man, a man familiar in my dreams from before. He was the dark man with the symbols painted on him; he sat alone with his arms up praying to the spirits.

As the others were performing dances under the silver moon, I looked off into the distance and saw a woman, her hair was black as silk and she looked just like Ms. Creed. She was tall like her and everything.

Her eyes glistened in the moonlight, and her stone glowed like sparkling diamonds. As I approached her she looked at me and spoke in her language.

"O Si Yo, A yo li." which means "Hello, young brave."

I opened my mouth to speak but I couldn't. She told me the great spirits are watching and that there was no need to worry. As she walked away I noticed that even under a moon so bright the dark got darker. Eerie sounds came from the woods and I could see the glowing eyes of the wolves.

They were gathering in groups watching our every move.

I could see a white mist moving behind them and there was a shadow of a man walking. I turned to see who or what he was but the mist was too thick. It raised its hand and the wolves retreated into the woods.

"Who are you?"

I called out to see if I could get a response. No answer. I called out again.

"What do you want?"

This time I got what I asked for. Its voice was deep and eerie, my stomach dropped to my feet when I heard it.

"It's not what I want, it's who I want." Who or whatever was moving towards me fast, the smell of burnt skin hit my nose, I was paralyzed motionless. The sounds of wolves grew closer; no one else could see them but me. I could sense shifters all around me. Suddenly I felt a cold hand on my shoulder; I was being pulled backwards by something or someone.

"I'm sorry young man but the library closed ten minutes ago, you can turn your books in at the front." The little old lady was pleasant and sweet.

"Yes, maam, thanks."

I smiled and walked away. I gathered myself together trying to focus on my recent event. Perhaps this was a premonition of some kind. I started to walk home and noticed how full the moon was, so big and bright. My mind was plagued with so much all I could think about was how much I looked like Liwanu the warrior, he was definitely after me.

Just blocks before my home I was startled by a noise off into the distance, I looked up to see a dark cloud cover the moonlight. I kept walking thinking about my vision, then another noise of rustling trees. I stopped to look around and nothing. The wind blew a little and I thought I could hear whispers, a shadow passed by me quickly then another to my right.

I had a gut feeling I needed to start running and to run fast so I did. I ran as fast as I could, I could feel my back burn a little I could see glowing eyes following me in the woods nearby.

The sounds of wolves in the distance seem to grow closer. I know now that I'm not dreaming I am being hunted. I ran so fast down the dark road I stumbled and fell, I got up to see a dark being coming right at me, I rose to my feet and off in the distance behind the dark being wolves were running towards me as well.

My adrenaline rush was in overload, I pushed myself hard only to see lights coming towards me. A fast moving car was headed right in my direction, I could get killed either way, I did not know who was in the car but it was very strange. Evil in front and behind me, this is not a good way to die young. I turned to see if the chase was still on and yes it was the car did not seem to slow down at all.

I did not know what to do the pain in my back started to slow me down a little. The car sped up and drove past me only to turn around in the middle of the road. Then the car sped up in my direction again, this time putting space between me and the wolves. A woman's voice called out to me.

"Jump in, hurry! We don't have much time!"

I couldn't tell who she was so I dove head first into the car and we took off down the street. I tried to talk and catch my breath at the same time.

"Who are you?"

She was in disguise so I couldn't see her face.

"You can start off by saying thank you for saving your life back there."

Still breathing heavy I replied. "Thanks! I still would like to know who you are!" The strange woman spoke as she notified the driver to keep going. Looking over her shoulder to see if we were still being followed she said she would tell me more.

"Once we are safe I will tell you, but now we must keep moving, they will not stop so we must keep moving."

My head started to spin, my back burned with fire, the woman placed her head on my head, and spoke in a foreign language.

Someone else touched me and I felt a sting in my arm. "Ouch!" What is going on here?" My eyes got heavy real fast then I was out.

Chapter Seven

STRANGERS MEET

I don't know how long I was out but, my head was pounding. The pain in my back must have moved to my head. As I groaned in agony, I heard a voice coming from inside the room speak to me.

"Don't worry son; it will wear off soon. You had a close call back there."

Her voice was soft and pleasant but I still had no idea where I was.

"Where am I? What am I doing here?"

I felt her place her hand on my shoulder, telling me to just rest and she would explain later.

I tried to sit up but my hands were restrained.

I couldn't see either; they must have put a blind fold on me.

"The shot you were given had a few side effects," She explained. I could hear more footsteps approaching before hearing the door open as she spoke.

"I see he is awake; you can leave us now."

I wondered who she was, or what they wanted with me. Had I been kidnapped?

What about my parents? Surely they would be worried sick. I had to do something. But the pain in my head would not allow me to.

"I do apologize for this Kyle but it was the only way we could be sure," she said.

"Be sure of what? How do you know who I am?" I tried to sit up again but all she wanted me to do was rest.

"Just rest a while Kyle. I will tell you more in the morning."

I didn't want to rest I needed answers so I made my demands.

"No way! You tell me now!" I tried not to yell, but it was too late.

"Once the effects from the shot wear off, I will let you know."

"Well can I least see the face of my kidnapper or are you going to kill me for doing that?"

I could hear her laughing, I didn't find anything funny.

"Son, I am here to help, not to hurt you."

I could hear her move towards me, her hands on either side of my head removing the blind fold. I rubbed my eyes waiting them to adjust to the light.

"Ouch! What the....? My eyes...my eyes!"

The woman explained to me that this would happen; she placed the blind fold back on my eye. I wondered how many others they have done this to. The woman, whoever she was, told me to just give it a while for my eyes to re-adjust.

After what seemed like hours my blind fold was carefully removed again, she said one of the side effects is temporary blindness.

As the blind fold fell from my face, I saw a beautiful fair skinned woman smiling at me.

"Hello Kyle." She said.

I replied with "Hello...whoever you are."

She started out by saying that I needed to call my parents to let them know I was safe. She apologized for not taking me home but there was no time; they had to act fast. I told her that they would actually freak out.

"Go ahead give them a call; I'll be back in a moment." She said, smiling at me.

She left the room and summoned someone named Lou. Before I could ask who she was, the door had closed already.

This house was the size of a mansion; it was so big.

I constantly wondered who she was.

Well whoever she was, she's very beautiful.

I looked around the house at all the expensive paintings and statues; this house must cost a fortune. I figured I'd better contact my parents and tell them I would not be coming home. I am with total strangers and no one knows where I am. How do you explain that?

I picked up my cell phone and called my mother. I knew she would be hysterical, not knowing where I was.

They must have left for their trip the phone just rang and rang only to receive a message that the person you are trying to reach is out of the service area.

I didn't know who these people were, but my gut told me I was going to be okay. Even though I felt awful; I wondered why they just didn't kill me.

Well anyway, I'm not dead yet. I owe whoever she is a debt of gratitude for saving my life.

Those wolves tried to kill me, if they had not had been in the area, I would have been wolf food.

After calling my parents, I thought about calling Elsha and Tony. Something deep inside of me told me not to though. If they knew where I was, they would try to find me and I did not want to endanger them.

I had to trust my gut knowing I was about to find out something that others have been refusing to tell me.

I was feeling tired and weak, then a knock at the door. The beautiful woman entered the room. I could tell she was Native American; her skin was like caramel, her hair like silk, and her cheek bones were high.

"So what's your name and what tribe are you from?"

She just smiled at me politely saying.

"My name is AiYana. I am part Cherokee part African American and a little bit Mexican."

As I looked her, over admiring her beauty, she looked like someone you would not reckon with on any given day. Being in the situation I was in, I didn't really care.

"Well you look more Cherokee to me."

She gave me an odd look and chuckled a little.

"Well thanks for not calling me a mixed breed, or dirty blood."

I did not mean to offend her so I apologized quickly asking her what her name meant.

"My name means "Forever Flowering; Eternal Blossom. No need to apologies, we all have some sort of mixture in us. However; in your case more than others but what some people desire."

She said trying to be discrete.

Astonished by her comment, I was shocked and curious as to why she would say something like that. How much did she know, and what did she mean by it. So I asked her.

"What do you mean by that?"

She pretended she didn't hear me so I asked her again. She just pointed the way for me to exit the room.

"You will soon find out, this way please.

My patience was wearing thin. I didn't know how much more of this I could take. I was tired and very aggravated.

We walked down a long hallway to a room at the end with a uniquely painted door. It had very detailed carvings of strange symbols on it. Elsha would get a kick out of this big time. I examined the door very close trying to make out the symbols.

AiYana told me this is where I would be sleeping tonight. She opened the door to a room with a bed fit for a King, the paintings on the wall told stories of ancient warriors, some on horses riding toward the setting of the sun.

Something about this room mesmerized me and instantly I was in a trance. While I was in such deep thought and amazement, I did not hear AiYana calling my name.

"Kyle...Kyle," she continued, waving her hand at me to get my attention.

"Oh sorry, I just couldn't help myself there for a moment."

AiYana reassured me once again that I would be safe here and there was no need to worry. By her telling me that I would have what I am looking for soon.

I was curious as to why exiting the room she locked the door. I found it quite strange that she would lock me in.

Am I a prisoner here? Or a threat to her and whoever else is here.

Looking around the room there was a tray sitting on a desk along with a note. I uncovered the tray to see that dinner had been prepared for me. I wasn't sure if I should eat it or not. Regardless, my stomach was making enough noise to wake the dead.

The note was an apology about the blind fold and the secrecy. I was instructed to get a good night's rest and I would be informed in the morning of more details.

The note was not signed by anyone but I was very tired.

After being chased by the wolves, my body was really starting to feel it.

I ate some of the food and climbed into bed. Staring at the portraits on the wall of the tribal warriors; their faces were so life like. Examining every facial expression, their faces seemed familiar to me.

The more I stared, my eyes got heavy then I drifted off to sleep. My dreams took me to a place of peace and of war.

In my dream, I could see two tribal chiefs of different tribes standing in the middle of an open valley, each of them marked with symbols of circles and pitchfork like drawings, one of them wore a headdress of an eagle, the other of a bear. They spoke in their native language to each other staring at the heavens.

The stars were glistening in the night and the moon was full. Both men watched the night as if the stars were telling them stories. One of them pointed upward just as a shooting star passed by in the distance. Then, one after another, all of them were headed in the same direction, like a meteor was falling. I had never seen anything like this before.

As the chiefs watched the sky, one of them said,

"Time grows near my friend. Our fallen have sent us a sign that we should gather in the west and that is where we shall meet them."

Holding his staff, the chief with the bear headdress replied to him saying.

"I agree my brother. We must go there and soon. The moon will be full and we must be at the great gathering where heaven and earth shall meet."

Looking at each other, they nodded their heads in agreement. The sound of growling was off in the distance and drew closer. The men stood their ground until they found themselves face to face with a huge beast.

Staring at it, the chief with the eagle headdress could see eyes glowing in the dark. He knew there were others around and they were no longer alone.

The smell of shifters was in the air; they had made their appearance. I could never forget the smell of burnt skin. As awful and sickening as it was, the smell was unforgettable.

Moving closer to the men, the shifter had no problem trying to intimidate them with revealing its hideous appearance.

One the tribal Chiefs spoke to the grizzly beast.

"No matter how the Aniwaya grows, you will never defeat us."

Exposing its long sharp teeth, the beast stood up right. Howling out loud it spoke to the others behind him that were waiting in the darkness.

The trees began to snap at the top as a dark mist moved around them. The chiefs closed their eyes and prayed to the heavens.

"Great spirits, evil is upon us shield us with your protection and cover us in the night"

As they prayed a white mist moved quickly surrounding them. Unable to move the beast could not get close to them the barrier would not allow the beast to come any closer.

As the men stood their ground, I noticed there were others with them. I could see the silhouettes of shadows standing behind them. They must be the spirit guides; never before have I ever seen them in human like form in my dreams. They stood as giants, motionless, and very intimidating.

The beast stepped back, looked at the men almost growling as he spoke.

"I have tasted his blood. He is a part of me and I am a part of him. He is a direct descendant of me; his blood is my blood. You cannot protect him from me much longer."

Moving backwards into the night, all I could see was its eyes glowing in the night. Then the beast was gone.

I trembled in my sleep; my mind went back to that night I escaped the cave and I received the mark from the beast.

He had left me scarred and scared; surely that is what he meant. My blood was his blood; Liwanu would drink the blood of his enemies to make himself stronger.

Trying to wake myself from this nightmare, I just couldn't something was keeping me in this dark place. I found myself running down a long dark road again, being chased by the darkness.

Falling to the ground, a dark shadow covered me. My heart nearly jumped out of my chest. I screamed out loud but the eerie sound from the woods was even louder.

Crawling backwards on the ground the shadow was the hideous shifter that had haunted me for years.

Weighting down my body, I could not move, all I could do was tremble with fear. Once again, I was stuck in a nightmare that left me scared for my life. I could not move my legs at all. Its dark black eyes stared at me, looking deep into my soul. My breathing increased and I hyperventilated in my sleep.

Gasping for air, I felt as if I was being choked to death. The weight on my chest and throat blocked my breathing. Flashes of light hit my eyes and blinded me. The more the light flashed, the shifter quickly retreated into the darkness.

I heard a voice call my name.

"Wake up Kyle, wake up!"

Visions of Eric flashed before my eyes.

"Wake up! Kyle, you must wake up!"

I tried to pull myself out of the horrible nightmare, but something else was holding me down. The more I fought, the more I tried wake up. This time, speaking to my subconscious mind, I began to fight even harder.

I was determined that I was not going to die in this dream.

"Come on Kyle, fight! Wake up and fight!" I said to myself.

I was not going to die in this dream.

My eyes opened a little only to be pulled back into the dream staring in the face of darkness. I kept talking to myself, trying to force my way out of the nightmare, only so I thought. I couldn't tell what was dream or what reality was anymore.

Was I awake or still dreaming? I saw myself sitting up on the bed, gasping and choking. I reached for a glass on the nightstand and poured myself some water. I went to the bathroom to splash cold water on face. As I came up from the sink looking into the mirror I stood motionless unable to move.

Staring into the mirror I found myself looking at the most disturbing image. As I moved, it moved simultaneously. I was face to face with myself...only I was not myself; the person in the mirror was not me or was it?

Moving in close to the mirror, my eyes were dark as night, hands bigger than usual, and chest larger and full of muscle. My facial features were changing quickly. The closer I looked at myself touching my face, the more my fingernails grew long like claws.

A pain in my mouth caused me to clutch down on my teeth, only they were changing too. Long fangs, formed out of my mouth but, I remained human. There was no hair just wrinkled skin, wrinkled burned skin.

The nightmare was not over, it changed again, and I was not awake yet.

Immediately, I was surrounded by fire, tied to a stake, and looking at a crowd of people that were watching me burn. I could feel anger and hate consume me as I screamed at the crowd. Some of them danced around me waving staffs, while others chanted prayers. They appeared to rejoice over this.

As the fire increased, the Tribal Chiefs stood and watched. I screamed at them as loud as I could. I was being burned alive at the stake. I could feel the power of evil take control of my body.

I have seen this dream before only it wasn't me; it was someone else. Someone, who vowed to get revenge on those who betrayed him,

Looking up towards the sky, a dark mist hovered over me. I could feel it pulling me towards it. I tried not to look into its eyes but I could no longer fight it.

Evil was trying to enter my body through my dreams once again. Feeling my body weighted down, powerless almost; there was nothing I could do.

I heard voices all around me but I could not tell whose they were. I could see small beams of light flashing into my eyes. Hearing the voices getting louder, I fought to wake up.

"Kyle! Kyle! Can you hear me?"

.....

"Kyle, wake up!"

I couldn't explain what was happening to me but it was not the first time a dark entity tried to enter my body. The sound of war drums were increasingly loud, the singing was as if someone was casting a spell over me.

"Kyle?" A soft gentle voice said to me. "Kyle, come back to us.....
please."

Waking up screaming, I grabbed a hold of someone. With my hands around her neck she ordered me to release her.

"Kyle...your hurting me, please let me go."

I must have had a tight grip on her, as she struggled trying to break free from me. She spoke in her native language for me to release her.

"Lou! Lou! Come quickly...help!"

I awakened quickly to find my hands around the neck of a woman. I realized the woman I had attacked was AiYana.

She was choking and gasping for air trying to breathe again. While others rushed in to see what was going on, she rose to her feet waving her hands letting them know she was okay.

Lou rushed into the room nearly tearing the hinges off the door.

"Is everything alright in here?"

Although, AiYana was still coughing while getting herself together, she spoke very quickly to him.

"Yes...Lou...everything is fine; everything is under control."

Lou was not too convinced that she was okay. He gave me a hard look, never taking his eyes off me, as he asked her again.

"Are you sure you're okay? Did he hurt you?

Walking towards him putting her hands on his shoulder, she reassured him that she was alright. Lou looked at AiYana and nodded.

"Yes ma'am, I'll be close if you need me."

Lou was a big strong man, built like an ox. He reminded me of Big John, only his arms were massive with muscle. After he had left the room, I felt horrible for what had just happened. I lost control, that nightmare scared me I did not know what I was doing.

AiYana looked at me hard while trying to collect herself. I could have killed her but I was coming out of a horrible nightmare.

"You okay now...you awake...completely!" AiYana asked as she rubbed her neck.

I quickly replied. "Yes.... I'm fully awake."

AiYana kept clearing her throat and rubbing her neck; I must have really scared her. As I kept apologizing to her, she told me it was no problem. She said she should have been more careful.

She went on to explain that there are serious steps to take when trying to wake someone out of their sleep.

Looking at me she had a great concern on her face.

"How are you feeling? I mean….how are you really feeling? That must have been a terrible dream"

I had to let her know it was more than just a dream. I took a deep breath and told her to brace herself.

I sat there telling her when my dreams began, not giving much detail about anything. I told her that I suffered from nightmares for a long time. Though bothered by the dream, I was glad to be awake. Even when I talked, I was haunted by what I saw.

AiYana more concerned than ever, felt that she had to share more chilling information. Clearing her throat again she began to explain.

"At first, we thought we heard strange noises coming from outside, only to realize it was just the wind. I was in the study down the hall doing some research, and Lou was making his rounds," She started. "I thought I heard screaming but didn't think much of until they got louder. The wind was blowing so strong; it nearly knocked out the power. And when we entered your room….."

She stopped in mid sentence.

"What!" Go on!"

Hesitating to speak, her voice cracked, she took a deep breath and started again.

"I've never seen anything like it before."

Anxious to get the truth out of her, I grabbed her by her arm.

"Never seen what! What did you see?"

She asked me to let go of her again, I apologized. She went on talking.

"Not seen, Kyle heard! There was a noise coming from this room, none like I have ever heard before. When we entered the room, we couldn't wake you. No matter how we tried, we had to use a softer approach."

"You keep referring to we, who else is here? Who are you referring to?"

AiYana paused for a moment and then I lost it. I yelled and screamed at her, looking at everything around the room.

"What do you people want from me huh? What do you want?"

She raised her hand to me to calm me down. But it didn't work; I needed to get answers and no more games. I turned to AiYana and asked her who runs this house and who did she work for.

She told me I would find out in due time, we just need more time. My patience was running out. I grabbed a glass from the table and threw it across the room.

The glass shattered, AiYana jumped and asked me to control my emotions. She told me that if I didn't calm down I would not come back from my anger. I turned to her in such haste walking towards her, she grabbed her throat.

"What do you mean, not come back?"

As I gave her a long hard look, she backed away from me slowly.

"My grandfather told me that anger is like poison. It can over take you if you don't control it. The more you fuel it, the stronger it gets."

Turning my head in slow motion towards her, it hit me like a ton of bricks.

"Who the heck are you?"

AiYana was silent, with a disturbed look on her face. Her expression let me know there was more to her than what she was saying. Her words made me think back to when I first met Chief Spearhorn; he told me the same words. AiYana just stared at me her eyes fixed up on me watching my every move.

I asked her again, only this time no matter the consequences, I approached her. I could feel my blood boiling.

It didn't matter anymore nor did I even care. I was brought here for a reason and I was going to find out why. She was hiding something and one way or another she was going to talk. I thought to myself for a moment trying to figure things out.

I'm here for a reason; I could feel it in my gut. If I were not important to them, they wouldn't have brought me here; they would have taken me home. I was nearly killed in my dreams again. Looking at the pictures on the wall, I recognized one of the men from my dream. This could not be possible but it was.

I stood to get a closer look at the painting on the wall. I was almost certain that this was one of the chiefs in my dream watching me burn.

The elders were responsible for the death of Liwanu. The more I thought about it, the room seemed to spiral. Things couldn't get any worse so, I asked AiYana again, this time grinding my teeth.

"Who are you?"

AiYana, though hesitant to speak, opened her mouth to talk only to be interrupted by someone walking from the back of the room. They looked right at AiYanna and said.

"Eliquv, adanvsdi I tsu la a yv"

I took this interpretation as she wanted AiYana to leave immediately. AiYana looked at her nodded and left the room.

In my anger, I looked to the woman speaking rudely.

"I guess you have come to settle things down in here, huh?"

She smiled at me shaking her head.

"Well Mr. Green, you were shouting and throwing things around. What are we to expect of you; you are a guest here."

Talking in a calm voice, she never took her eyes off me while she spoke. Although she looked very mysterious, I know I had seen her from somewhere before. But I wondered how she knew my last name.

How much did they know about me I wondered? That is what I am determined to find out so again I asked.

"How did you know my last name? Are you some kind of reporter?"

Putting her hands behind her back she said.

"You spend your time looking for answers but when it stares you in the face, you can't even recognize it. Your anger has blinded you Mr. Green. I'm sure you have been told to be careful for what you seek, for one day it may seek you."

With my heart still pounding, I dared not to ask who she was. All of these riddles, I swear it felt as if Chief Spearhorn was in the room.

She asked me to follow her and that she would explain things over breakfast.

Food was the last thing on my mind, my blood was still boiling but I didn't like the way it made me feel.

I knew they were right. All of a sudden, I felt sick to my stomach. I rushed to the bathroom and hit the floor. The adrenaline rushed to my head so fast the room was spinning. The woman knocked on the door, she was very concerned. I told her I was fine but I don't think she bought it.

This time she pounded on the door questioning me again.

"Are you okay in there? Kyle, Kyle!"

I stammered a little when I spoke, telling her I was okay. I could hear the door handle jingle so I hurried and splashed water on my face and opened the door.

She stood at the door staring at me. I tried to shake it off but I just couldn't.

I tried to give an excuse.

"It must have been something I ate; I'll be fine."

I could tell she didn't believe me. The look on her face was quite puzzling.

"Well you don't look okay, you look pale. Come, I have breakfast waiting for us. You need to get something in your system."

I kept trying to tell her not to worry, but she was very persistent. Looking at me as if she was giving me some type of examination she asked.

"How long have you had these anxiety symptoms?"

I raised my eyebrows to her.

"What do you mean symptoms? What are you my doctor now?"

The symptoms I just experienced in the bathroom. I wondered how much she knew about me and why she asked so many questions.

I gathered myself together and told her I would ask the questions from now on.

"First of all, who are you? Second, what do you want with me? Third, how long do you plan on keeping me here?"

She laughed she asked me to follow her to her study.

We got to a room on the far side of the house with an incredible view of the mountains. The room was gorgeous, and there was a huge patio that led to the outside. I followed her through the French doors and we sat down to talk.

"Kyle.....I do believe that you and I have a lot to discuss. I apologize for any inconvenience to you. Shall we start over?"

She kindly said ushering me to sit down. I had a strong feeling I was about to get the answers I have longed waited for. Whoever this woman was, I felt she was no stranger and that our meeting like this was no coincidence.

Chapter Eight

PROPER INTRODUCTIONS

While I sat at the other end of the table, so many thoughts were going through my mind. Whoever this woman was, she must be very important. As she uncovered the food for us to eat, she explained that she felt it best to eat outside. She figured some fresh air might do me some good.

I looked at the beautiful scene of the mountains; it reminded me of Elsha's place. Except there were no horses or dogs running around.

A beep from the woman's cell phone alarmed her for a moment.

"Eat up, I'll be back in a moment," she smiled.

I did what she said only until she had left the room.

Once I made sure she was gone, I walked back into the study to take a quick look around. This place was like a library; books and newspapers were everywhere.

I wondered what kind of research she was doing.

I could tell by the notebook on the desk she was looking for someone.

She had names and addresses, maps, and phone numbers written down. I wondered who she was looking for.

As I kept looking, I stumbled upon an unpublished report that read:

Mystery surrounds the children of the Spearhorn reservation.

As I read the report it talked about missing children as well as others that are all connected to the reservation.

According to the birth records on some of the children, at least half of them shared the same DNA which meant they were related. However; only two of them shared the exact Gemini gene which meant they were identical twins.

Though mystery surrounds the reservation about some of the once found missing have now disappeared again; gone without a trace. Some speculate they are on distance reservations or staying with relatives.

Those who remain on the Spearhorn reservation are under heavy and strict protection. Reporters are not permitted on the reservation unless they are given permission.

As I read, chills went up and down my spine. Nothing could prepare me for what I was about to read next.

Strange events have been reported of sighting of a dark entity. The most recent event took place at Rocky Point where a victim was attacked. A local physician from Patagonia by the name of Dr. Morgan was on assignment to assist but later was dismissed when the victim he found was taken away.

The victim, whose name is being protected, had claw marks on his chest and back. My sources tell me that the blood samples taken from him linked this victim and others to the Spearhorn reservation.

I stopped reading for a moment to think to myself.

"This is why he was interested in my blood; he was doing a comparison; but, why?"

As I kept reading, I learned that other victims were taken away by Chief Elders from distant tribes. The report stated the reporter has a source that gives inside information about everything and how reports leaked out about some of the people killed had abnormal blood. Some blood was even similar to a wolf's blood which brought up the superstitious rumors of the Suhnoyee Wah.

An ancient legend told long ago that a warrior turned evil would drink the blood of his victims in order to devour their souls.

This warrior believed by doing this act it would give him eternal power. He killed many that were enemies to him, and it had been rumored that he defiled a Chief Elder's daughter.

I could not read any further, this was too much for me. There was a lot of information in this report. Hearing someone coming, I quickly placed everything back before noticing the initials VB at the bottom of the page. Quickly exiting the room, I hurried and went back out onto the patio.

With my mind plagued with so much, I had to act normal and keep my cool. Now knowing how each child is connected also meant that I was somehow connected.

I ate more food to make it appear that I was actually eating so when she entered the room she would not suspect anything, so I hoped.

When she arrived, she apologized for being gone so long. She explained it was not her intention for me to eat alone.

I told her that it was no problem.

It was funny how even under these weird circumstances, she was very friendly. Unfolding her napkin, then pouring herself a glass of juice she looked at me, took a deep breath and spoke.

"Now, let's start over. I apologize for us meeting under these circumstances and to answer your questions I will start at the beginning."

I didn't know what to expect or what she was going to say, but this is what I needed so I listened.

"Well Kyle, I am part of a research team on tribal cultures. Second answer, my associate brought you here because of the attack; if they hadn't been in the right place at the right time you could have been killed. Third answer, I don't plan on keeping you here; you can leave whenever you want."

I still felt she was hiding something from me.

I thanked her for saving me and she interrupted me by telling me that it was no problem. But there was still one question remaining. I did not know who she was; neither did I know her name so I decided one more time to ask her.

"Thanks for your hospitality, but can I at least get your name before I leave."

Lowering her head a little she responded.

"I believe you already knew who I am."

She stood up from the table and walked towards me, extending her right hand.

"Allow me to introduce myself, my name is…."

I stopped her before she could finish her sentence.

"Veronica Banks, the missing reporter." She shook my hand at my answer.

"Well I don't know about missing; but, yes I am Veronica Banks."

I could not believe it; it's actually her. I had been trying to find this woman to get some answers and here we are, face to face.

Now that we have been properly introduced, it was time for Veronica and me to get down to business.

Excited and nervous at the same time I didn't know where to begin. I started out by asking her why she left her job. She responded by telling me it was due to her getting too close to the truth.

Veronica explained how she started receiving threatening phone calls that if she didn't stop her investigation of the missing children she would be the one missing.

"How did you handle such a threat?"

"I don't take threats; especially when I was so close to revealing the truth."

She went on explaining that she had received many threats and she knew that someone wanted her to stop her investigation. However, she stated she did feel the threats didn't come from someone on the reservation, but someone else.

"How can you be so sure about it?"

"Chief Spearhorn was also being threatened; it made me feel comfortable that I was not the only one."

This did not surprise me at all; he is very protective and would do anything to keep the peace with his people.

So I asked her to continue, surely she knew a lot and I wanted to know everything. As she spoke, she ran her hands through her long hair saying.

"Apparently, someone felt that Chief Spearhorn was not doing enough to protect his people. Though some of the people on the reservation were very afraid they relied upon him and the others to keep them safe."

She stopped for a moment and chuckled a little. I had to ask her what he had to say about all of the speculation behind the missing people.

"Though the people were scared, Chief Spearhorn has such a way with words."

She sat back in her chair, looked at the sky as she replied.

"In the words of Chief Spearhorn, a man that stands alone is an army of one, but when he is joined together with his brothers, he is an army of many."

Veronica said that he was a man of many words, and I agreed. She said there was something about his words that made her feel mesmerized. He was a peaceable man, but she knew he was hiding something.

So during her investigation, she learned the real reason why the children were taken from them and why the Chief and his followers worked hard to get them back.

Sitting back in my chair with my hands on top of my head, I braced myself for what she was about to say. Not knowing what to expect, I then tried to get into a comfortable position so I eased forward a little in my chair.

Veronica Banks sat across from me explaining that there was a connection between the missing and the ancient legends. Her research started when there were reports of people disappearing at first she thought it had to do with hate crimes.

But the more she researched she learned that there was trouble brewing on the reservation.

"Sometimes you have to pay close attention to what seems bizarre or too good to be true. There is a prophecy that says during the season of the high full moon, there will be a great gathering of tribes."

"How can you be so sure of the legends?"

"The noise coming from your room last night was proof enough."

I quivered in my seat. I should be used it by now but unfortunately I wasn't.

I knew deep inside me I would never be free from the evil that haunted me until I confronted it face to face instead of my dreams.

As I sat and listened to Veronica, something shifted inside me. A cold feeling came over me. Looking over my shoulder, I felt the wind upon my face. With a puzzled look upon her face Veronica stopped talking in midsentence.

"Kyle, what's wrong…you're looking pale. Do you feel well?"

I didn't respond. I sat there staring off into the distance, the wind howled even stronger. No clouds were in the sky dark shadows moved swiftly across the mountain. The sounds of whispers were in the wind as I sat there paralyzed unable to move. Shooting stars flew across the sky like bullets, all heading in the same direction.

By the time the vision had past, Veronica was calling my name waving her hand in front of my face.

"Yoo hoo, Kyle……hey come back to earth. Are you okay?"

Snapping out of it, I responded.

"Yes, I'm fine. Sorry, I spaced out for a moment."

Before she could say anything else I gathered my thoughts. I felt that she needed to know the reason she was threatened. I explained to her that whoever wanted her to stop investigating the reservation was keeping her away from danger.

She asked me what made me so sure and that she was not going to stop until she found out the truth.

She went on telling me how she had heard more about the legends and how the chosen ones would one day assemble with others.

This gathering would symbolize a nation of people coming together to thank the great spirits for protecting all living descendants of every tribe.

Those chosen would purge the land of a great evil but it would take the power of many joining together from the four corners of the earth.

She looked at me and took a deep breath.

"Which brings me to my next point; I have reason to believe that these children were sent away because they were the chosen ones. Their parents felt that they would be safer away from the reservation that on it."

"Perhaps it was for the best."

Veronica explained that she didn't think so. She believed that the families that gave up their children felt if no one knew or had knowledge of their background they would be safe. That is why her team had been following me for quite some time.

She said she was close by watching the night Elsha went missing. When she heard the news, it frightened her that it was going to be another sad ending story.

Listening to this brought back the memories of that horrible night inside the cave. She continued telling me that later she heard that I too had been trapped. She tried to get close to the scene but was not allowed.

That night she said she could feel such eeriness in the air, that she could hear the sound of drums. She said she knew deep down inside there was a battle going on.

That is why she surrounds herself with people of knowledge that can explain what some people call myth and others call truth. Of course, by now you notice my staff is of different cultures which caused me to research my genealogy. Come to find out I am also one fourth Blackfoot Indian. It's amazing what you find out about yourself while searching the history of other people.

Some people dismiss the tribal legends as just that, legends. There are some that follow you home. According to her sources, she later learned that these children had more than just special gifts.

Some had the gift of prophecy, to tell when events would take place by seeing visions in the heavens. These children had the ability to sense when evil was present; some of them as they grew into their teen years spoke of seeing dark shadows in their sleep.

From generation to generation, these stories have been told for each member of the tribe to say prayers, and watch their children. Some chose to ignore this only to live normal lives but yet some have paid the price.

The more I listened to her talk; I wondered how much more she knew about me. I then started putting two and two together, the strange car in my neighborhood, the car that passed us on the road, the strange black car that was seen in Rocky Point.

Shaking my head at her, I slid my chair back from the table; there were just a few things I had to let her know.

"Veronica, you have no idea what is going on out there, I believe this research is more than just a story, it's a personal one."

The startled look on her face let me know that I had her attention now.

"Go on, I'm listening."

I sat there telling her how I felt that the reason she was risking her life was because she wanted to know if she also was connected somehow.

Researching her genealogy to discover she is part Native American, she wanted to know about the legends to see if she also had ties to the reservation. I told her if I was way off the mark she could stop me at anytime.

Only the chosen ones can tell when evil is near because it is drawn to them because of the bloodline. Last night, I had a horrible nightmare of the Shah-wa-nee warrior named Liwanu who was killed by the tribal Elders because he killed his own people and became very evil.

I told her exactly what she wanted to hear, that we all were in danger.

Just a moment ago I saw dark shadow pass over the mountain along with bright lights headed in the same direction. I know what this means from my dreams, and I must be prepared for it.

Now that I know the what, the why, I needed to know the how.

Though intrigued by my story, Veronica was amazed; I just had to know more though. I poured on the questions and asked her why the bodies are taken after an attack.

She said from what she knows, the bodies have to be heavily guarded in fear of the individual turning into a shifter. I asked her if she believed that the shifters are real, she says she wasn't certain but she knows there is an evil upon us.

That is why she had to learn her heritage and learn all she could about the bloodline.

By this time AiYana approached us, she had been listening and apologized for ease dropping but she had some news and thought we both should know.

Veronica asked her to sit down; though AiYana was very upset I asked her if she was okay.

"You seemed disturbed. Are you alright?"

With shaking hands, she poured herself a glass of water.

"There has been another attack, this time two tribal elders in Poteau, Oklahoma," Veronica clutched her chest as she spoke.

"When did this happen?"

AiYana replied in slow breaths.

"Late last night, they were traveling up in the foothills and never returned home. Their bodies were discovered a little while ago....chest ripped open."

She struggled to talk as tears ran down her face. She buried her face in her hands crying.

"They were my great uncles," she said. "My family is preparing to travel back home for their burial ceremony."

With tears in her eyes, she turned to me.

"I wish I had your gift, you have no idea how many are after you for it."

Veronica tried to stop her from talking, by grabbing her arm but she couldn't. AiYana jerked away from her. AiYana was determined to tell me more and she did.

"I believe it's time you tell him the truth of why we brought him here," AiYana said.

Veronica was shocked and so was I. What else could there be, what was left to be said? The women quarreled a little. I asked both of them to stop and just tell me.

AiYana was sobbing even more now then she brought the truth to the light.

Chapter Nine

SHAPED DESTINY

"You being here is a sure sign to us that you are indeed one of the chosen. Last night, when we heard the noises coming from your room, I held my stone to the door and it lit up."

Turning her head towards Veronica she pointed at her.

"She knew it the whole time! Her stone lit up as well!"

AiYana's crying had turned to anger. She spoke harshly to Veronica telling her that, even though the wolves were after me, it was wrong for her to bring me here. Veronica had to be sure though.

Veronica suggested we leave the balcony and go inside. AiYana was very upset so we tried calming her down first. Veronica received a report that there had been more attacks. She made a few phone calls and sent her team to investigate. AiYana began to yell even louder as her anger escalated. She lashed out even harder and revealed more information in her rage.

"After watching the video tape, it was enough proof." She went on, "But no, she had to get you here and that thing almost killed you in your sleep! It tracked you here! Kyle...the wound on your back will never heal, as long as your blood runs they can smell you!"

I don't know how much more of this I could take; but, now it was my turn. I questioned them both. It seems there are more people involved than I thought, but whatever was going on I had been lied to long enough. So I asked them both.

"What tape? Veronica what is she talking about?"

Veronica looked at me very strange. I walked towards her and she stumbled backwards falling onto the couch. I leaned into her and spoke.

"Start talking. Now!"

AiYana left the room to pack for her trip. Veronica took a few short breaths and started talking.

She said that she had learned about me when my parents brought me to Dr. Hill's office. She said some of the children reported seeing dark entities in their sleep. She knew Dr. Hill kept video tapes of his sessions so he could further study his patients.

Veronica stated that, during her investigation, she found out several children suffered post traumatic disorders after being treated by Dr. Hill. Apparently, he was doing his own research on children who suffered from the nightmares. He was sending mild shocks to their brains to trigger and affect. She also discovered that each child had a connection somehow and he was being forced to give their information to outsiders.

"Outsiders? What outsiders?

She continued by saying.....

"That, we don't know yet. We believe they are part of some secret organization that has been following the children who were adopted illegally. My team had a good lead on them but their trail went cold. I suggested that they kept searching until they found the source. I suspect whoever they are; they had knowledge about the children and took them away to hide them."

I asked her how she could be so sure, when her team couldn't find them. I had to prepare myself for what she said next.

Veronica began by telling me her investigation started years ago which would have put me around the age eight or nine years old. When she first learned about the children that were illegally adopted from the reservation it was around the same time when people first started disappearing.

She learned of Dr. Hill when some of the names started showing up on his visitation log. I went to speak and she raised her hand to stop me.

"Don't ask, it wasn't easy. That's why I had a private investigator."

I wondered how she got her hands on his visitation log; she must have been reading my mind. Veronica continued by saying her investigator was at the clinic the same day I was there with my parents.

"How did he know about me?"

"He didn't at the time," she stated. "He thought he was seeing double for a moment. After you had arrived with your parents, he swore he had just seen you moments earlier with someone else.

As she talked, my mind went back to that day that I talked to Eric through the vents. Veronica told me her investigator noticed when the young boy came from the quiet room.

"Quiet room? What's that?

Veronica continued.

"The quiet room is where they placed children before each procedure, to give them a sense of calmness. Though you can't see or speak to anyone, the room is somewhat like a relaxation room to prepare you and relax your mind."

I shook my head, laughing a little. I always felt it was more like a prison cell. My room was different though. I told Veronica to continue I needed to know more.

As she went on, I learned that before Dr. Hill could see Eric, a man came and took him away. His mother wanted him to stay and get treatment, but the man was very persistent. Dr. Hill tried to argue with him but it did not work. The man took Eric and his mother outside to talk. She said as her investigator followed the commotion, I was being taken to the exam room. She said he did a double take, he could not believe it.

"They must be twins." She said. "That's what my investigator said about you, they must be twins."

Thinking about my brother, I whispered his name.

"Eric…"

She must have heard me then she said.

"Yes, his name was Eric."

She got up, walked over to her desk and picked up a stack of papers. Looking at it, I realized it was the report I had read earlier on her desk.

"Yes, here it is. Eric…Eric Spearhorn." She said, running her fingers over the file. "You two were about the same age at the time we were watching out for him. Due to the stories that surrounded him, we had to be very careful. He had reported to another doctor that dark scary things were chasing him in his sleep. We wanted to keep a close watch on him, and see who else was watching him as well."

She stopped for a moment and, with a puzzled look, spoke again.

"Come to think of it, you two are so identical, I wonder if you share a rare gene called the Gemini; his blood type is different though."

I asked her how she knew that, yet again she said her investigator. I told her how illegal it was to access someone's medical records; then she asked me what my blood type was. Looking at her, I just had to go there with her.

"What, you don't know that by now, perhaps your investigator missed that one."

She looked at me saying.

"Good one, I can see you're full of jokes as well."

She told me it would help her to continue her investigation, and why others were trying to figure out the connection between the victims.

"Others, what others? I asked.

Veronica stated that she was not the only one seeking answers. She felt she was getting too close and that's probably why the threats were made against her. So I told her my blood type was AB negative. She looked at me and asked if she could continue her story and I told her to proceed.

Veronica went on telling me that while outside hospital others joined in the conversation, the young boy's mother was furious telling them they had no right. She wanted him to stop having bad nightmares and the tribal stories were not helping. But whatever this man said to the boy's mother, she could not argue with him any longer. The boy was taken away by the man who we know as Chief Spearhorn.

CHERYL LEE

She said other children were taken as well, at the time they did not know about me. Somehow, they received information that the other children would be there, and Dr. Hill would be conducting their sessions.

Then she paused for a moment, looking for something on her desk. She pulled out a notebook.

"Come to think of it, your name was not even on the list that day. It was very odd; Dr. Hill never sees anyone without an appointment."

She pulled her long hair back around her neck. Looking over her notes; she asked me if I remembered anything about that day.

I told her yes, it was a day I would never forget and one I did not want to relive.

It sounded crazy even though I have been reliving this nightmare for as long as I could remember.

"AiYana mentioned a videotape; she said it was a taped of a session with another child."

"I never told AiYana about the child on the tape because they haven't figured that out yet. I can only speculate that AiYana thought it was you. I'll tell you more in a moment." She then continued her story.

At the time Chief Spearhorn learned that Dr. Hill was seeing Native American children only that day. This made Chief Spearhorn furious. She said her investigator reported that Dr. Hill was experimenting with the lives of children and Chief Spearhorn would stop at nothing to shut him down.

When she had proof that Dr. Hill was secretly giving over files on certain children, she decided to keep a close watch on him.

"Why would he give the files away to these people?"

"Someone else was also watching the children, learning about their backgrounds. I felt that it might have been someone from one of the reservations, working to track the children down to return them." She continued telling me she hoped that they were safe. Sometimes as a reporter you have to be careful what you report.

"Do you have regrets?"

"People will do anything to protect the innocent, no matter how we reporters feel that the truth needs to be told. There are some things the public should never know about. In this case, however, when people that have a connection are dying and no one seems to know why, somehow one can only wonder."

I agreed; this was very strange.

We all must be crazy. Who will believe you when you say something you can't see is chasing you or trying to smother you in your sleep? I had asked myself that question for years and finally, I meet people who have knowledge about my nightmares.

I continued to ask Veronica if she felt the threats on her life ever made her think twice about moving forward or just backing off.

"I only thought about it for a moment. I just couldn't back off but I did feel driven almost."

I could see how sympathetic she was and how it took a toll on her for a moment. She became almost emotional.

"Do you have any close relatives that have been killed since this all started?"

"No." I did not believe her.

I was very satisfied that I finally got the answers I was looking for. Veronica had given me more than enough but I knew there was more yet to be revealed. She answered questions for me that I couldn't even get Chief Spearhorn to tell me. It made me wonder why he just didn't take me as well when I was younger.

The more I learned, the more I needed to know. I had to ask Veronica about the tape again. She said it was a tape of a little boy but the tape was not very good.

"What's wrong with it?"

"The picture is too dark and fuzzy and the audio is full of static."

I asked her the name of the boy and she did not know there was no name on the tape; she was trying to find that part out. Her investigator was busy listening to Dr. Hill, Chief Spearhorn and Eric's mother that day.

"Why have me followed then?

"It was the only way to be sure if there was a connection."

"Connection....connection to what?"

Searching through papers on her desk she said.

"Connection to the missing piece of an ancient puzzle."

She really had my attention now. I joined her at her desk to look at the report perhaps I missed something when I read it earlier.

"How did you know about this?"

"My investigator, of course."

Whoever he was, she was very good.

"By now, you know that your parents are not your real parents."

"I was adopted as an infant and my parents are the only set of parents that I know."

"Kyle…do you know anything about your birth parents?" She turned in her chair as she spoke.

I replied "No."

With a serious look on her face she started again.

"Would you like to know?"

Shock waves went all through my body, my heart beat increased and my palms were sweaty. With a nervous voice I responded.

"Yes, yes I would like to know."

She proceeded to tell me that for all of the children that were adopted, the state turned over their sealed records to the reservation. There I will find in their archive room all of the names of the parents that gave up their children from the reservation.

"I tried to get the information from Chief Spearhorn but I didn't have much luck."

I found it quite odd she would tell me this so I questioned her about it.

"So am I to be your investigator now to get this information for you? Or is it that you just wanted me know the whereabouts of my birth records."

"Kyle, I would never ask you to do that. I just thought you would like to know. That's why I have an investigator, remember? Despite that, even he can't get on the reservation unnoticed. I just felt that if you wanted to know, perhaps Chief Spearhorn would tell you; you do have that right."

She was right, he owes me. I am his grandson but he treats me different in an odd sort of way. I wonder why they kept me away from Eric; why not allow us to see or get to know each other? So many questions swarmed around in my head.

I must have had a confused look on my face because Veronica was trying to get my attention.

"Kyle, earth to Kyle! Hey you're spacing out again."

I snapped out of it to get myself together. By this time, AiYana returned with suitcases in her hand.

"I'm all packed, my flight leaves in a few hours. Lou is driving me to the airport." She told Veronica.

AiYana was still saddened by the death of her uncle's. I felt real sorry for her. She stared at me for a moment then apologized. I told her there was no need; we have to express ourselves in some way.

I should be leaving as well. The last 24 hours have been hectic and before AiYana could say anything else she looked at me and said.

"I really hope you find your way, and learn how to defeat this enemy."

"Do you believe I am the chosen one?"

I also asked Veronica the same question.

"What about you? Do you think I am this person destined to stop this evil entity?"

Veronica paused, looked at AiYana for a moment, and spoke.

"Kyle, we all have some kind of shaped destiny to fulfill, some more than others. I don't know what to think sometimes about all of this. What we have uncovered during the investigation has left even the Chief of Police scratching his head."

I had to agree with her but I listened as she continued.

"I believe we all have a part in this. Our great ancestors knew of this great evil and the protectors that vowed to be sure we would be safe."

AiYana though saddened agreed as well. Veronica said she believed that somehow I have been chosen for this task to face the evil.

"The only way to be free from this is to confront it." She held her necklace in the palm of her hand, talking softly.

"They said this would keep us safe. Now what do we do?"

Veronica wore a rare silver stone around her neck; I asked her where she got it from she stated from a direct descendant. AiYana also had one; she too clutched hers tightly as well.

I knew about the stones, and the legend behind them. I warned both ladies to keep them on, regardless of whether they believed in them or not.

I sat there thinking for a moment, trying to piece all of this together. Everything began to unfold in front of my eyes. I couldn't help but think when Elsha and Tony went with me to pay a visit to the doctor. There was a strange car that passed us. Elsha saw it again when she was spying on Dr. Hill. Everything was coming together now: the car, the strange woman, all of it.

I looked very hard at both of them.

"What kind of car do you drive?"

Veronica wanted to know why. I began by describing the dark colored sedan with the dark tinted windows. Veronica stated that was her investigators car and it is used when she is keeping a low profile or from being recognized.

I was a bit relieved to hear that I was afraid of another psycho out there following me. Not that Veronica is crazy but she does put herself out there to reveal the truth.

Veronica asked AiYana about the bodies.

"As far as I know, they were taken to the reservation for preparation." She apologized again for her outburst. Veronica apologized for putting her in a compromising position.

By this time, there was no need to say anything else. AiYana was leaving for Oklahoma but not before she shared something else with me.

"Be very careful out there."

"What do you mean?"

She had such a scared look upon her face. I was almost afraid for her to continue. She took a deep breath and looked at me with tears welling up in her eyes.

"There are some that would kill for your gift, maybe even kill *you*. Kyle, I believe in the legend of the Suhnoyee Wah and if you are one of the chosen ones then you are going to need protection."

Looking straight at her I said.

"Protection...protection from whom? Don't I have enough protection already?"

I scratched my head as I listened to her talk about the legends. The fear and anger in her eyes let me know that she was very serious.

As she continued, a stream of tears ran down her face. She struggled to talk. Veronica told her that she did not have to tell me, but she insisted.

AiYana sat down slowly on the couch and proceeded with her story.

"My great uncles told me stories about our people and how for centuries there have been secret societies of followers that bare the mark of ancient symbols. These symbols represent the four directions of peace; others carry the symbol of life and death. These are just to name a few; they vowed to keep watch over the chosen ones. Some symbols identify the tribe in which they are in. Others have symbols of sacred prayers upon them as well."

She told me to take care of myself and follow my instincts, as she stood up extending her hand to me with her palm forward she said.

"*Anasgáti ekua didanádo adasehedi nihi*"

"This means, *may the great spirits be with you.*"

Veronica walked her to the door and hugged her as Lou came into retrieve her bags. Lou was a big strong fellow with muscles like Hercules. His voice was deep and stern. He nodded at me and I waved at him. He was a very intimidating guy; I don't think he even smiled.

I also needed to get home. Surely my parents were home by now. Veronica offered to take me home she said she has more research to do since AiYana is leaving. She also explained to me that the she felt that the spirit guides are with me, protecting me.

"Did you accomplish your quest in getting your answers?"

"No, I fear the deaths will continue to rise until the evil is stopped."

"What about the bodies that go missing after an attack?" She paused for a moment.

"There are things that have the power to turn someone into the attacker." She went on to say, "I had heard strange rumors that bodies were missing from the morgues around town. I fear that we will find whoever or whatever is responsible soon enough."

As she drove I stared out the window, thinking about my life and how deep down I could feel something deep within me changing.

"Veronica, do you honestly believe that I am the key to all of this?"

Shaking her head she said, "No doubt, kid. We watched to see what would happen since your attack and so far you are still human. Besides, you must follow your destiny, where ever it takes you."

I turned to look out of the window again; we were almost to my house when I forgot to check my cell phone to see if anyone had called. Sure enough, I had a ton of missed calls.

Now I knew I was in big trouble. Mom and dad are going to kill me.

We pulled up to the house and luckily no one was home. I thanked Veronica and I told her that no one would know her whereabouts. She thanked me and, before she drove off, gave me a number. She said she would be close by if I needed her.

I told her I would hold her to that. As she drove away, she honked the horn; I waved then walked into the house. It was very quiet and peaceful.

Chapter Ten

CRIES OF THE WOLF

I checked the messages on my phone to see what I had missed. My parents had stated that they would be home late tonight; Tony called several times as well as Elsha. I wanted to tell them what had happened but I promised Veronica I wouldn't say anything.

Before returning Elsha's or Tony's call, I contacted my parents. According to their messages, lightening struck one of the towers so they were not able to use their cell phones. With mom's strict instructions however, I was told to leave a message telling them both that I was okay and did not burn the house down.

After nearly being killed by a pack of wild wolves, rescued by a woman who I had been searching for, surely there is no doubt that my destiny is unfolding. Looking out the window, I could see the mail man doing his deliveries. It was Mr. Peterson. He was a nice old man.

Mr. Peterson had been with the post office since it opened. I remember when I was a little boy; he used to give me peppermints. He did that to all the kids in the neighborhood.

Mr. Peterson was a tall, thin man. He was bald on top and had sparse hair on each side. He wore glasses that made him look smart, like a professor. He was in great shape for his age; I remember he used to challenge the kids in the neighborhood to race him.

Everyone loved Mr. Peterson; he's nice to everyone. As he approached the house, I walked outside to greet him.

"Hi, Mr. Peterson. How are you today?"

Walking towards me with his bright smile he patted me on the shoulder.

"Well hello there Kyle, good to see you." I smiled and shook his hand.

Wiping the sweat from his forehead he said, "Doing well son, I'm glad to be back at work. Whew! It's a scorcher today."

"Yes it is. This desert heat is no joke. Are you ready to retire yet?"

"Nope, this job keeps me busy enough and I love to keep busy. I have thought about retiring but I would have to find a new hobby though."

He was a funny old man; I enjoyed talking with him he hasn't been around much I wondered if he was sick. I didn't want to ask so I made up something.

"So Mr. Peterson, I haven't seen you in a while. Were you on a different route?"

"No, young man. The wife and I went to visit the grandkids up in Utah for a couple of weeks. My son and daughter-n-law have a ranch house up near Payson Lake."

His story fascinated me, so I continued.

"Wow that sounds exciting, I'm glad you had fun and got the chance to see your grandchildren."

"Yeah Kyle, Payson Lake can be a good getaway spot."

"Did you get the chance to get some fishing in at the lake?" I remembered that Mr. Peterson enjoyed fishing. He'd been on a few trips with my dad.

"Oh yes, plenty of fishing, rest and relaxation until, uh, well...." Mr. Peterson stopped talking for a moment. He seemed a bit disturbed.

"Mr. Peterson, are you alright? Did something happen?"

He scratched his head with a puzzled look.

"Well it was kind of strange. My son and I were out on his balcony just talking and then we heard the strangest sound. It was almost like a wolf baying at the moon, the moon was not even full though. Strangest thing I'd ever heard had the dogs barking all night."

I wanted Mr. Peterson to tell me more.

"Did anything else happen that night, did you hear any other sounds?"

His facial expressions told me that something else did happen that night. He looked as if he'd saw a ghost.

"Well the oddest thing about it was the way they cried, like they were calling to something. I know it sounds hard to believe so we started to investigate. My son grabbed his rifle and I grabbed my shotgun. We told the women to stay inside and bolt the doors. Before we could get out the door though, the noise had stopped. I mean it was dead silent, not one sound."

I was intrigued by his story; I could tell that he was shaken up too. Maybe it was nothing at all but perhaps just nature doing its thing. But the look on Mr. Petersons face told a different story.

"So you're glad to be home?" I tried to change the subject.

"Yeah son, I'm glad to be home. You know, that is one night I will never forget. It's funny though. We stood outside for almost ten minutes looking like night guards, defending our territory, and heard not one sound. The night was so still and quiet, you couldn't hear anything."

I just had to ask, trying to play it off as if I didn't know what he was talking about.

"What do you mean, the night is always quiet."

Mr. Peterson dropped his head, his eyes peeking over the top of his glasses and said.

"Not this night. When you live around nature, you hear every cricket, frog, or any other critter running around. But on that night, it was dead silent. Like I said before, we stood there on guard and I could swear something was watching us; I could feel it in my bones."

I could feel the coldness come over me as Mr. Peterson continued to talk. He told me there was usually plenty of commotion because his son has a lot of cattle and horses.

However on that night, he and his son could feel something eerie in air.

Shaking his head back and forth he said.

"When nature stops talking son, something evil is on the move."

He continued as he handed me the mail.

"Well son enough of my ghost stories, time for me to get back to work, this mail isn't going to deliver itself you know."

He walked away smiling and greeting the neighbors on the sidewalk.

As I went into the house, I thought about his story and had no doubt about what he and his son had experienced. The last twenty four hours have been unbelievable. It just kept getting better and better.

I felt a little tired, but wanted to do more research. I sat the mail on the table and an article from the local news paper caught my eye. It was about local hunters setting traps since more wolves have been spotted.

There have been reports of wolves crying throughout the night. There were reports as far as Montana, Wyoming and even Utah of howling wolves causing quite a disturbance. Some authorities have ignored this stating that it's just the nature of the wolves.

Even a local zoo reported they could not get their wolves to calm down. One worker reported that the animals just went crazy one moonless night.

A few scientists have decided to travel to some of the sights to record the sounds. Some, however, have been denied access due to private property. Others have reported a change in the activity of some of the wolf packs.

As I read, all of the reports were similar. Wolves howling in the night, for hours at a time, one scientist reported the cries of the wolf seemed scarier. Some natives considered the wolf song as music, but not lately. It seemed different somehow.

They described the wolf cry as more of a deep growling sound; it was a sound they had never heard before.

However people have been warned not to approach any wild animals.

As I read the paper I checked for other articles to find any similar stories. To my surprise, there were more about missing people, even the discovery of more mutilated bodies. I cringed at the thought. Fear was spreading across the land and people were still dying.

I couldn't help but think about my close call with them; I could have been wolf food. I decided to go to my room when the door bell rang.

Perhaps it was Mr. Peterson forgetting something; then again who knows.

I opened the door and to my surprise Elsha and Tony looking at me with scolding eyes. They walked in quickly, Elsha started the conversation, upset that I had not returned any of their calls. I spoke in a calm voice and told them both that I was okay.

"Why are you so upset? I am a big boy; I can take care of myself."

"I know you are a big boy. I just have important news and we need to talk; haven't you been watching the news?"

Shaking my head at them both I replied, "No, I didn't watch television last night; I was busy. What's up?"

Tony walked over to the table to pick up the remote and turned on the TV.

Breaking news was all over the network about the attacks. Police Chief Morgan was about to address the community about the most recent attacks.

Elsha looked at me with her arms folded.

"I'm glad to see you…I was a little worried," She let me know. Tony said the same as he punched me in my shoulder.

"What's been happening?" I had to ask them.

When I was at Veronica's I knew there were more attacks but not here in town but in Oklahoma. Tony started to talk when Elsha interrupted.

"Hey, quiet! My uncle is talking, listen."

We all sat down on the couch and I turned up the sound on the television. Police Chief Morgan was about to give a press conference about the recent events. I nervously sat and listened as he approached the podium.

Chief Morgan, his brother Dr. Morgan was by his side, thanked everyone for attending the press conference. He asked everyone to hold all questions and comments until his statement was finished.

He stated that during the recent events around our town and neighboring states they first thought they had a serial killer on their hands. Giving the timeline, and after working with fellow law officers, they now have come to know what or who they are dealing with. He went on saying how within the last twenty four hours there have been twelve deaths reported all happening at the same time. He had the sound of frustration in his voice as he explained.

"Unfortunately this is not the kind of news we like to report, however we must continue our jobs as law enforcement to serve and protect. From what we know, we are dealing with an occult the murders took place almost simultaneously and we feel that whoever they are may strike again."

I must have been shaking; Elsha held my hand and whispered.

"I'm scared, Kyle...really scared."

Police Chief Morgan continued.

"The town curfew will remain until the perpetrators are caught."

There were a lot of reporters in the crowd, eager to get answers, once Chief Morgan had finished the question poured in.

One reporter asked, "How do you know that it is an occult group committing these murders?"

"We know because of the timeline of the death of the victims. They all also died the same way."

"Chief Morgan, you say the deaths occurred at the same time, could this be a religious group sending a message, or someone trying to confuse law enforcement?" Another reporter asked.

"Well until we obtain more information, we are talking with religious leaders and keeping our eyes and ears open. We are encouraging everyone to report suspicious activity."

I could tell that this was getting to him; it was difficult for him to answer the questions. Chief Morgan responded to one last question.

"Chief Morgan, I heard that one of the victims survived an attack. Can you give us any information at all? With the recent deaths of two tribal elders in Poteau Oklahoma, are these attacks connected somehow?"

Chief Morgan cleared his throat but Dr. Morgan interrupted quickly.

"Yes, the victim did survive the attack; however, the victim is in critical condition. We cannot release the name of that victim until the family has been notified. And, as far as we know, we need more information before we can connect these attacks."

Dr. Morgan stepped away from the podium as Chief Morgan came forward, telling everyone to keep watch and secure their homes.

Before closing the press conference, another reporter quickly asked another question, changing the atmosphere of the press conference. Something about this reporter though seemed different and looked very familiar.

"Chief Morgan, can you tell me if this is an attack on Native Americans only? Since these attacks began, all of the victims have been of Native American descent."

I leaned forward whispering under my breath.

"It's her; it's Veronica."

Chief Morgan adjusted his tie, cleared his throat and harshly responded, "We are not trying to start a worldwide panic here; we are keeping the identity of the victims and their families safe. I can't say if there is someone out there targeting just Native Americans."

Turning his head toward the camera he sent a serious message.

"Whoever you are, we will catch you! We will prosecute you to the fullest extent of the law!"

Chief Morgan walked away from the podium as the reporters kept prying for more questions.

I turned off the television and sat quietly for a moment. I wondered why Veronica came out to the press conference. I wondered why now? I thought she was in hiding. I sat there trying to figure out why she would come out in public this.

"Are you okay?" Elsha seemed to have seen that I had a confused look on my face.

"I'm fine..." I just wanted all of this to be over.

"I have new information but if you're not ready for it, I understand." Elsha sat down next to me.

"I can't stop now. It's my destiny to keep going and the more answers the better."

Elsha went on and pulled a folder out of her bag.

"My research has led me to believe that we are not the only ones seeking answers about the killings." She started to explain.

According to Elsha's research, the person who owns the mysterious car yet remains a mystery. Aside from that though, she received a message from Professor Jones; she stated that she was in town completing her research and wanted to meet with us later.

Elsha went on to say that Professor Flynn's discovery has led her to our town where her great ancestor might have disappeared. She told Professor Jones she would contact her when we were ready.

Tony also stated that it would be a good idea for all of us to get together and compare notes. I looked at Tony with a shocked look on my face and said.

"Now that's a good idea, it just might be what I need."

Elsha replied by saying, "It will be what we all need. I want to know more about the land were my house is. I know that my research about Jeremiah Flynn has a lot to do with that cave."

"What makes you so sure? He disappeared decades ago." I turned to her and said.

"I'm sure," Elsha replied, putting her hands on her hips. "Because what other reason could Professor Jones be here. She has been searching for answers which have brought her to our town. Why would anyone come to a place where people are dying and missing? It all makes perfect sense."

"You'd be foolish to come to a place where mutilated bodies seem to be the number one topic," Tony agreed with Elsha.

Elsha was right; it was time for us to get together and compare notes. We would be helping Professor Jones continue her research regardless; but, I just hope she wouldn't think we were crazy.

"I'll contact her and set up a meeting," Elsha told us.

I wondered if I could also get Veronica involved in this meeting as well.

"Can you take me home so I can gather all of my paperwork," Elsha asked Tony.

"Sure, should we meet at the library?"

"I don't think so; we needed to meet at a more private place… where we won't be disturbed." I explained. "I'll call you guys in a couple of hours with a location. I have a few phone calls to make first." They both agreed but Elsha gave me a very strange look. "What is it now, why the strange look?"

She only stared at me for a moment before turning to Tony.

"I'll be a minute," she sent him on his way before walking towards me with her arms crossed.

"What are you up to? We always meet at the library. You're hiding something from me, aren't you?"

Shaking my head, I assured her I wasn't.

"I just want to be in a more private setting. We have a lot of work to do and no one needs to know what we are doing."

I could tell that Elsha still didn't believe me. If Tony wasn't honking the horn for her, she would have hounded me with more questions. Elsha was just like her uncle Police Chief Morgan, when it comes to asking questions.

"I'll wait for your call," she told me as she left.

I just had to be sure my plan would work. I just couldn't tell Elsha and Tony what that plan was yet.

After they had left, I started gathering everything I had. My notebook, the video I took from Dr. Hill, the envelope I received from Benjamin, everything I could think of I packed into my backpack.

"Now to make a list of who I want to be at this meeting and the first person in mind is Veronica. Her place will be perfect for this meeting."

I gave her a call but only seem to get her voicemail. I settled on leaving a message. I only told her that is I wanted to meet and that had some very important information that would help her in her research.

Then it was onto Ms. Creed; I hoped that I could get in touch with her. I sent her an email explaining that I had vital information and needed to meet with her right away.

As I finished, my cell phone rang; it was Veronica.

I quickly reiterated my message and asked her if I could meet at her place.

Through the past years Veronica has kept a low profile up until her public appearance at the press conference. I still wondered why she did it.

Regardless, she agreed to meet with me and that she would call to give me specific instructions and directions since I was sedated and blind folded when I was first taken to her place.

I still needed to make a few more calls though.

While I waited from a response from Ms. Creed, I noticed an envelope on the floor. Being in such a rush I must have dropped it while putting things in my bag. I picked it up and remembered it was from Benjamin. He had gained access to the archive room on the reservation and sent me some information he felt I needed to know.

One of the items was a report about the adoptions and the names of the parents that had given up their children.

It was reported that the children were illegally adopted from the reservation but according to this report, that was only partially true. Another report listed the names of parents and their children's birth records. My hands started to shake, holding the paper in my hand I could feel my body break out in a sweat.

This is the moment I had been waiting for; my life has been filled with unanswered questions about my past and where I come from. This was my time to discover who I was; I couldn't help but wonder why Chief Spearhorn would keep this from me.

I kept reading and found several names of parents who gave birth to children around the time I was born.

The birth record stated that there were two twin boys born to a couple by the last name Tsosie from Great Falls, Montana. I looked through my bag to search the newspaper article to see if they were connected to this story. And, to no surprise there was an article along with a full page report dated July 10th 1995.

According to the police report, the injured bodies of a young couple were discovered on Canyon Creek road near mile post thirty-one. They were traveling north when their vehicle struck some kind of animal. The driver of the car must have gotten out of the vehicle to access the damage only to be attacked. The local authorities are not sure if the attack came from the wounded animal or another

The woman also got out of the car to assist him when she was attacked as well. Also traveling on the same road that night were a group of hunters returning home from a trip. They came across the scene and they reported seeing huge wolves leaning over the injured man and woman. Not knowing if the wolves would attack them one of the men immediately grabbed a shotgun from the gun rack in the truck and fired off a few rounds.

This startled the wolves and they ran off into the woods, there was no sign of the injured animal the couple struck with their car.

The other men got out of the truck with rifles, loaded to stand guard just in case the wolves tried to attack again. The others loaded the injured man and woman onto the back of the truck and rushed to a nearby hospital.

The hunters reported the accident to the local authorities. The man had a gaping wound on his chest and was losing a lot of blood. The hunters noticed the woman was pregnant and also had a wound across her abdominal area. The police investigated the crime scene and found no sign of foul play.

After reading the article and the report I just had to know more, could this be my parents? So many questions plagued my mind. I searched the envelope to see if there was more information but there was nothing. I had to find out more about what happened that night so I decided to pay Benjamin a visit. I only hoped he was at his tribal shop.

I grabbed my bag and rushed out of the door.

While driving to Benjamin's, I thought about my birth parents. None of the reports stated if they were alive or dead. Perhaps Benjamin could shed some light on things for me; he has helped me since I was little. I arrived at the tribal shop, praying he was still there. I went inside and there was a lady behind the counter.

"Can I help you young man?" She asked with a smile.

Calming my nerves, I approached the counter.

"Yes ma'am, I'm looking for Benjamin. Can you tell me if he's still here?" She was very nice, pointing to the back of the store she replied,

"Yes, he is here. You can find him just through those doors."

I nodded, and thanked her as I walked towards the back of the store.

Benjamin was unloading boxes with another worker. I didn't want to disturb him but I just had to talk to him. I cleared my throat to get his attention. He looked up at me with a surprised look.

He greeted me with open arms and much excitement. I was glad to see him too. He instructed his worker to finish unloading the boxes and met with me in his office.

Benjamin came in sat down and placed his hat on the desk, leaned back in his chair.

"So I see you received the information I sent you. Your presence here lets me know you read the article and reports."

As nervous and anxious as I was, I replied slowly.

"Yes, I read the report; but, I need to know more about my birth parents. That's why I'm here."

Benjamin smiled at me.

"I knew you would follow your instincts and come to me. It wasn't easy getting access to the archive room; it is only used for research of family history. There many sacred documents that they keep protected."

Benjamin told me he always knew there was something about me that night I came into his tent. After watching me that night, he said there was no doubt that I was one of the missing children.

Benjamin stood up to walk over to his file cabinet, unhooking keys from his belt he looked at me.

"Kyle, I know what you are going through is a lot; but, what I'm about to show you I pray it will give you peace and help you move forward."

As Benjamin stood there, I could tell this was also affecting him as well. He almost seemed as if he didn't want to show me. He also had a compelling look on his face. He proceeded to unlock the cabinet and took out a box; it was very old and dusty. He sat down in his chair looked up at the ceiling.

"Ekua didanádo adanedi ayá nulinigágá"

Benjamin was just as nervous as I was. He placed the box on the desk in front of me.

"I knew this day would come… one day I would have to tell you about your family."

I just wonder why Chief Spearhorn was so secretive. He was definitely hiding something but what I wonder.

As I watched Benjamin open the box, his hands were shaking.

"Are you alright?"

"I'm fine." The memories inside the box were coming back to him. He then started to tell me what I had longed waited for.

He pulled a photo out of the box, stared at me for a moment without a word. His eyes were filled with sorrow and joy. Then he stared even harder at me as if he saw something in my eyes. It was the same look my mother gave me when she swore something in my eyes moved.

This made me nervous and I didn't know how to respond to him. He looked at the photo, then again at me, what was he doing? Who was on the photo? I wondered. Then Benjamin sighed, shook his head.

"You have your mother's eyes."

He slid the photo across the desk in front of me, and for the first time, I saw my mother's face. She was so beautiful, just like a flower that blooms in the spring. She had a smile that glowed like the sun, and her hair was long and black like silk.

Benjamin left the room to give me a moment alone; he told me he would be back in a moment. I sat there staring at the woman who gave birth to me; I didn't have time to think about why this has been held from me for so long. Now I knew who I was and where I come from.

I wonder what my birth name was or if Eric even knows about her. Anyway, I have come so far in searching for the past that I now finally have received the truth.

Benjamin entered the office and asked how I was doing. I told him I was speechless and didn't know where to begin.

"Well then let me start since I owe you an explanation anyway." he started as he took a seat.

"Explanation, you don't owe me anything, it is I that owe you a great deal of thanks. Ever since I was little you have always watched over me, helping me discover who I am. That night inside your tent I felt so safe. I knew something was after me but I did not know what it was. But something inside me told me I was safe with you. You don't owe me anything at all."

Benjamin smiled at me, shaking his head again he said.

"Yep, you are definitely your mother's child."

Laughing at him I replied, "Now what's that supposed to mean?"

Benjamin stood up and said.

"Come with me; it's time I tell you about your parents."

We walked outside to the back of the store Benjamin said he wanted to take me on a short drive. I got into his truck, which by the way was very nice. Benjamin drove a silver Dodge Ram fully loaded with navigation system, satellite radio. It definitely had all the bells and whistles you could pull a house with this thing; it was so huge.

Benjamin was not a small man so I guess a guy like him needs a truck like this.

I told him how much I admired his truck. He told me that he liked it too and that he took it off road sometimes when he went fishing. He continued to drive and we continued to talk about things that we liked to do. I told him how I always enjoyed the outdoors. Then I asked him how he knew my birth parents.

"They were very special people, very active in the community and always helping others."

I could tell it was difficult for him to talk about after reading about the accident there was no information about how they died.

As Benjamin drove he took a side road up a mountain. We drove up and around curved bends way into the hills. We came to a spot that overlooked a scene right from a post card. I was amazed at how beautiful it was. I had never been up here before so I was a little curious.

"So what do you call this place?"

Benjamin looked at me with a smile on his face.

"It's my backyard."

As we got out of the truck, Benjamin pointed to the view. He stated that the land belonged to our ancestors and how this property was a part of his backyard. I was amazed at this; I could not believe it. He said for generations they fought the government from coming in and taking the land from them.

They wanted the land as is. Many companies had offered millions for it but he would not sell. He believed that the land was meant to be left alone for the animals to roam free in their own habitat. If developers came in they would destroy the land, pollute the air and contaminate the water. The animals would be driven out and into communities where people live; therefore, some things are just better left alone.

I couldn't help but agree.

"Why did you bring me up here?"

"Follow me," was all he said as he led me through the woods on a small path.

At the end of the pathway, we came across a little valley of flowers and huge rocks with streams of water coming out of it. This place was breathtaking; I was amazed at how peaceful it was up here. I stood there overlooking everything and said.

"This place is so beautiful and peaceful."

Benjamin walked toward me putting his hand on my shoulder.

"That's what your mother said; she liked it here too. I remember the first time I brought her up here. She had the same look on her face as you do." He pointed to a big rock and spoke again. "Come sit down, son."

Chapter Eleven

CRY OF THE WOLF PART II

I sat down on a huge rock that looked like a throne; Benjamin sat across from me on a little handmade rug. He took a straw from his hat and put it in the corner of his mouth.

"It's time for me to tell you who you really are. Back then though, I, he had to be sure you were indeed one of the missing."

Before he got started he crossed his legs and, with both of his hands up he prayed to the heavens. He thanked the spirit guides of our people for bringing me to him. As he prayed, the wind blew a soft breeze and eagles flew overhead announcing their presence.

It seemed like a déjà vu, straight from one of my dreams.

After Benjamin said his prayer, he began by telling me about my mother.

"She was a very loving person. Ever since I'd known her, she had such a graceful presence about her. When she was little, I used to bring her and the other kids from the community up here for a little field trip."

In the words of Benjamin, my mother enjoyed the outdoors and she loved nature. She used to pick flowers to make hair pieces for their festivals and carnivals. She could light up any room she entered.

"Her name was AdSilah. It means *blossom*," He told me. "It matched her personality as well as her beauty."

With such sincerity he continued to tell me how much he enjoyed watching her grow up into a beautiful young lady.

"Some of the local boys used to fight over her. Not because she was beautiful but because she was smart. She had no problem showing how strong she was, out hunting the other kids. She had a fire inside her that no one could tame, until she met your father. He fell in love with your mother the first time they met. They were a match made in heaven; he loved and respected her from day one."

He smiled as he explained to me. "And she played hard to get."

I couldn't help but laugh while Benjamin talked about my parents. She reminded me of another woman I had heard about: Lei'Liana.

I listened as Benjamin continued.

"After your parents were married they moved to Montana. Charley, your father took a job working for an oil company but the two vowed to keep in touch. AdSilah always told me that her heart, as well as her spirit, would be in this place."

He looked around as he spoke.

That was why he named it after her, in her honor. Benjamin called it **atsilásgá Ama Ganugogá** which meant *Blossom Springs*. That was why he brought me here; he said it was what she would have wanted.

"She felt connected to this place and he felt that her spirit was here. AdSilah told me if anything ever happened to her she would want to be buried here. She spent a lot of time here when Charley's job had him away on assignments."

Benjamin took a deep breath as a tear rolled down his face. He turned his head away from me looking in another direction saying,

"She knew something was going to happen to her. When she found out she was pregnant she was both happy and sad. When she got the ultrasound she was happy to see life growing inside her; however, she knew she was going to be in for the fight for her life."

"What do you mean?"

I asked as I looked over him. He went silent for a moment.

"At one of her doctor's visits, the ultrasound showed a dark spot near the fetus. The doctors didn't know what it was but he said it shadowed the fetus. It was too early to tell but they thought it was the machine but that was not the case."

Benjamin never looked me in my face. His reply was a chilling one that brought back memories and opened up old wounds.

"Kyle, one night I got a call from Charley saying that AdSilah was experiencing horrible nightmares. There were times that he had to wake her up from her sleep. There were also times that he couldn't."

I had that feeling coming over me again; I slowed my breathing and kept calm. Benjamin continued on telling me about that night Charley called him about AdSilah.

"Kyle, your father was so scared that night. When AdSilah would wake up she would scream out,"

He explained.

"*You will not take my baby from me,* was only one of them. Charley didn't know what was happening to her. He thought perhaps she was under stress about the ultrasound so he took her to see one of the tribal elders to get a blessing."

As curious as I was I had to ask him.

"What happened to my mother? Is she dead?"

Benjamin just told me to hold on, that he would tell me about her. I guess he wanted to break it to me as gently as he could.

"The nightmares continued until Charley took her to see Chief Ahwahnee one night."

Before I could ask Benjamin said that Chief Ahwahnee was known as one of the spiritual leaders on the reservation in the foothills of Montana.

Charley took AdSilah to see him to seek his guidance out of fear for his wife and unborn child.

They arrived on the reservation and met with Chief Ahwahnee. He told them he would perform a spiritual ritual over AdSilah, other tribal elders joined him and prayed the sacred prayers over her. He said that as the elders began their prayers, they were halted by a strange disturbance.

Raising his staff over her, he told Charley that his wife and unborn child were in grave danger. An evil entity is trying to destroy the unborn child.

Shocked at the news, Charley told the elders about the dreams AdSilah was having. The elders had explained to Charley that he must leave his home and take his wife to see Chief Spearhorn. He would know what to do.

As the Elders prayed, the sounds of wolf cries were off into the distance despite the moon being only half full. Charley needed to hurry. Charley was told that the great spirits would guide him and that the child his wife carried was special.

The elders looked at AdSilah and were all startled by what they saw in her eyes. According to Benjamin, AdSilah's eyes were shifting from deep within. The elders told her that she must fight to save her unborn and that her time was very close.

AdSilah explained her dreams to the elders. She told them how she saw a man who stepped into the night cloaked in darkness. His eyes peering through the night like stars.

She said it looked deep within her and she felt paralyzed as if this creature was looking deep within her soul. She explained to them how hard it was to turn away from him. He spoke in a growling tongue and she said she could feel her unborn child shift inside her.

The elders continued their prayer but, as the night grew darker and quieter, they stopped. Charley was told that the balance in the air was stable for the moment, but it wouldn't last.

"That is why they were coming here to Patagonia; they were escaping,"

Benjamin explained.

"Your mother's nightmares were getting worse. She started to lose control of herself, saying that she could feel evil following her. One night Charley heard her screaming and ran to see what was wrong. By the time he had entered the room, AdSilah's arms were stretched across the bed, she tried to move but couldn't."

He told me that she raised her head, speaking in her native tongue asking the spirit guides to help her. Charley could even feel an evil presence in the room. There were imprints on the bed where she laid but they were not hers.

Startled by this, I interrupted.

"What did Charley do?"

"There was nothing he could do. His wife was being attacked by something he could not see."

Benjamin went on telling how Charley stood there in horror watching his wife scream out. He rushed to her side only to see her belly moving up and down. He thought she was going into labor but whatever this evil was it was surely trying to kill her.

He grabbed her silver stone off the nightstand and held it up. It glowed very bright that night. He moved toward his wife and it seemed to drive out the evil.

Once AdSilah's arms were free, he grabbed her and left immediately.

Benjamin explained how Charley called him and told him what was happening. Charley told him that they would be leaving immediately. Benjamin told him it was too dangerous and that he would come to them but Charley disagreed. There was no time and the elders demanded that he bring his wife to see Chief Spearhorn.

Placing the stone around his wife's neck, Charley grabbed what belongings he could and left. Charley drove all night until they were about ten miles from the reservation. Benjamin went on saying that Charley called him to meet him at the front gate. He asked how AdSilah was doing. Charley said her stone had not stopped glowing since they had left. It had never seen it do that before.

Benjamin rushed to meet them when he heard AdSilah scream.

"Charley watch out!"

Then there was a loud crash. Benjamin's voice trembled as he explained the horrifying details. He drove fast to get to them but, by the time he had got there, the only thing he could find was the car wreckage.

Blood was all over the ground. The police told asked him if he knew the victims. Benjamin explained that he did; he was coming to meet them near the reservation. They told him the victims were taken to the local hospital.

Upon hearing this, Benjamin was on his way. When he arrived at the hospital, Charley had been taken to the emergency room. According to the doctor on call, he had a gaping wound on his chest and he'd lost a lot of blood.

AdSilah was taken away as well; apparently she had suffered the same injury across her abdomen.

Benjamin struggled to talk but he pressed on.

He said they had to perform an emergency C-section on her. She too had lost a lot of blood. While Benjamin was waiting to see about AdSilah, he got word from the surgeon that Charley had passed away during surgery.

Another doctor had also approached him about AdSilah; he was told that she was in stable condition but not out of the woods yet. When Benjamin asked about the baby, the doctors said that they were fine. One of them had suffered an injury during the attack and was sent to a pediatric trauma unit.

This made Benjamin worry because the doctor told him that one of the babies had a rare blood type and his body was rejecting the blood transfusion.

Benjamin was confused. He told the doctor that AdSilah was only carrying one child. The doctor informed him that, unless he was just hiding, this must be a miracle baby. She gave birth to two twin boys. One of the babies was in ICU, we have named them babies A&B so we can identify them.

Benjamin was allowed to see AdSilah but only for a moment. He went in to her room to see her laid there with tubes hooked up to her. He sat down next to her and started talking.

I sat there soaking all of this in; it overwhelmed me a little. I was puzzled by Benjamin and just had to know more. Who was Benjamin to me? Why did he go through so much trouble to tell me all of this? I didn't know if I could take anymore. I had to ask him about his relation to Charley and AdSilah. Before I could, however, he stopped me. He said I needed to hear him out first.

Benjamin went on. He told me that he sat there talking to AdSilah, letting her know that he was at her side. He said that AdSilah recognized his voice and she spoke softly to him in a whisper. She asked about Charley and Benjamin told her not to talk. She also asked about her babies but the nurses came in and Benjamin had to leave.

He stayed at the hospital all night with AdSilah and prayed. Benjamin watched over her until morning. When she was strong enough to talk, she had a few last requests. While at her bedside she asked for her sons so she could properly name them.

The nurses brought them in and she named Eric first, she stared at him crying and called him "Jonathon Michael Tsosie" his native name was "**ganayegi sakuu**" meaning fierce one.

Benjamin said when they brought me in AdSilah screamed out in pain. She said her dreams were real, she knew she had another child within her so she named me "Charley Benjamin Tsosie" my native name is "**asuyedá sakuu**" meaning chosen one.

Benjamin explained that AdSilah stared deep into my eyes for a long time. Whatever was in her was now in me. AdSilah's last request was for Benjamin to care of us, he promised that he would always watch over me and my brother.

She asked for her silver stone to be held up in front of her, but Benjamin did not have it. He asked the doctor for her belongings and the nurse came in with her purse and a few other items.

Benjamin looked inside and found her silver chained necklace with the stone around it; it was much larger than any he had ever seen before. AdSilah wanted Benjamin to give me her journal. She always kept it with her. She also wanted my brother to have Charley's silver stone as well. AdSilah requested that Benjamin hold the stone up to her head so she could look into it.

Benjamin knew she was slipping away, he really didn't want to tell me but he had to keep his promise. He went on saying that when he prayed, AdSilah asked the great spirits to carry her spirit into the sacred stone so she could watch over her children. While doing so, however, her eyes were changing; they were getting darker and this had Benjamin worried.

He spent as much time with her as possible. Though her life was fading away, her will to stay alive was still strong.

Holding the stone closer to her; he pressed it into her forehead and spoke in his native language. She fought hard with her last breath, saying she could see the great elders sitting on the wings of eagles coming for her.

She sang a song, *"The eagles have come to carry me away"*.

As the tears rolled down her cheeks, she closed her eyes for the last time and died. Benjamin told me she fought to keep us alive; he said they never saw the animal; it just appeared in the middle of the road.

Benjamin said he knew it was the Suhnoyee Wah that attacked them. Looking at me with teary eyes he said.

"That's why I brought you here, she wanted this for you. Your mother is here with us."

Benjamin pulled a small black pouch from his pocket and took out a silver necklace. Placing it around my neck he said

"This stone is of our people, my **ayoli tsulitsyasdi.**

"This means, young brave."

"Before your mother died, she asked the spirit guides to link her soul to the stone. This is a gift from her."

The stone was beautiful. Overwhelmed with emotions, I fell to the ground and cried. My puzzle had come together. Remembering something from my dream, I spoke.

"It was her all the time guiding me away from the shifters in my dream. There was a white mist guiding me the whole time."

Benjamin placed his hand on my shoulder telling me how she much she loved her children. I questioned him about Eric again.

"What about Eric? Why he didn't get the stone?"

Benjamin explained.

"Because I was the strongest and she knew I was in her womb even though the ultrasound showed one baby." Looking at me he said. "That is why she called you her special one, her gift. Your mother believed the great spirits sent you here for a purpose. Your destiny awaits you, my son."

I looked at Benjamin and asked him what did AdSilah mean to him? What was she to him that he took the time to look after her so much? Placing his hands on both my shoulders he said.

"AdSilah was more than just another child I watched grow up; she was my great niece, which makes you my great nephew, my family."

I backed away from him slowly shaking my head I could fell a wave of emotions come over me.

"Why? Why now, you knew this whole time and you tell me this now! Why Benjamin? Why?"

He replied by saying.

"I had to be sure it was you. Something happened after your mother died. Since I was next of kin you and your brother were supposed to be placed in my custody."

Shocked by this news, I asked Benjamin about it.

"So what happened? Why were we separated at birth?"

Benjamin paused for a moment then he told me how my brother and I disappeared during the burial ceremony of our parents.

He said while both my brother and I remained in the hospital, the doctors noticed an abnormality in our blood. It caused us to stay in the hospital a while longer. The doctors couldn't understand why there were more than three blood types in my system.

Though we were born healthy, they wanted to run more tests, but Benjamin refused. They explained that it was the only way to find out how and why. Benjamin would only agree until after the burial ceremony of our parents.

So my brother and I were placed temporarily in states custody and were to be taken to the reservation until custody could be given.

There had been rumors and talks of wolf attacks and strange things happening to people in our community. It was only then that Benjamin heard the rumors of people starting to disappear around town. Therefore, he thought it would be safe for us to leave. Natives were afraid that the legends about the Suhnoyee Wah were coming true.

The ceremony took place here in Blossom Springs, AdSilah's favorite place. He continued to tell me when our people die their bodies are washed in lavender and oil to clean away the impurities. Then they are wrapped in sacred white sheets. An eagle's feather is then placed on the body, before it can be buried. Benjamin said all burial ceremonies must take place at sundown so the bodies can be given back to mother earth.

As Benjamin talked my mind reflected on my dream of a man being burned alive. He was so full of anger and rage, that he did not get the type of burial Benjamin was talking about. I wondered since this type of burial was custom, who chose to burn Li'wanu at the stake? He died such a horrible death; but, in the midst of him dying something dark and scary hovered over his body.

It transformed him into the night; he was dead but yet alive. I shivered at the thought of it.

I managed to focus back on Benjamin; I did not want to think about that right now. He continued telling me that on the night of the burial ceremony. Sacred prayers were spoken over the bodies of my parents. Then they were buried here in a sacred garden of my mother's favorite flowers.

Benjamin pointed to a small path that was just beyond the big rock that looked like a throne.

"Follow the path of flowers and there you will find their grave stones," he told me as he looked over. "I will give you a few moments then come back for you."

Wiping away the tears, I was trying to be strong.

"Thanks, uncle. This means a lot to me."

"It means a lot to me also son," he told me as he placed a hand on my shoulder. "I must go get my radio from my truck; I will return momentarily."

I walked down the path and came to a tiny grave site. The trees were covered in vines and had beautiful flowers on them. Two huge stones on a rock wall marked the spot where my parents were buried. The rays of the sun shined on them both. The wind blew softly. I did not know what to say. I fell to my knees.

Each stone had their names carved in them with sacred symbols on the top and bottom. They were diamond shape stars circling the moon. I had never seen this symbol before.

As I placed my hands on both of the stones, a wave of emotions came over me. I cried and cried. I pulled their picture from my pocket and rubbed my finger over my mother's face.

I know they were beyond this world but, I talked to them any way.

"Hi mom... hi dad. I'm your son, Kyle...well Charley Benjamin Tsosie. I'm sorry I don't remember you but I know you are watching over me. I wish you both were here. I could use your help right now."

It was hard to talk without getting choked up again, there were no more words I could say; all I could do was just cry.

Just then, a breeze came and covered me like a blanket. It felt like someone had their arms around me.

With the sun shining through the trees, I could feel the warmth and a sweet presence embraced me. As I cuddled the ground and lay there, I listened to the wind very close. It seemed to call my name. I closed my eyes and focused on the voice in the wind. My body fell into a trance; I could feel myself floating into the air.

I opened my eyes to see a place so serene and wonderful. Bright lights were all around me. I was standing in a meadow filled with tall grass with tall trees all around. I remembered this place from my dreams. Looking toward the ground, I could see a white midst at my feet. As I followed it, I came to the edge of the forest.

There, a tall man stood in full native attire. His headdress was filled with a rainbow of eagle's feathers. The head of an eagle stood out from the base. Around his neck he wore a beaded white and topaz necklace.

His jacket and pants were decorated in all types of symbols with tassels hanging from the side. His caramel colored skin was painted with brown and white stripes and his eyes were bright like copper. In his hands, he held a staff with a huge round stone at the top.

I slowly walked closer to him in small steps. With his arms crossed over his chest with the staff I stopped in my path. Looking upon him, I could see he must have been some type of warrior. Reflections of the moon and stars were in his eyes. As I stared deeper and deeper until I saw what looked like reflections of me.

It was as if I were staring into a mirrored image of myself. He did not move only he stood there like a guard on post. Then without warning he spoke.

"My young one, who do you seek beyond the boundaries of the dead?"

I nearly jumped out of my skin, he scared me. Struggling to talk I said.

"I, I don't know, where I am. Or what I am doing here. I was called to this place. Who are you?"

Looking at me he spoke words of an ancient language, more and more I could understand the meaning of it but only in my dreams. He told me he was one of the many guardians at the gates of the spirit world. He told me it was not my time to be here, only those who have crossed over shall pass the realms. I told him I was brought to this place and did not know why.

Nodding his head he said.

"Your spirit is very strong. You also bare the gift of the moon and stars. Only the chosen ones have the gift to see beyond the realms of earth."

Looking at him with curiosity I said.

"What does that mean?"

He uncrossed his arms and held the staff out in front of me. The silver stone around my neck began to glow. He told me to look deeper and watch closely.

"The stone you wear around your neck, is a symbol of our people, centuries ago seven were chosen to place their souls in the sacred stones to expose the evil that tries to harm us. All that you need is in you, trust your heart and remember the ways of our people."

The more I looked into the round stone; it felt like something was pulling me deeper inside of it. Unable to break free, I fell into a realm of moons, stars and clouds. Spiraling downward I landed on what appeared to be a space a rift between two worlds. Clouds and stars filled the sky were me. As whispering voices grew louder around me, the stars began to form silhouettes of two bodies.

Then within a blink of any eye AdSilah and Charley stood before me smiling. I became paralyzed, unable to move. There were no words to speak; I just stood there staring at them both. AdSilah approached me placing her hands on my face, her touch was soft as silk, and her smile was brighter than the moon.

Charley placed his hand on my shoulder and said.

"My son, my heart rejoices to see your face."

Still speechless, I could not utter any words to say. Overwhelmed with emotion, I could not believe what was happening. This was surely a dream; AdSilah looked at me with tears streaming down her face and said.

"Asuyedá sakuu asdá adanádo adasehedi"

Which means, "Chosen one of the spirit guides"

"My son, we have watched over you all of your life. You are the special gift that hid inside me. It is your destiny to fight against the evil one. We love you and always will. Keep your stone close to your heart it holds a great power."

My head filled up with so many questions to ask them both. I didn't want to wake up from this dream. I wanted to stay here with them forever; both of them must have read my mind because Charley said.

"No, son your place is not here. It is time for us to go now."

As they both turned to walk away I said to them.

"No! Please don't leave me again; I have so much to ask you." AdSilah turned to me placing her hands on my face.

"No dear, we are always with you, but it is not safe. You must go."

She paused, looked up to see the stars shooting across the sky, then her countenance changed.

"Son, you must go now. Remember we love you; you will see us again."

They turned and walked away, I tried to follow them. I needed to know more, and something prevented me from going any further. I took another step and fell through a cloud then I found myself back at the grave site. Trying to remember everything AdSilah and Charley told to me, I looked at the tombs and shouted.

"I wish you were here, I don't want this, any of this!"

Feeling my grief turn to anger, I beat my fist against the stone, and screamed out loud. As the sun hid behind the clouds, darkness was soon near. I could hear the sound of a wolf off in the distance. I didn't care; I was stricken with grief so I yelled out again as loud as I could. The louder I yelled, the more the wolf cried, this time it was different.

This cry was more of snarling and growling. I rose to my feet, and trembled with fear, I looked at my stone and it did not glow.

I followed the pathway back up to where I entered to look around. I reached for my phone to call for Benjamin but I must have left it in the truck. There it was again, louder and deeper, it seemed at first the wolf cry did not bother me, but when I heard it the second time something changed. I decided to walk back to the path Benjamin showed me, the wolf cries seemed to be getting closer.

I had to get out of there and quick, the sky looked grayish, something was different. The wind blew a little stronger and then it hit me. The smell of burnt flesh was in the air, from what direction I could not tell. Fear and panic was settling in on me, turning around in circles I tried to find the path that lead out of the clearing when I found it. I walked as fast as I could.

Slipping on rocks, I tried to keep my balance; the sounds were getting closer and closer. Hurrying down the side of the mountain, I slipped and fell on my back, looking up into the sky; I swore I saw the sky moving. The smell was getting stronger and stronger. I could hear noises in the wind, like in my dreams.

I felt compelled to get up and keep moving, just as I reached the bottom; Benjamin met me with a disturbed look on his face. He asked me if I were okay and I told him we must leave this place now. Benjamin looked over my shoulder and said.

"Yes it is time to go. Something has shifted in the atmosphere and it is not safe here."

The look in his eyes, were very disturbing. His eye brows came together and he gave a mean look as if someone or something was standing behind me.

"Benjamin, let's go. Come on, we've got to get out of here." I tugged on him as I spoke.

Benjamin looked as if he saw something; he slowly walked backwards handing me the keys to his truck. Looking in one direction he stopped moving.

"Get to the truck as quick as you can. Whatever you hear, don't get out! Go now!"

Not knowing what to do, I ran back down the hill to the truck. I did not know what was happening but I was afraid for Benjamin. I did not want to leave him, but I trusted him.

Chapter Twelve

THE HOUSE GUEST

Once I reached the truck, I locked the doors, everything was so quiet. Just as the clouds covered the sky, the wolf cries started up again. They sounded like they were calling out to something. I worried even more about Benjamin.

I wondered what he was doing, even though it had only been a few minutes it felt like hours. I wondered what he was doing up there. Then I heard something hit the back of the truck making a loud noise. Gripping my stone I softly whispered.

"Benjamin I sure hope that's you."

I turned around to see what it was and no one was there. As I slowed my breathing, I could hear my heart beating very loud. I spoke softly to myself.

"Calm down, Kyle, just calm down."

Looking around, I could see the clouds dropping; it appeared like fog all around the truck. I could see something glowing as it moved toward me. It looked like eyes peeking through the clouds. I looked around the truck to see if Benjamin had a weapon of some kind. I checked the glove box and found a handgun I kept it close to me.

As whatever it was got closer, I realized it was Benjamin, he jumped in the truck and sped off real fast. I asked him what was wrong and he just kept driving. Once we were back on the main road Benjamin pulled off to the side and parked the truck.

He placed his head on the steering wheel mumbling something. I called to him.

"Benjamin, hey uncle are you alright?"

Benjamin noticed I was holding his gun. He gently took it out of my hands and said.

"You might want to give me this, it's still loaded."

Surprised at myself holding a loaded gun I said.

"Oh sorry, what happened back there? Why are you acting so strange?"

Benjamin relaxed himself and pointed toward the sky.

"Look there; tell me what you do see?"

I looked up toward the sky to see the thick clouds moving swiftly across the sky. Only they appeared to still be dropping though we are no longer in the mountain.

"The sky looks weird; the clouds are moving fast and falling settling over the mountain."

Benjamin replied.

"Those are more than just clouds moving, evil is moving. I apologize for not coming back sooner; I had a few important calls to make."

I told him that was fine; it was nice to have time alone to say hello and goodbye. However, I wanted to share with Benjamin what happened up there but I think he already knew. I watched him as he kept his eye on the sky, he whispered something and I asked him if we were going to stay on the side of the road or keep moving.

Then he said.

"**Asegi ganolásgi agasgi.**"

I replied.

"What does that mean?"

"It means *strange storm* surely something is coming, I can feel it."

Benjamin started the truck and headed back to his shop so I could get my car. He told me when he was a little boy, his father and grandfather said they could tell when something bad was going to happen. The sky always told the story, even though Benjamin kept saying, the words strange storm.

He even told me there is a legend of a man, a dark skinned man who is said to be wandering the hills casting spells to protect the chosen ones. He said some claimed to have seen him in their dreams or even in the hills.

Benjamin says his father and grandfathers claimed that when a strange storm is on the horizon he appears in the hills and sometimes you can hear his prayers. Some believe that he is one of the guardians left to live his life on earth to protect us from evil spirits. Others say that he is one of the guardians of the dead.

Benjamin says his eyes are crystal blue and he has ancient symbols tattooed in his skin. Benjamin had no idea I too have seen this man in my dreams and each time he has helped me. That's why I have decided to tell him about my encounter only it wasn't an encounter just the smell of danger.

Once I got up the nerve to I told him about my experience, and how I saw Charley and AdSilah. I even explained the man dressed in native attire, and how I felt my spirit leave my body only to be in a place between space and time.

When it was time to come back that's when I noticed the smell and the strange storm approaching. Benjamin said he was in his truck and noticed the clouds settling on the mountain where I was and headed up the hill when he heard the wolves. Benjamin said he could feel something was not right and had to get to me as quick as he could.

I told him, I knew they were close because of the smell of burnt flesh but it was hard to tell which direction. He said when evil is near it's in every direction; he knew I would be safe going back to the truck alone. I asked him why he ordered me to the truck alone, the look in his eyes was kind of scary. Benjamin said he vowed to keep his promise to my mother AdSilah that he would watch over me.

He said he could smell the evil in the air. I asked him why he ordered me to leave. He said I have a strong connection with the spirit world. Something about my blood also has me connected to the Suhnoyee Wah. Benjamin said the claw marks on my back are a true sign that whatever evil is lurking around it wants more of my blood.

I looked at him saying.

"What do you mean?"

Benjamin answered slowly.

"The blood that is in you runs deep within our heritage. When Running Bear was killing anyone who defied him, he would cut off the head of his enemies and drain their blood. He felt that if he drank the blood of his enemy it would make him stronger."

I told him I remember reading about this. So then I asked him something else.

"What does he want with me? I know my blood is different, but what is so significant about it?

Benjamin replied.

"He wants your blood because it is a part of him. No one knows what real type of blood you have. Only a true test of your blood will tell."

Now this conversation is getting weird I dared to ask but I did any way.

"Test. What test?"

Benjamin said it was a test that would prove the strength of the blood line. When a brave was born or when he reached a certain age the elders would cut a line across his hand into a bowl filled with sage leaves. They would then let the blood drip until all the leaves were covered.

Once this was done they would blow smoke from a chanupa pipe over it then light it. If the flames rose high, it meant the bloodline is powerful and would be for generations to come.

This same ritual was done between blacks and Native Americans centuries ago. To test the strength of our races it was proved through the blood. That is why when blacks and natives intermarried; the elders would perform these rituals to test the strength of the bloodline.

They believed there was such a strong connection between the two races, that no matter what happened as the world changed, the two would always come back stronger together. The flame would tell, even through the children.

Benjamin said he believes, my blood is the same way. That's why he has to protect me, even if it means dying for me. I told him not to talk like that, sometimes it's hard to believe all of this is happening but he assured me that nothing would happen to me as long as he was around.

I thanked him for that, but I told him the look he had in his eyes earlier was very threatening, and I wondered what took him so long. He said sometimes you have to stare evil in the face and let it know that you are not afraid.

Benjamin seemed very different, I told him I also saw the dark skinned man in my dreams, which brought back a memory of a woman giving birth to two twin boys. Benjamin asked me to tell him of this dream so I did. He said going back in history, from what he read and heard, a fierce warrior kidnapped the daughter of one of the Tribal Elders, but what they didn't know was that later on she would become pregnant.

Chief Wah'tayo knew that War Eagle was very fond of his daughter. So for his bravery she was given to him for marriage. I asked Benjamin was this true or just another legend. He asked me when I dreamed about it did I believe it. I told him yes I did. I told him I felt as if I took a step back in time. I didn't know what it meant then, but I do now.

Then he told me that he believed the story to be true. Once we got back to the shop, the hour had grown late and I needed to get home. Benjamin said he would follow me home just in case. I told him it was not necessary, but then again I knew he was going to do it anyway. The sky was covered with dark clouds and the winds were blowing out of the north.

Before I drove off Benjamin gave me my cell phone, I must have left it in his truck. I headed home and of course Benjamin followed, by the time I had made it to my house he parked his truck behind the car. He told me he would call me later and said he enjoyed spending time with me then he said.

"You sure have your mother's eyes."

As Benjamin drove off I went inside to relax awhile before returning any calls. Mom and dad left a message they were on their way back from the cabin and would arrive late. But before I did, my body told me I needed to eat something. The way my stomach sounded I needed food and fast.

I went into the kitchen, sat my phone down and listened to my messages as I fixed myself something to eat something didn't feel right. Elsha was right on top of things of course; she had managed to get Professor Flynn to meet with us. All I needed to do was get everyone else on board. While in I was in deep thought about my day, the beeps from the microwave reminded me my dinner was ready.

While I retrieved my dinner from the microwave, suddenly I had an odd feeling come over me, the kind of feeling you get when you are not alone. I tried shaking it off but I just couldn't, my gut instincts told me that something was not right.

I walked toward the den, until a dark shadow caught my eye near the corner of my mother's curio cabinet; with trembling hands I grabbed a baseball bat from the closet. I could see the shadow moving across the floor. I moved my hand along the wall trying to find the light.

I slowed my breathing, and walked slowly into the dining room. The sounds of little whimpers and heavy breathing came from over by the window. I called out.

"Who's there? Is anyone in here?

Not a sound. I found the light switch and when I flipped it no light. I forgot dad needed to replace the fuse for this room. When I went to move in closer, something dashed by me fast in the dark.

I followed it into the living room only to discover a little girl crying behind the couch. Turning on the light and looking at her tear soaked face I spoke to her.

"Are you okay, how did you get in here?"

She had a terrifying look in her face; I laid down the bat, keeping my distance from her. She had to be around seven or eight years old, her hair was long brown, curly and she had big brown eyes.

I sat down on the floor and said

"My name is Kyle, I live here, and you're safe now. What's your name?"

She didn't move or make a sound, the look in her eyes told a frightening story, and the little girl was scared. I didn't know what to do, I heard a car outside then the garage, my parents have returned home.

I didn't move I wanted to keep the little girls attention, she was already scared, I told her that my parents have returned home and I needed to meet them. Her eyes were so full of fright, whatever scared her had her in serious shock.

My parents called out to me and I told them I was in the living room, but they needed to walk in slow. Then I heard my dad say.

"Kyle, did you know the back window is open? We sure don't want anyone breaking into the house."

So that's how she got in. I explained this to both of them as they walked into the living room that our guest was already here. When they saw the frightened little girl, instantly my mom moved toward her.

"Well who have we here?"

Still scared and in shock, the little girl backed up against the wall, digging her nails into the carpet. Then dad looked at me asking who she was. I told him I didn't know I found her like this. Mom was worried about her; she noticed the sleeve on her dress was torn.

Dad stepped out of the room to call the police, as he walked out of the room I heard him say.

"This has been some kind of night."

I wondered what he meant by that, I would have to ask him later. Mom also left the room to get the first aid kit. She told me to stay close to her until she returned. This little girl was so frightened I doubt that she would let anyone close. She started crying as she looked around the room.

I sat down on the floor and told her how afraid I was when I was little, not wanting to disclose much to her I said sometimes things happen to us that scares us, even in the dark. And when I said the word dark, her eyes widened and she softly cried out.

"Please don't let it get me, please help me."

I had a feeling I knew what she meant, whatever it was scared her so bad it traumatized her. As both my parents re-entered the room, they saw her crying, mom wondered if the little girl would allow her to get next to her. Dad said the police were on their way and would be here soon. Looking at me he whispered.

"I wonder where her parents are. Poor girl must have been through hell."

I couldn't have agreed with him more. As mom moved in closer to the little girl she knelt down toward the floor. Trying to communicate with her she extended her hand out to her.

"Honey, I know you're scared, but you are safe now. Tell me, what's your name?"

The little girl looked at me and I nodded giving her a friendly gesture that it was okay. She looked around the room, then at my mom and said.

"Becca, my name is Becca."

Mom replies.

"Is that short for Rebecca?"

Becca slightly shook her head no and said.

"No ma'am, just Becca."

Mom smiled at her introducing herself.

"Well Becca, my name is Helen."

With her hand extended, mom asks Becca if she was hungry and she said yes. She takes her into the kitchen to give her some food. Dad asked me how long had I been home I told him not long. I asked him how were things up at the cabin and if it was okay he said there had been reports of bears invading cabins searching for food.

Dad said that didn't bother him so much it was the wolves that gave him the creeps. Surprisingly I looked at him asking him what he meant. He said the rangers stopped by the cabin to tell them that along with the bears there had been reports of wolf sightings in the area and we needed to take precaution.

Well dad said he didn't think anything about until one night he couldn't sleep because of the storm. He said he there was something very odd that night. The wolves must have been gathered on the ridge high above the cabin. He said it sounded like hundreds of them howling at once.

He then retrieved his gun from the gun rack in the living room; he said mom was still asleep. Not wanting to alarm her he closed the door to the bedroom and walked toward the back door. Peeping out of the window he could see movement up in the hills, the moon was half but bright enough for him to see.

He said the more the wolves howled, the more they gathered as if they were calling out to each other or something else.

He said there was a weird feeling in the pit of his stomach that told him it was time to leave, but the storm knocked out the power.

Dad said he was glad he installed custom wood indoor and outdoor shutters that would completely cover the windows on the inside and out. He must have made a lot of noise due to the fact she woke up asking him what he was doing. Then she heard the noise from outside and asked what it was, dad told her to stay away from the windows.

He didn't want to alarm her but the sound of the wolves already had her nervous. Dad described the sound as eerie cries. He said it sounded like the wolves were crying out to something, the more they gathered the more the sounds increased. Dad explained how his fear began to grow as he closed the shutters.

He wanted to get out of there and fast, as he listened to the radio he could hear other people talking about the wolves. Hunters had set traps to capture them so people were warned to stay inside their cabins for the night due to the slick roads that could cause a slide offs down the steep canyon. So that's why they stayed another day before driving down the mountain.

Dad shrugged his shoulders scratching his head he looked into the kitchen at mom and Becca, and then he looked back at me and said.

"Did she say anything to you?"

Looking just as surprised I said.

"No, dad the only thing she said was….she was too scared to talk."

After I responded I thought back to my childhood and how scared I was when *I* felt no one would ever believe my story. I had a feeling this would satisfy him but I don't think it worked. Dad looked at me and started sharing his feelings about me when I was little. He said he didn't believe me when he asked me about Becca.

Dad told me one night when I was about five years old he found me sitting in the corner of my room with my nails clawing in the carpet. He turned to me and said.

"Son, I knew something was wrong with you that night, so don't tell me that little girl in there didn't tell you anything."

There was no pulling the wool over his eyes so I replied.

"What do you mean dad."

He asked me to sit down in the living room for a little chat while we waited on the police to come. I sat down on the couch, placed a pillow on my chest and leaned back while dad talked.

"Son, there is a scared little girl in there and I know what's wrong with her."

Dad looked over his shoulder at mom and Becca; he didn't want to talk too loud so he just lowered his voice a little. I sat and listened to more of what he had to say. Dad continued.

"Kyle, whatever that little girl has been through, somehow I feel you can relate to her."

Surprised by what he just said I asked him.

"Relate to her how, what can I do for her."

Then dad said.

"Son, something sure scared the hell out of that little girl, she had the same look on her face just as you did the night I found you in your room."

I leaned forward and thanked him, sometimes when you see something so scary it is hard to talk about. Dad interrupted me for a moment telling me there was more he wanted to share with me that mom doesn't know about.

I looked at him asking him what he meant. He said, while listening to the radio he heard Chief Morgan's press conference about a possible serial killer on the loose. He said he tried calling me but he couldn't get good reception on his cell phone service.

Dad sat there and told me while he was out fishing at the creek he felt as though he was being watched.

He looked through the trees and thought he saw something but shook it off. Then he said he heard another weird sound, a sound of a wolf howling at first then something else.

He said it was so weird it sent chills up his spine, never before had he ever heard anything like that and never wanted to hear it again.

He said for years people have claimed to have heard Bigfoot not that he believes in it but strange things began to happen in the hills that night.

Dad said he kept his eyes on the sky and watched the clouds settle down on them like fog; whatever those wolves were calling out to it must have come through that. Because he could have swore he heard growling and snarling moving in it.

As he headed back to the cabin he ran into Mike Reeves, a good friend of his. Dad said Mike ran past him so fast he almost knocked him down.

He said the look Mike had on his face was as if he saw a ghost. It was the same look Becca had on her face. Dad said he asked Mike if he was alright but he just kept running, looking over his shoulder.

Something in his eyes told me he was scared out of his wits. Whatever he saw, or encountered in the woods scared the living daylights out him. Dad tried to reach Mike on his radio but didn't get an answer.

Dad decided to head back to the cabin to check on mom, everything was okay when he arrived but he was worried about his friend. When they were leaving, he noticed Mikes truck was still parked at his cabin he wanted to check on him so he knocked on the door and called out to him but he didn't answer.

Mom asked if everything was okay but dad didn't want to alarm her but he told her what happened at the creek. She agreed with him that something weird was happening up in the hills that was creeping her out especially the eerie sounds coming from the woods and the wolves.

So they decided to come home once the cabin was sealed tight and the roads were clear and safe.

The sound of the doorbell told us that the police had arrived; dad and I went to answer the door. Police Chief Morgan arrived with a few of his officers and asked to see Becca, we led them into the kitchen and Chief Morgan talked to her. He asked us if she told us anything or where her parents were.

Mom told the police so far we knew nothing about her. So Chief Morgan asked to speak to mom and dad alone. I stayed in the kitchen with Becca to keep her company looking at me with her big brown eyes she said.

"Is the police man going to take me away now? I don't want to go outside."

I was glad she was talking but I needed to know what scared her.

"Why? No one is going to hurt you."

With her saddened eyes she held her head down and started crying again. She struggled to talk I told her to take her time. Then she revealed what happened.

"We call them *el, noche Diablo,* the night devils."

I encouraged her to go on.

"I was playing in the park when."

She stopped, looked around and said.

"Los lentes oscuros son suyos. It means I heard a voice in the dark.

This did not surprise me at all; this little girl was so brave to open up to total strangers. I just had to ask her how she got into the house and what happened to her.

She said she was in the park playing with her parents when the she saw the storm coming. Her mother told her to gather her things and take them to the car, it was then she heard the voices and remembered the stories her grandfather used to tell her father.

As she was putting her things in the car, she heard her parents screaming, the night swallowed them and she said she could see eyes peering through the night. She ran as fast as she could and did not look back. She said her father always told her if anything was to happen she was to run.

Becca was trying to be strong; she looked at me and said.

"I ran as fast as my papa told me, I didn't know where I was going I could feel them following me, so I saw the open window to your house and hid hoping that el noche diablo wouldn't find me."

Then she started crying again, not knowing what to do I went to comfort Becca and she leaped into my arms. I put my arms around her and told her she was safe now. I heard my parents and the police enter the house and they saw me holding her.

She took Becca and said she was going to take her upstairs for a while, to get her to calm down. Dad asked me to sit down while Police Chief Morgan had something to say.

"It's good to see you again Kyle, I wish under better circumstances though."

I told him it was good to see him again as well. He asked me if Becca had told me anything about what happened to her. I only said that her parents disappeared and she was left alone and scared.

Chief Morgan took off his hat, scratched his head and explained the details.

"I hate to be the bearer of bad news, but about an hour ago, two bodies were found up past the park deep into the woods. We believe they are Becca's parents."

I sat back in my chair, while silence filled the room. Chief Morgan said someone reported screaming coming from the woods and when his officers arrived on the scene they noticed a car in the parking lot with the door left open. They ran the plates and found it was registered to Albert and Sonja Pedina.

Chief Morgan believes Becca saw her parent's murdered and would like to talk to her but he wanted to see if she had disclosed anything to me first. I told him perhaps he should talk to her. Helen came back down stairs with Becca and Chief Morgan said he wanted to talk to her alone.

He takes Becca into the living room to talk when his cell phone rings. He answered his phone, and then he breathed a heavy sigh. He told Becca to stay put on the couch. He walks back into the kitchen very disturbed. Dad knew something was wrong.

"Frank what's going on?"

"Sorry to have to do this to you all but....Tom, Helen. I don't know how to say this but. The park rangers just found another body up at Mountain Peaks. It appears to be Mike Reeves."

Dad drops his head; mom puts her hand over her mouth.

"Oh, my dear God, no. Mike. Poor Charlene and the kids must be devastated!"

Dad told Chief Morgan what happened when Mike came running by him. Chief Morgan asked dad to come down and give a statement. He also asked if Becca could stay with us until her next of kin could be located. He also asked them not to say anything about her parents he felt she had been through enough.

Mom said that would be fine, she asked me to take Becca upstairs for a moment while she spoke with Chief Morgan.

"Frank what is going on around here?"

Frank responds.

"I don't know, I wish I knew my officers have been busy trying to solve cases they can't even explain."

Dad told Chief Morgan he would meet him down at the station in a little while. With a frightful look on her face, mom was not too happy with dad at all. He knew she was upset about Mike and wondered why he didn't tell her. He explained she was scared enough up there and did not want to make matters worse.

He told Helen, the last time he saw Mike he was running away from something, whatever or whoever it was must have scared him. He thought perhaps he was being chased by a bear, but there was nothing behind him.

Dad told Mom not to worry, which he knew that was going to be hard for her to do. Before he left he asked me to make sure the house was locked up and to double check all the windows and doors. He was also worried about Becca; mom said she would take care of her. He kissed her on the cheek and said he would return later.

While dad left for the police station, I kept Becca company for a while as mom searched for clothes for her to wear. I wanted to make her feel comfortable so I asked her questions like what her favorite games were, what type of music she liked. She just shrugged her shoulders and said she didn't know. Her parents didn't allow her to watch much television.

She stared at me for a moment with an odd look on her face.

"You have strange eyes, not like most people do, but different."

I smiled at her.

"Yes, I get that a lot."

Becca was still trying to be brave and hold back her emotions. She was also a little curious about me as well.

"You've seen them haven't you, your eyes tell a story."

Her glaring look, sent chills through me, I asked her how could she tell. She said her mother had the same gift. She could look at a person's eyes and read them. She explained it was kind of hard to explain but you will know what a person has seen. Then her countenance changed.

"They're not coming back are they…my parents are dead."

I didn't know what to say to her, I sat there hoping for a miracle. Becca cried again mom must have heard her and came and sat down beside her. Comforting her she told Becca how difficult this must be for her. Then she took her to get her ready for bed. With so much happening the time really went by fast.

While mom took Becca to her room I prepared the guest bedroom for Becca to sleep. Thoughts went through my mind about everything that happened today. Then I realized Becca was just like me, she too had seen the shifters and she was terrified. She witnessed her parents snatched by the darkness then come after her.

Once I finished the room I went back to mine. Then something on my dresser reminded me about a soon coming event. The bonfire on the reservation, I think this would be great for all of us. Becca could sure use some cheering up though. After a while dad returned home, mom stayed in Becca's room until she fell asleep.

Later that night I thought I heard the faint sound of crying. Mom must have heard it to we went into Becca's room and there she was underneath the bed. I called out to her and she said she was scared. Mom decided to stay in the room to comfort her, it brought back memories of my childhood and how scared I was. I knew what she was going through, and I really felt scared for her. Perhaps a night on the reservation will make things better.

With strange things happening once can never tell.

Chapter Thirteen

NIGHT DEMONS

This is it; the day I was waiting for had finally arrived. I was going back the reservation once again to see everyone including Chief Spearhorn and my brother Eric. Though thinking about it had me very nervous and a little scared. I wondered how Big John and the others were also doing.

I decided I'd better pre-pack for my trip. It's funny how things happen in life. You try to figure out why dreams haunt you, only to find out who you really are. My life has surely changed since all of this has happened.

Now someone else is affected by it, after last night I couldn't help but worry about her. Mom slept in Becca's room all night, poor girl it took her forever to fall asleep.

Perhaps dad was right; maybe I can help her with her nightmares, I know how terrifying it can be to see something or not see something trying to kill you.

I'm also worried about dad as well; he just lost a good friend of his. Last night he got in late, and asked how Becca was doing. I told him how mom stayed with her all night until she fell asleep. I asked him how Mike died. Dad went very cold; he swallowed hard then clearing this throat.

"I just can't get over the look he had in his eyes, the man looked as if he'd saw a ghost. The look Mike had sent chills through me."

Dad was very bothered by this. I didn't know what to say, but I thought it was time to tell dad what I think that killed his friend. But before I did I again asked him how Mike died. He told me they found him in the woods lying against a tree. Park Ranger noticed his truck still parked in front of his cabin. They were making sure everyone was leaving the mountain before any mud slides happened.

As dad talked he trembled he said someone else must have seen Mike running; he never made it back to his cabin. When they found him, dad couldn't go on any further. He just said it must have been a wild animal attack. Dad sighed deep as he tried to tell me more. He said the police think they have a serial killer on their hands.

My gut instinct told me dad thought something else. He said he was going to visit with Mike's family and help them out for a while. He asked where mom was and I told him she decided to take Becca shopping this morning to buy her some clothes. He said the Police couldn't find any next of kin at all so she will have to stay with us a little while longer.

I told dad mom how mom was doing a great job taking care of Becca, she seems to be doing okay but she has her moments. Dad was headed out to Mike's place to meet with his, while on the other hand I also had a few things to do today as well.

I decided it was time to check my emails and messages, Ms. Creed agreed to meet along with Veronica. Now I just needed to contact Elsha to see so we could get everyone together. I also called Benjamin asking him if he could pick me up later. So many things ran through my mind. Eventually I am going to have to introduce my parents to my family. I just need to wait for the right time to tell them, with dad mourning the loss of his friend, and mom taking care of Becca; I figure it's just better to wait. Perhaps after the bon fire would be a good time.

I picked up my phone called Elsha and of course she was on one again. She told how she had been speaking with Professor Flynn and she has new information. The meeting would take place today around noon.

She asked if anything interesting was going on with me and I told her she should know me by now something is always happening to me. She laughed and said she would see me later. Something about her just warms my heart, her voice, and her looks.

Since the first day we bumped into each other our worlds collided as if it was our destined for it to happen.

While I packed a few things for the meeting, mom had Becca returned from their shopping trip. Police Chief Morgan was right behind them; he parked his patrol car and met them in the driveway. Mom told Becca to go inside and wait for her because the nice policeman wanted to speak with her alone for a moment.

I heard Becca come into the house, it was nice to see her smile, but yet she was still sad. I asked her how she enjoyed her shopping spree; she told me how mom let her pick out a few of her favorite things. Becca was very brave; I couldn't imagine what it would be like to see your loved ones taken away from your right in front of you. She looked out of the window at mom and Chief Morgan.

"Have the policeman come to take me away now?"

Looking at her, I wasn't sure what to say.

"I'm not sure Becca, we will have to wait and see. Don't worry; things are going to be okay."

Becca frowned turning her face away from me.

"I know my parents are dead, they are not coming back. That thing took them because."

Becca stopped talking and held her head down again. I encouraged her to keep going and that she didn't have to be afraid. Before she continued mom and Police Chief Morgan came into the house. He wanted to talk with us and Becca dad had also just arrived to pick up a few things he had borrowed from Mike, he wanted to return them to his wife.

Chief Morgan said it was good we all were together, he told us throughout his career as a police officer has faced many things in life. But the hardest part about his job is telling someone their loved one is gone. Chief Morgan sat down and asked Becca how she was doing. Becca just shrugged her shoulders telling him she was okay.

Chief Morgan sat down next to Becca and took off his hat. Before he could tell her the truth about her parents she showed great strength and told him what she already knew.

"You don't have to say anything; the great eagle took them away to their final resting place."

Chief Morgan was surprised at how she knew her parents were dead. This gave him relief and then he asked her how she would like to stay with us. Becca smiled and told him she would like that very much. Mom and dad felt since Becca had no other family would she have to go to a foster home. Chief Morgan told them that a social worker would contact them soon to get the paper work started.

Mom and dad looked at me and asked me how I felt and I told them I was okay with it, besides it would be nice to have a little sister around. Becca was happy that she didn't have to leave. Mom and dad asked me to take Becca to her room and help her put her things away while they spoke with Chief Morgan.

Dad wanted to talk to him about Mike. I walked Becca to her room and hung out in the hallway. I wanted to listen to see what Chief Morgan had to say, something told me there was more going on out there. As I stood in the hallway, I overheard Chief Morgan tell mom and dad that he sent a few officers to Becca's home and his officers will bring some of her things.

He said he feels Becca may need counseling because of what she has gone through. They both agreed that they will get her help. I hope it was not to Dr. Hill, I will not see her go to the crack pot of a doctor. That uses little kids nightmares to further his career. The more I listened more I could hear dad telling Chief Morgan that Mike's wife and kids are holding up but they are seeking answers.

Chief Morgan said his officers are doing everything they can to keep our town safe, however he feels that the curfew may not go away and will remain in place. He can't stress it enough for people to be safe then he said something that shocked me.

Chief Morgan said he was having a hard time explaining the unexplained. Even we as The Chief of Police even he does not have all of the answers. He talked about the gathering on the reservation and stated he even sent Chief Spearhorn a message to cancel the event.

But it got him nowhere, he was told that all of the reservations are on alert but local police have no jurisdiction on the reservation unless a crime has been committed.

After listening, I learned that there was going to be a town meeting a little later and he wanted my parents to be there. Dad asked him if there had been any leads in the case, but Chief Morgan said right now they are calling it an animal attack.

Dad asked about Becca's parents and he said the case was identical. Then he said something else.

Chief Morgan said according to the coroner report, all of the victims died the same way. When they were found, their hearts were missing. The Chief feels there is a serial killer out there outsmarting the police.

He also said that he wonders if Becca saw her parent's killer, or killers. Just for safety he was going to place an unmarked car in front of the house as a precaution.

Dad told him that was not necessary, but Chief Morgan insisted. He didn't like the idea that they have so many cases and not one lead.

And this made him very angry, everyone wanted answers. He told them the town meeting would be at the local library around noon.

They told him they would be there but only for a short while since they too had an invitation to the reservation. By this time Chief Morgan received another call and had to leave, he said he would check up on Becca and gave them a few numbers in case they needed help.

Dad asked mom to accompany him to Mike's house to help Charlene move some of Mike's things. She was moving out of town to stay with her sister. Mom asked how she was holding up and dad said Charlene told him how for a week Mike couldn't sleep. She said he keep saying he was seeing strange things in his dreams, things he couldn't explain.

Then dad asked mom if Becca had told him anything about her parents or if she saw anything. Mom said no, Becca just gets quiet and doesn't say much. Mom feels she will talk when she is ready.

After standing in the hallway, I turned to see Becca standing there looking at me. She was looking very scared; I should have stayed in the room with her. I wondered how much she heard, by her expression everything.

I put my arm on her back and took her back to her room. I looked at her and tried to comfort her, but Becca said she knew how Mike died. I asked her how and she said the same way her parents died.

I told her she didn't have to talk about it but she did anyway.

"I heard your dad say Mike had bad dreams, he was dreaming about the night demons."

I sat there listening to this little girl talk to me about dreams and night demons. She was so discrete giving me every detail about them. I wondered how much she knew.

Becca continued.

"I heard my mamma and papa talking about the night demon one night. They worried about me because I saw them in my dreams too. My mamma told me I have a special gift that would keep me protected."

Becca talked more about her parents. She had the same dreams as I did. How she survived that night is a miracle within itself. She said she felt safe around me, but also felt danger following me. Becca had a special gift to sense danger, but I wondered how much. Earlier she explained why she stopped talking; she said she knew why her parents died. I asked her to continue.

"My parents died because the night demon told me he was going to take them. He came to me in a dream, there was a dark mist moving all around me. I couldn't see its face. All I could see was its eyes glowing in the peeping through the night. Then it spoke to me and told me I wouldn't be able to save them."

I could see how this made her sad, but she was yet strong. As I sat there listening I realized that Becca was just like me. Perhaps destiny brought us together, but I yet wondered how many more of us are there out there. I told Becca she was very special and how I found her gifts to be very unique.

Then she asked me about my nightmares and I told her I would tell her some other time.

As I stood up to leave the room Becca told me something that stopped me cold.

"You can't run from them you know, they will find a way to get to you."

Then I turned around to face her.

"What do you mean?"

Becca starting drawing circles in the floor with her fingers as she talked. Her eyes fixed heavily on me; she seemed to be in a trance.

"Your blood is as strong as others, but different. To kill a shifter you must be as one, move as it moves, see what it sees, and know what it knows."

Her prophecy was strong; she spoke of things I did not understand. I know my blood is different but she didn't know that. She went to say more, but her trance was broken by mom entering the room.

"Kyle, honey your father is calling for your please go to him before he blows a gasket."

She asked how things were going with Becca and I told her we were just bonding.

I quickly ran down stairs to meet dad, he was in the garage moving boxes around. I asked him what was he looking for and he said an old key. He located a box on the top shelf removing a silver key. I asked him what was the key for and he said it was to and old safe he had.

Dad unlocked the safe and took out a thirty-two caliber pistol. He said he was going to give it to me as a graduation present. But felt it was time to give it to me now. He also got one for mom as well.

"Son before you leave I want you to have this. Just remember to take the safety off before using it okay. There is just too much happening and I want you to be safe."

I told dad, that the gun was not necessary but I didn't want to start an argument. He insisted that I keep it in my car. He had it registered awhile ago and said he will do anything to protect his family. Now that Becca is staying with us we can't be too careful, if she did see something someone may be looking for her.

I told him I had a ride to the reservation, he thought perhaps with Tony or Elsha; I told him that Mr. Benjamin from the antique shop was taking me. Dad thought for a moment then he remembered him. I explained to him how Mr. Benjamin has ties to the reservation and he agreed to drive me so I wouldn't have to.

Mom and Becca walked out into the garage to let dad know it was time to head to the town meeting. Mom asked if I was packed for my trip, she had such a worried look on her face. I reassured them I would call as soon as I arrived on the reservation. Mom still looked worried.

"Call me as soon as you get there so I will know that you are safe."

It was hard to tell her not to worry but that wouldn't do any good. She kissed me on my forehead and then they left. I double checked my bag to be sure I had everything I need for the road trip while I waited on Benjamin.

Later Benjamin phoned and said he was on his way. I called Veronica and asked her if we could meet up I had something very important to discuss with her but I needed to know if I could come to her house.

Since I was sedated and blind folded I have no Idea how to get there. She gave me an address giving me specific instructions on how to get to her place.

Once Benjamin arrived, I told him I would explain things on the way, but we needed to make a stop first.

Though it would take us a while to get there, we talked about the incident at the grave site. I told him about my dad's friend and how he was killed. Then I told him how strange the wolves were acting up at Mountain Peaks.

Benjamin was not surprised, he said there has been many things happening and we must stand together in order to defeat it. I told him how can we fight something we can't see?

Even though no one knew what was happening in our town. Benjamin said what we can't see is the gift inside of us sees it for us. We will know what to do when the time comes. I told him I hope he was right. Then I thought about Becca's prophecy and I had my answer. I asked him if he also heard about a couple that was found dead in the woods.

He said he also heard about that as well. Then I told him how I found Becca hiding in the house. I told Benjamin that she too has the same dreams as I do and how she called the shifter el noche diablo. Benjamin said there are many cultures that have different names for the Suynoyee Wah. It is still the same dark entity that has plagued our people for centuries.

The bloodline runs deeper that what I think. I told him I would introduce them later. He said he couldn't wait. Benjamin continued to drive while I called Tony, Elsha and Ms. Creed and gave them Veronica's instructions. Benjamin drove to an old country road with a huge lake. He asked me why I had him bring me to such a desolate place.

I told him this was a private meeting on private property and I felt it was very important that he learns what I have come to find out. Just then, we saw a car approaching, it was Tony, Elsha and Professor Jones. Shortly after that Ms. Creed arrived.

As Benjamin and I went to greet everyone, then a black sedan with dark tinted windows drives up toward us. Tony and Elsha look at me very strange. I told them it was okay and that I would explain everything soon.

Elsha gave me such a hard look, she hated when I kept things from her. But this is what we have been waiting for.

The car approached then stopped, the door opened and Lou stepped out. He asked everyone to follow him, but stay close.

We followed him through the countryside on an old dirt road. We came to a huge gate where we were met by a security guard. Waving his arms he ushered us through the gate as we drove up to a big beautiful mansion.

Once we parked our vehicles, Lou took us to the main entrance of the house, and to my surprise, AiYana was there to greet us.

"Well hello Kyle, it is very nice to see you again."

The last time I saw AiYana her great uncle's had been killed.

"It is good to see you again as well."

She invited us to come inside, and we followed her to a private room in the house. She opened the doors and there was Veronica waiting at a table filled with maps and books.

"Welcome to my home, I am Veronica Banks. Please sit down."

Everyone sat down at the table and began to properly introducing themselves. I started by thanking everyone for attending the meeting. I shared with them how important it was for us to meet since we all are trying to get answers.

Shocked by this, Elsha was not happy that I had kept this from her. I promised her I would tell her later but right now all of us must put our heads together and share what we know.

Chapter Fourteen

THE GATHERING

Elsha started off by introducing Professor Jones, as she did she passed around a book that seemed very familiar to me. Elsha must have worked hard on this. On the front cover was a photo of the cave and on the inside were the photos and symbols. She even had notes of the last whereabouts of Jeremiah Flynn.

Professor Jones was very pleased with her research; she even mentioned to Elsha how this was going to help her own research even further. Professor Jones explained to us how her research brought her to Patagonia. She said she was at a dead end until she received Elsha's package.

Veronica asked the professor what her ties were to our town, the professor told her about her third great grandfather Jeremiah Flynn who spent the majority of his life exploring caves and visiting native villages.

She felt that our town holds the clues to his disappearance. Ms. Creed asked why I invited her to the meeting, she felt her presence there might not be of any help. I assured her that her help would be greatly needed.

Since Ms. Creed was good at family ancestry I thought perhaps she could share any information on Jeremiah Flynn or the history of our town.

Veronica suggested we take a look at a map she had put together. She stood up, walked over to a wall and pulled down a huge map of the United States. Each red pin indicated how many people had died.

The blue pins marked the reservations. The white pens marked how many people are missing.

This sent chills through me. Veronica went on to explain how tribes from other states have arrived on the Spearhorn reservation not only to gather for the festivities but to hold a council meeting.

Benjamin stepped forward agreeing with Veronica.

"What she is saying is true, many of my fellow brothers and sisters are gathering on the reservation. Our people fear that a great evil has somehow been resurrected among us and it seeks to devour our souls."

Ms. Creed asked Benjamin will he be among those in the council meeting. He said he was not sure but he would be close by. The great elders will meet to discuss their plan; he called it the gathering of the great eagles.

Everyone had something to say at his meeting, talking about the symbols, to the lost tribes and the most recent deaths.

Professor Jones was more interested in the cave she asked Elsha if it were possible to take her there.

Ms. Creed suggested the cave be left alone, Benjamin also agreed. He explained that the cave almost took the lives of me and Elsha. Professor Jones indicated that she did not want to enter the cave, only to see it from the outside.

However Ms. Creed did have some knowledge about the people that dwelled there proving Elsha's theory. She told Professor Jones that her great ancestor was a true explorer. Looking at the book, she confirmed that the symbols were correct.

Ms. Creed went on to explain that centuries ago the Shahwanee tribe dwelled here almost in the same exact location as the cave. Since Kyle and Elsha's cave incident the cave has been sealed and is under heavy protection by Chief Spearhorn. No one is to enter the cave unless a sacred ceremony is being performed. Since the cave is unstable, it will be far too dangerous to enter.

As Ms. Creed points to the symbols she further explains their meaning.

"This symbol here of the wolf incased inside the circle means imprisonment. The diamond shaped stones are the ancient guardians. The diamond shapes represents a spell to keep evil entombed for all eternity."

Professor Jones asked why the symbol is in the shape of a wolf. Ms. Creed replied by stating long ago a great warrior named Liwanu fought and killed a giant bear. It was said that the spirit of the bear entered him which gave him great strength.

Ms. Creed went on explain to everyone how Liwanu would later fight off a pack of wolves some would say that he sustained some type of injury from the wolves. Professor Jones was fascinated by this.

She even told us how in her research she had heard many legends about his followers and they worship him like he was a god. She even talked about what had been happening in town and how people are afraid. As I sat and listened, I felt something hit me in the pit of my stomach.

An overwhelming sensation that sent my blood boiling, I had such a thirst for something but I didn't know what. I tried to shaking it off but it was too strong. I sat there trying to control this feeling of power, my hands turned red like blood; I could feel the sweat forming on my brow.

Elsha knew this look on my face, she had seen it before. She acted quickly.

"Why don't we take a break, we have been talking for a while, I could use a breath for fresh air."

Everyone agreed, we took a break and I followed Elsha out onto the balcony. She was worried.

"Kyle, you have that flustered look again, take a deep breath."

As always I obeyed, she touched my forehead and I was a little warm. I told her not to worry the fresh air would do me some good. Then Benjamin came outside he must have felt something was wrong he asked Elsha to give us a few minutes to talk.

Benjamin looked me in my eyes, and asked had I had any unusual thirst lately. I told him how sometimes I get the urges of overwhelming strength and increased eating habits. Benjamin had a worried look on his face, I tried to play it off by telling him I would be fine but he didn't buy it.

As everyone started returning to the room; Lou and a few others of Veronica's staff had prepared food for us. I looked around the room to see how everyone was getting along on a social level. Ms. Creed was talking Professor Jones while Tony was busy stuffing his face with food.

It never fails that kid will always find the time to feed his face. Speaking of food, I was starving; Elsha was nice enough to bring me a plate. I thanked her and she told me she didn't want me to pass out on her again.

She still found a way to remind me that I owed her an explanation. I told her I would tell her in time.

Elsha couldn't help but notice the fine paintings of Native American warriors Veronica had. While Elsha admired the paintings I couldn't help but notice Benjamin watching me

As he approached he had that worried look in his eyes again.

"Kyle, are you sure you are feeling alright?"

I stuffed food in my mouth nodding my head up and down.

"Sure uncle just needed food."

I knew he was worried about me but I had to get past this odd feeling. As we sat down to wrap up our discussions on old ghost. Veronica thanked everyone for shedding a lot of light on the mystery that hovered over us. As she continued talking, AiYana entered the room and whispered something in her ear. Veronica's face was pale looking, and very disturbed.

She quickly walked over to her desk picked up the remote to her giant wide screen and turned it on. And to our surprise breaking news coming out of South Dakota where bodies were discovered at a campsite near the badlands.

It appeared the attack happened at night when everyone was either sleeping or camping out near their fires. There had even been reports of several people missing.

The reporter stated how local authorities think this could be a copycat of what has been going on in other states including ours.

More and more reports from different parts of the world were coming in. People were starting to get into a state of panic. Religious groups calling for repentance, one person even told a reporter.

"There is a beast walking among us, and he must be destroyed."

Professor Jones sat down in her seat in shock. The reality of the news must have hit her real hard.

"What is happening, all this talk of animal attacks, people missing. What is going on here? I know we are dealing with something far beyond our beliefs, pardon my outburst I guess I wasn't expecting to hear more news like that."

I felt it was time I shed some light on things with Professor Jones. The world we live is in under attack by evil, no one will be safe until we come together and meet with the council of elders.

While everyone sat down to talk AiYana told us how when she went home to attend the burial ceremony of her uncle's many were seeking the spirit guides for help.

She told us the day her great uncle's died they went out into the fields to pray over ancient caves that were found up in the foothills near their homes.

She said her uncle's made a great discovery of ancient scrolls which she would explain later.

She said her aunts told her they were not themselves that day as if they knew their time had come.

Listening to AiYana tell her story about her uncle's saddened me and also I felt something else like her uncle's were with me somehow.

Their presence was very strong and though I had never met them, I knew they were among the eagles.

AiYana pulls an envelope from her front jacket pocket she took a deep breath and said a short prayer for strength.

"My great uncles must have known their time was coming to an end, they left me this note explaining when the time was right I should read it. And since we are all gathered here I feel that I must read it now."

She opened the envelope and took out a folded up piece of paper. She stood up and told us how the death of her great uncles was a true sign that evil is upon us. She said the night before the ceremony her uncle's came to her in a dream telling her that she should deliver a message to a gathering of people.

170

Not knowing that her aunts would give her an envelope she was told when the time was right she would know when to open it.

AiYana unfolded the paper and she began to read it to us.

"By the time you read this we will have passed from the earth into the spirit world. I want you to know that when the eagles gather in the west we will be there. There is a war coming that is going to test the very strength of mankind. Our people must come together in great strength and numbers. Follow the stars that settle on the high mountain where the earth and sky meet. Don't worry our brave ones, sometimes the strongest of this world has to leave in order to keep the living protected. The spirits guides will ever watch over you. As our lives ended it was our duty and our calling, as you gather together so will we."

The room was quiet, no one made a sound. My mind reflected on my dream of my parents AdSilah and Charley. Seeing what looked like stars shooting toward the western sky. AiYana shed tears and Ms. Creed comforted her.

But there was more to come, AiYana asked if I remembered when she told me that some people will kill for the gift I have.

And I told her yes, she went to say that there is another evil who seeks out those who can expose the Suhnoyee Wah.

Professor Jones was having a hard time taking all this in she questioned AiYana about the discovery her great uncles made.

AiYana told her that she would explain it in a moment, she encouraged the professor to listen carefully for she felt the information she had was very important. AiYana walked in front of the huge conference table and began to explain her uncle's discovery. She said it was her uncle's who discovered an ancient cave with the writings and drawings identical to the ones Elsha had in her books.

She said they had been working day and night uncovering artifacts, and translating the symbols. AiYana said that what they found next shocked them deeply.

She said her uncle's discovered skeletal bones and fragments in one part of the cave, which was sent to a research institute center to determine if the bones were human or animal. As they continued one of them came across a huge pouch made from cowhide. Her uncle's carefully unraveled it finding the well preserved ancient scrolls.

By this time AiYana moved toward the wall and pulled down a projector screen, she asked Elsha to assist her by setting up the projector with her laptop. The scrolls were too delicate to bring so she had them scanned. Professor Jones asked AiYana how she was allowed to even show this. AiYana explained that in both her uncle's last will and testaments the scrolls were to be used for research purposes only, which gives her the right to use them when she does volunteer teaching at the university sometimes.

This made Professor Jones pleased to hear this. As AiYana continued she explained that there were about six scrolls, what they learned from them was very important.

AiYana stated that one of the scrolls had drawings of people standing around a sacred stone with seven diamond shaped symbols around it. The people appear to be worshipping someone or something, and offering sacrifices to it.

The next slide showed seven people stand in a row with a bowl in front of their feet. These seven must have been chosen as a sacrifice to whatever was on the other side of the stone. Photos of the seven were carved in stone, each one dressed and prepared for the ritual. One of them looked different; his skin was painted all white and he had hair on his face. While the other individuals were red skinned and had their face and arms painted with white stripes.

As Professor Jones saw this she asked AiYana to stop for a moment. She quickly picked up her brief case and pulled out a huge binder. Everyone watched and wondered what she was looking for. Professor Jones binder was more like a scrap book, putting on her glasses she searched through her book.

"I've just got to know if it's him or not."

AiYana, moved toward the table.

"Know what professor?"

Looking in the back of the binder Professor Jones finds an old photo and holds it up.

"I've found it, Sorry everyone but I believe the pale faced man in that drawing is my great, great, great, Grandfather Professor Jeremiah Jones."

AiYana looked at the photo asking Professor Jones how she could be so sure. Professor Jones responded.

"The last known whereabouts of my third great Grandfather was somewhere near this area almost two hundred years ago. I was able to find photos of him with the people that dwelled here long ago."

Elsha opens up her book and shows the professor the location. "Professor I believe this is what you are looking for."

Professor Jones thanked Elsha then continued looking for the photo of her great ancestor. AiYana asked her if she felt the pale face man in the drawing could be her long lost relative. One photo in particular shows him with a small group of Native American villagers. According to Professor Jones research her ancestor spent of lot of time away from home learning the ways of native people and the land.

Once she located the photo she asked Elsha to up load it for her and project it onto the big screen. As she did I kept noticing my uncle Benjamin staring out of the window from his seat. His eyes fixed on something. Professor Jones and AiYana compared the photo to the drawing and it was an exact match.

Every detail about Jeremiah Flynn was captured in the drawing, this confirmed her research and she was pleased but needed more clarification on what actually happened to him.

According to the petroglyphs seven people were chosen to be offered as a sacrifice to a warrior. It was said that the followers of Liwanu would be granted his strength and power. By this time Benjamin walks over to the window and looks out, I wondered what he was looking at. As everyone was focused Professor Jones and AiYana Ms. Creed shared her thoughts on what happened to Jeremiah Flynn.

Ms. Creed believed that Jeremiah Flynn became a victim of his own research. Ms. Creed was very knowledgeable in ancient history and she knew a lot about the Native American culture since she herself is. I had no idea that she knew about the Jeremiah Flynn, Benjamin was still looking out of the window and hadn't moved.

Everyone was so caught up on the new discovery no one paid any attention to him. Ms. Creed went on explaining that the tribe that Professor Flynn dwelled with was considered outcasts because they worshipped the ancient warrior Liwanu also known as Running Bear. Legend says that centuries ago the Shahwanee tribes and others split because the people feared him and were afraid.

Some of them felt that if they worshipped the warrior a sign of respect their lives would be spared.

Ms. Creed continued on telling us about the many stories of people that just disappeared once and no one knew what happened to them. She felt that the paintings and drawings are those of the missing Shawanee's and Professor Jeremiah Flynn.

She also stated that according to the map there was plenty of proof that tribes dwelled in hunter valley. The cave that Elsha and I were trapped in is one of many. There are others that are welled hidden deep within the woods some possible underground.

As Ms. Creed talked it all made sense, there were many chambers inside that cave. Some we didn't even get a chance to see because we were trying to get out.

More talks of legends and strange deaths, sparked up a new conversation about the legend of Suhnoyee Wah, *night wolves*. Professor Jones said she had been following the stories and first thought it was a cult or serial killer performing the rituals offering sacrifices to a pagan god. But then she also wondered it her late ancestor fell victim to the same fate.

That is why she is so fascinated with the legends; she wants to discover the truth. The hour grew late and as everyone talked Benjamin was still at the window, I kindly excused myself, Elsha and Tony joined me.

"Uncle are you oaky, you have been staring out of this window for a while. What's up?"

He didn't respond, he just stared out of the window as if he was in a trance, his eyes were glossy looking and it appeared as if he was not breathing. Tony and Elsha had confused looks on their faces. I whispered my uncle's name softly and he didn't move, the clouds covered the sun which darkened the room.

Talks of people disappearing and strange deaths seemed to escalate in the room. I looked at my uncle once again and his eyes glistened in the little darkness that overshadowed him.

With the sound of wolves off in the distance, Benjamin did not move. His eyes squinted, focusing on the wooded mountain. Whatever he was staring at must have been staring back at him because he still did not move.

I didn't want his trance disturbed so I asked Tony and Elsha to leave me with him so it would appear we were having a conversation.

I tried one more time calling out to my uncle but before I could, he moved. Slowly turning his head he spoke in a very slow tone.

"We must leave this place and get to the reservation, there is not much time left. The gathering is taking place."

Chills ran up and down my legs, Elsha and Tony didn't say a word. Benjamin turned his focus again to the mountain his eyes fixed on something, or someone. The sounds of the wolves were gone. Not knowing what just happened here, it must have been serious. Veronica turned her attention to us and asked if everything was okay. Benjamin nodded and said everything was fine and it was time to go.

She looked at him for a moment giving him a hard stare; AiYana also questioned him about his actions. Benjamin began to tell them about how for centuries our people always could tell when something was coming by watching the movement of the clouds, the darkness that followed, and the sounds from the animals in the wilderness. He said when the earth speaks we should listen. But only those who are gifted can hear and feel a shift will know.

This confused Professor Jones for a moment, she turned to Benjamin asking him to carefully explain since we were all gathered together.

Benjamin looked at everyone, and then turned his eyes toward the ceiling; he lowered his head looking around the room.

"I think it's time my nephew and I leave, but before we do let me tell you this. I too have studied the lost tribes of our people; many of them have sold their souls to become scouts for the enemy."

This time Benjamin turned his focus on Ms. Creed. He looked at her and she appeared very nervous.

"Some of us have heard the sacred call; we must leave, to gather with our brothers and sisters. Though we are faced with many dangers, we still must come together and celebrate the lives of our people. Many of us are born with the gift to sense the unknown. But I am afraid there are those who have chosen to follow evil to destroy our gifted ones."

I looked at AiYana for a second, so that's what she meant that there are some that will kill for my gift. There must be a secret society of some kind watching people like me working for an evil to find and destroy the gifted ones. It all make sense now, then I thought about Becca's parents, how do the shifters know when and where to strike? Are they summoned somehow and then they attack?

It appears I am still in danger, I even thought about the interest in my blood. I still need to meet with Dr. Morgan since he has such an interest in my blood I wonder what he has discovered.

Well once Benjamin finished talking about the ancient tribes of our people, he kept his eyes on the outside. I wondered what was going on and why the rush for us to leave. I figured I would question him on the way to the reservation. But Veronica beat me to it.

She told him how she watched him near the window, and was wondering why he stared so long and hard out of it. Benjamin told her there are some things she will not understand. Being the person that Veronica was she stepped to him and whispered.

"Try me."

While Benjamin and Veronica talked I wanted to be close to them to know what they were discussing. I wanted Tony to go over and try to be nosy but he must have left the room. Ms. Creed approached me and thanked me for inviting her to the meeting, I asked her if she was going to the celebration and she said she would not miss it for the world.

I asked her how her family was doing and she said they were doing well.

She told me she was glad I was going to the reservation it would give me a chance to learn more about our culture.

I asked Ms. Creed if she could set up a meeting with Dr. Morgan. I explained to how I would like to know more about the survivors and what he found out. She thought maybe I should ask Elsha but I told her I didn't want to involve her. Ms. Creed did say she had a friend coming into town to meet with Dr. Morgan. She would let me know when and where to meet her.

Benjamin's conversation was over with Veronica and he seemed quite disturbed. I felt this short trip was going to be a long one. I had a feeling I was going to find out how long.

Chapter Fifteen

DARKER SECRETS

It was time for us to leave so we all set out to the reservation. So many thoughts plagued my mind. I wanted to question him more but since Elsha and Tony were in the back seat I thought I would ask him when we were alone. The road trip went well, we listened to music, cracked jokes, and talked about are plans after high school. Then Tony asked how I met my uncle and Benjamin gave him a bit of our family history.

Then another question came, but this time from Elsha, she asked Benjamin why he stared out of the window for so long. Her curiosity just had to be satisfied; Benjamin did not mind her questions. He knew she was an inquisitive person just by looking at her. He did tell me that it is good to have friends that care. That is something you just don't get often, Elsha and Tony are my best friends and I don't want anything to happen to them.

Benjamin talked about how we are connected to nature, and if we listen to the wind and the animals the animals will tell us a story. But Elsha was determined to get into his head. Being who she is she just had to go there.

"So you say your people have a way to communicate with the wilderness, do you think there is a connection with what has been happening lately?"

Benjamin sighed first before he responded.

"Animals can sense danger, just as a person can sometimes sense or feel when something bad is about to happen. We just have to listen, but also respect the wild by giving them their space."

Elsha was curious to know more, she kept asking more questions. The look that Benjamin gave me he knew she was not going to stop. So he told her she would learn more once we arrive at the reservation. He said there was a lot planned for us, and that he wanted us to have a good time.

Benjamin looked at me giving me a wink and a smile. Once we arrived at the reservation a welcoming party met us at the main entrance. It was Big John he looked even bigger that when I first met him. I swear these guys eat a lot of red meat, or work out a lot at the gym. Big John was the first to approach us.

"Welcome back Kyle, it's good to see you again."

His arms were massive, and his broad shoulders looked like mountains.

"I see you're still working out."

Big John flexed his muscles and told us to go on in he would catch up with us later. He said he was glad to see my friends and he told us to enjoy ourselves. He gave us a little lecture about wandering off into places that we shouldn't. He told us there was enough to see, and then he looked at Tony and Elsha and told them to have a good time.

He handed us maps, and a list of time and events.

"Have a good time, and I will see you all later."

We thanked him and drove in. We all agreed to stay together, the last time I was here I found out I had a twin brother, thanks to Tony snooping around. I really wanted my friends to have fun so once we were settled in our rooms I told both of them not to snoop. Tony agreed and since this was Elsha's first visit to the reservation she was already busy taking pictures.

We decided to look around first then meet up so we picked a central location which was the library. Tony came up with the idea and I reminded him to make sure he did not go into unauthorized places. Elsha was very excited she decided to go to the museum and look around. Tony decided to walk around sight see, I reminded him again about snooping. He told me he would abide by the rules and not get into trouble.

While Tony and Elsha were off sightseeing, I decided to walk around myself and check out a few things. There were so many people here; the workers were busy hanging lights and décor. There were dance practices and booths being set up. Venders were cooking their favorite food to sell to hungry crowds.

As I looked at the license plates, there were so many people from out of town, some as far as Alaska, Oklahoma, Nebraska, and Montana Just to name a few. Some even charted flights to get here. Though everyone was gathering, however I felt something else was gathering as well.

I could sense tension in the air, something was definitely stirring. I hoped to meet with Chief Spearhorn but Benjamin said the chief would probably be busy since there were so many other elders that had arrived. He told me he would talk to Big John and see if he could arrange a meeting. I told him I would like that very much, he told me not worry about anything he wanted me to have a good time.

As he headed toward the counsel building, Benjamin looked back at me saying.

"Enjoy yourself great nephew and don't forget to show that pretty young lady a good time."

I laughed to myself a little and was surprised he would say that.

"Sure uncle, whatever you say."

As I waited for Tony and Elsha to join me, I decided walk around a while. I checked out a few vendor booths looking at the different items from each tribe. Some were telling ancient stories, while others shared their beautiful native attire. The reservation really went out of their way to make sure everyone has a good time. I watched one crew put up a giant Ferris wheel, while another crew was setting up booths for games.

I was looking forward to having a good time, I tried to think positive but something else was tugging at me. I finally heard from my parents, they were on their way with Becca; it appears that she is now a part of our family. Dad said the town is still on high alert and the curfew is still in place.

As I walked I noticed a group of men entering a building they were big, muscular and very tall. I followed them inside to see where they were going. I guess you can say curiosity got the best of me. The closer I got to them, something came over me. One of them looked at me and his eyes gave me a cold chill.

Although he kept his focus on his direction, I played as if I were a tourist just sightseeing. I followed the men to a hallway and watched one of them enter a code on a key pad. My swift impulse drew me closer; I watched them enter and waited for my chance. As the last person walked in I quickly snuck in behind quickly entering another room with an open door.

It must have been a broom closet or something because it smelled of cleaning supplies. Trying to find a place to hide my foot knocked over a bucket and made a small noise. I peeked through the crack in the door to see if anyone had notice but lucky for me they kept going.

I wondered where they were going and what type of room this was, I thought about what I told Tony and Elsha about snooping.

Now I know how they feel when their curiosity gets the best of them. I had no idea what I was getting myself into. But from here I knew there was no turning back. I followed the men to a private room. I had to find a way to get in there somehow. Looking around I found a stairwell with a ladder that led up to the ceiling. I climbed up and headed in the direction of the conference room.

I found a small crawl space right above them and listened. As more men entered this must have been a private meeting for the Elders because Chief Spearhorn was attending this meeting.

Each person introduced themselves and stated which tribe they were from. The main focus was the disappearance or killings of their people. They talked about ways to protect themselves but spoke more on a spiritual level.

One man stood up he said his name was Chief Redcliff from Elkhorn Nebraska, he stated that people were coming up missing in the town where he lived. Later their bodies were discovered up in the Black Hills of the mountains.

Chief Redcliff told everyone the spirit guides had spoken he felt a war was coming and how everyone needed to be ready. He went on saying how one night during a prayer vigil; eerie sounds came from the woods. With his sons by his side, a dark mist moved across the plain. He told his sons to take their places by his side, each facing the four corners of the earth.

Saying their sacred prayers Chief Redcliff stated how each one of them prayed to drive the evil away. He said that night felt like the longest night of his lifetime. Because he could feel a shift in the atmosphere as they called upon the spirit guides.

Though Chief Redcliff and his sons, encountered evil that night, the sounds they described made my skin crawl. One of his sons stood up and introducing himself and Bo, he was the one that gave me chills when I looked at him. There was something about him that I just couldn't make out. His deep voice was even creepier, he said that night when the dark mist moved across the plain. He knew from within it was time for all of us to come together.

He said the spirit guides have shown him that that he must be ready face the enemy. The Suhnoyee Wah has started a war with the living. They are killing our brothers and sisters. He asked the Elders how much more bloodshed must we deal with before the gathering takes place.

Chief Spearhorn stood up to address everyone. He started by saying he has heard the concerns of our people. He also stated that he is not blind to the fact that there is something going on. But everyone must be careful; though the bloodline strengthens our focus should be getting stronger. He told them he too has felt the shift, and knows it is time for us to follow the stars.

As Chief Spearhorn continued, I thought of my dream again when I met my birth parents. The stars shooting across the night sky, I had to know more about this location and where this great gathering was going to take place. Chief Spearhorn walked toward the front of the room, he cleared his throat.

"I know you all are worried about the events happening in our land. The stars have shown us the way. I fear there will be more bloodshed therefore we must gather in the far west at Devil's Tower."

There was a lot of conversation in the room now, Chief Redcliff also stood up and voiced his opinion.

"I'm afraid Chief Spearhorn is correct, we must meet with our other brothers and sisters in the far west. For centuries we have met at Devil's Tower it is one of our most sacred sites. Though it possesses the power of the great bear, we must use caution. The spirit of Running Bear has left its mark on our people long enough."

The men agreed and Chief Spearhorn said he would make the announcement. Chief Redcliff looked turned and looked at Bo and he immediately left the room. Even though he didn't say a word something told me his eyes spoke for him. I decided to get out of the tiny crawl space when I heard something.

One of the other men asked Chief Spearhorn about his grandson Eric, Chief Spearhorn stated he was doing much better.

They asked if he would be attending the ceremony and he said yes, and how he was looking forward to performing his war dance. Someone else asked another question about me and my whereabouts but the Chief was very hesitant. He asked him why the interest and the man stated he was just a little curious.

Chief Spearhorn took his seat asking the young man his name and he replied Jeremy Hawk. Chief Spearhorn leaned back in his chair rubbing his chin and stared at him for a moment.

"Last I heard he was doing quite well."

Before Chief Spearhorn continued, Big John entered the room, walked over to the chief and whispered in his ear. Chief immediately adjourned the meeting and told everyone to join him for the fellowship dinner later that evening.

Then men exited the room which gave me time to make my getaway before anyone saw me. I waited until everyone was gone, before climbing down out of the ceiling. Looking around to be sure no one was near. I headed toward the exit door, only to be met by a janitor named Sam.

"Excuse me young man, are you lost?"

I looked at him and smiled.

"No sir, just looking for the restroom."

He scratched his head and pointed the way.

"Well son it's just down the hall to your left."

I thanked him, and quickly headed in the opposite direction. My thoughts were on Jeremy Hawk and I wondered why he had such an interest in me. I had to know more about him, although I didn't like the feeling that came over me. Chief Spearhorn seemed a little hesitant, and knowing him he looked a little suspicious of him.

Once I exited the building I met up with Tony and Elsha. We decided to check out a few venues, and learn the ways of other Native American cultures. Elsha was having fun snapping pictures while Tony was making new friends.

Elsha asked what I have been up to in the last half hour and I told her nothing much; I didn't want to tell her what I just heard in a closed door meeting. So I told her how I checked out a few places and met a few people.

As we walked I couldn't help but admire her beauty. I heard about a trail that we could take that led to a river stream. I asked her to go for a walk with me and Tony decided to hang out with his new buddies. But before we started on our walk we ran into Big John, he asked to speak with me alone for a moment so I asked Elsha to give me a few minutes while I spoke with him.

She help up her camera telling me she would take photos while I chit chatted.

"Hey Big John what's up?"

With his massive arms he folded them and gave me a serious look.

"Are you enjoying yourself?"

"Sure, yeah, I'm having a great time."

Big John looked a little worried, and I told him a big guy like him should never look worried it should be the person standing in front of him. He reached into his pocket and handed me something.

"You dropped this, when you were climbing down out of the ceiling. What were you doing up there anyway?"

My heart nearly stopped when he handed me my visitors pass.

"Crap."

Looking at him with a sorrowful face I had to apologize and sound very convincing on why I did it.

"Well I wanted to see the Chief and I saw these men go into a building and followed them. I didn't mean to cause any trouble."

Big John smiled at me and laughed.

"Look kid I know how you feel, but this will stay between me and you. There is a reason why I said no snooping. I want you to be careful around here okay."

Big John looked around and stopped talking for a moment. He looked quite disturbed.

"Kyle, listen I need to speak with you alone with your Uncle Benjamin a little later so make sure you and your friends are at the special dinner tonight okay."

After my nerves calmed down, I thanked him. Then I asked him why Chief Spearhorn had to leave so soon. Big John said he had an important business matter that came up. I also asked him about that Jeremy Hawk fellow. He did not know him, only that he is a visiting guest.

Now this time I gave him a strange look.

"Why is there so much mystery around this place? I mean why keep secrets?"

Big John took a deep breath, his eyes glaring for a moment.

"Son, there is a little bit of mystery in all of us, some darker than others. Everyone holds a secret Kyle; just some of us know how to get the truth without asking for it."

I walked towards him compelled to keep him talking.

"Now what's that supposed to mean?"

Big John seemed quite serious about this.

"You will find out soon enough."

Before he could answer I heard someone calling my name and when I turned around I saw my mom and dad along with Becca.

I was so excited to see them I hugged them tight and told them I was glad they were able to join us. Becca was excited to. Big John also gave them a warm welcome.

"Tom, Helen it's good to see you two again."

He looked down and smiled at Becca.

"Well who is this pretty little lady?"

Big John kneeled down to greet Becca.

"My name is Big John welcome to my place."

Becca stepped back for a moment, and then she smiled and said.

"My name is Becca; nice to meet you."

Mom told Big John that Becca was living with us now. Big John asked Becca if she would she like to visit the petting Zoo and feed the animals. Becca said she would like that very much. Mom and Dad said they would settle in and meet up with us later, Becca asked if she could stay with me and I told her that would be great.

Elsha greeted my parents also and told them there was a lot to see and do here. I told my parents I would meet them at the special dinner a little later.

I wanted to be sure I get some alone time with Elsha, I want her to know how I feel about her. Becca seemed to warm up to her right away, we took her to the petting zoo where she fed the animals. Then there was a kids' corner, where Becca got to dress in native attire and get her face painted.

It was nice to see her smile and be happy. Although she is still haunted by the death of her parents I do worry about her. Everyone seemed to be settling in on the reservation.

Elsha, and I ran into Tony and we all decided to take the historical trail by the lake.

There were signs along the trails of ancient carvings. Snap, snap, goes Elsha's camera. We came to part of the trail with a back drop of the mountain. Elsha decided to set up her camera to take an automatic picture of us.

So there we were the four of us taking pictures and having a good time. Becca enjoyed seeing a few deer along the way, along with other forest creatures. Once we reached the river we all sat down for a while and enjoyed the scenery. According to the history we read about the trails some of them lead to hidden caves.

This of course was sealed off by the reservation staff to protect the people. Warning signs were posted up for visitors not to wander off the trails but to stay on the paths. After that nice outing, it was time to head back to get ready for the celebration dinner. I still wanted to spend time with Elsha alone but Becca is having so much fun. Tony kept entertaining her with his silly looks and jokes.

Elsha loaned Becca one of her cameras so she could take pictures, they have already started to bond.

As we headed back to our cabins, I asked Becca if she was having fun. She said she was having a good time although she said she felt strange. When I asked her why she just looked at me then turned her head. Though this did concern me I didn't want to ruin her fun. I told her that I wanted her to enjoy herself, but somehow I felt that was easier said than done.

Becca was too busy looking around and we passed through the trails. She crossed her arms as if she felt a cool breeze. I was starting to feel sorry for her, I told Elsha and Tony to go on ahead and I would meet them later. I wanted to talk to Becca alone for a moment. Elsha didn't want to leave so soon, she kneeled down and asked Elsha is she was okay.

Becca began to squeeze my hand; I could feel fear all in her. Elsha was concerned about her and there was no way she was leaving us alone. Tony walked back and asked what was wrong.

"Hey little lady are you okay?"

Becca's bottom lip trembled, and then her eyes started to go dark.

"I'm okay I guess, I just miss my mom and dad."

Both Tony and Elsha did not know what to say, but they made Becca feel very comfortable.

Elsha placed her arm around Elsha asking her if she liked horses and she would like to take her for a horse ride. Becca said loved horses and always wanted to have one. Elsha told her anytime she wanted to go for a ride she would take her. Becca seemed to cheer up and told Elsha she would like that a lot. We all sat down for a moment and watched the clouds roll by the Sun. The winds picked up a little and Elsha shivered.

"Hey guys I'm having a feeling of déjà vu here."

I looked at her for a moment.

"What do you mean?"

Elsha said a couple of nights ago the animals on their property began going crazy. She was outside putting the horses in the corral when she looked up and watched the clouds roll in front of the sun. The winds blew from the north, but were not strong. She said for a moment something didn't feel right. She went inside the house to work on her photo books when she heard Tango and Boomer barking like crazy outside of the house.

Chapter Sixteen

THE BON FIRE

Even her dad couldn't figure why so he brought the dogs inside the house for a little while to see if they would calm down. Elsha said the dogs were onto something like bloodhounds. They ran around the house barking and sniffing and near the window like they picked up the scent of someone or something.

Her dad checked the house out and found no sign of anything strange. I asked Elsha if she could describe anything else that seemed odd that night. She couldn't. This made my blood boil when I heard this; I could feel that impulse of energy rising up in me again. In my head I told myself to calm down, and then the shifting wind sent a familiar scent to my nose.

Becca looked up at me with terror in her eyes.

"It's time to go come one. It's time to go!"

She nearly dragged me up the hill to the next trail; Elsha and Tony were right behind us.

"Please hurry we must leave!"

As we made it to the top of the hill, Benjamin, Big John, and a few others met us. They told us to head back to the cabin and wait until further notice. The look they gave was as if they knew something was out there. I knew it and Becca also knew it. There was no time to question what just happened, but it was clear enough to me when the wind shifted.

Once we got back, my parents were still out so I took the time to talk to Becca. I told Elsha and Tony I would see them later but it didn't work. They wanted to stay for a while, besides Benjamin told us to stay put for a while at least until the dinner.

"So what was that all about back there? Is Becca okay? She looked as if she saw a ghost or something. I hope my story didn't frighten her."

I told Elsha Becca is fine she is dealing with a lot, and perhaps it was a bad idea for mom and dad to bring her here. Elsha asked me why I thought that and I shook my head telling her I didn't know. Of course I forgot who I was talking to. Elsha is like the research police, if anything if out of place our balance she wants to know why.

She told me how she felt that something weird is going on around the reservation that security does not want people to know about.

I asked her what she meant by that, and she said while she was out sightseeing she noticed more men had shown up. And she overheard a group of men along with my uncle Benjamin talking about increasing security near the borders. Four men came from the woods and gave them updates. They said they have the borders surrounded and everyone was in place.

Elsha said they were talking as if an escaped convict was on the loose, whoever they were looking for or whatever they are preparing for must be very serious.

Especially when she heard my name, I asked her who asked about me and she said one of the men asked about me and my uncle Benjamin said I was safe. That's probably why they met us at the top of the hill.

Elsha said she wanted to do something nice for Becca since she felt that her story scared her. She said she saw a doll shop earlier and she would be back later on.

I told her to be careful we all needed to get ready for the dinner, I also reminded Tony not to eat so much but to save room in his stomach.

He said he was going to get ready and he would meet up with us later.

Becca asked when mom and dad were coming back and I told her soon. It was nice to hear her call them mom and dad. She said the last dreams she had of her parents they told her it was okay to move on and they would watch over her. She also said that it was okay for her to call my parents mom and dad.

I told her to go and get ready while we waited for them to return. As I thought about today's events I felt that energy rush again, the overwhelming sensation of hunger and strength.

I went into the kitchen to a grab a quick bite to eat when there was a knock at the door. It was my uncle and he wanted to talk for a moment.

I stepped outside and he asked me how I was doing. I told him to cut the chase and get to the point. I didn't have time for secrets. Benjamin told me to calm down and give him time to talk. He asked me if I were having a good time, and if I enjoyed walking on the trail today.

I told him I enjoyed my outing with my friends and Becca, and wanted to take a long walk on the trail again. He told me to use caution, and not to wander off too far. I found this very strange and felt that he was trying to keep me from safe from harm.

I wanted him to be honest with me so I decided to challenge him a little bit.

"What happened out there today? You looked as if you were looking for someone."

Benjamin didn't waste time responding, he got right to it.

"Some of our brothers received word of an intruder on the premises; we tracked him to the northern borders of the foothills. With a lot of prominent people here we can't afford for trouble to start. Sometimes we get protestors on the land or on the outer boundaries it's another way to protect ourselves.

I relaxed myself a little and told him that I didn't see anything out of the ordinary although I was a little curious of him.

"Since when did you become head of security around here?"

Benjamin laughed.

"Kyle, one thing that you are going to have to learn is when it comes to family we all must stick together no matter what."

I couldn't help but agree with him. He told he would see me soon at the dinner and also stated that we had assigned seating so look for our names. He tapped me on the back and said he would see me later. But before he left he touched my back again.

"Whoa, talk about working out check out your muscles.... solid."

Benjamin pressed on my back and arms; I thought to myself wondering what the heck was going on. I wondered how my body mass could increase so fast. Benjamin walked around me examining me from head to toe. He leaned in close to me and asked if I had experienced any changes lately. I glared at him hard and long.

"Changes like what?"

Benjamin didn't waste any time, hesitation he said I knew what he meant. And I told him, no more than what he is really telling me. Benjamin said he would see me at dinner and walked away. I didn't mean to be rude to him but I don't understand what's happening to me lately. But earlier my nose sure let me know there was something in the atmosphere that was definitely not from around here

Later on my parents returned and mom brought Becca a beautiful dress. It was white with a red belt and it had pretty flowers on it. She put her hair in a ponytail and placed a red flower in it. She looked like a little princess; I wore a nice dress shirt and black slacks. Mom said I looked sharp, dad agreed.

We all headed to the celebration dinner together. Mom looked stunning I complimented her along her with dad. Once we arrived there were so many people, the room was nicely decorated in Native American colors and flags. The ushers guided us to our table where we sat down for an eventful evening.

As I looked around the room I saw quite a few familiar faces. Veronica, AiYana and Joe were seated to my right, and then on the left was Professor Faye Lynn Jones. At the head table was all of the Chief Elders along with Chief Spearhorn. There were so many people here, Tony finally arrived but Elsha was late. I wondered what was taking her so long. She said she was buying a doll for Becca but she never came back.

Mom asked me about her but I said she was probably getting in some last minute exploring. I would give her a few minutes then call her. I asked Becca is she was excited about the festivities tonight and she said she was but judging by the sound of her voice she didn't sound so sure. After everything that she has been through I want to be sure he a fun night.

Big John approached our table saying hello to everyone. He asked where Elsha was and I told him I was expecting her at any moment.

Mom also asked about Elsha and suggested I try to reach her again; she looked more worried than I did. I excused myself from the table and walked outside to call her.

"Hi you have reached Elsha leave me a message and I'll call you right back."

I did not want her voicemail, I wanted her. I tried calling her again when I heard my name.

"Kyle, Kyle."

It was Elsha running in high heels towards me.

"You had me worried what took you so long?"

She grabbed me by my hand and pulled me away from the door. Her hands were shaking she was definitely bothered by something.

She was holding her chest trying to catch her breath.

Elsha said something weird was happening. She said when she left my cabin she went to one of the vendors to purchase a doll for Becca. One of the vendors was closing up their shop so she went to another one further up the trail.

While she purchased a doll for Becca she overheard a couple of men talking about an unauthorized visitor somewhere on the reservation. This visitor goes by the name Jeremy Hawk and was in a meeting today with Chief Spearhorn.

Apparently he was not supposed to be there; so they pulled Chief Spearhorn from the meeting. Before they could ask him where he was from or who he knew, he disappeared. As Elsha told me this she was nervous and scared I have never seen her like this before.

As she continued she told me that whoever this guy was he is bad news, men were all over the reservation looking for him. He seemed to have disappeared but the disturbing part was he has been asking questions about you and your brother Eric.

Then Elsha rubbed her head and appeared even more confused.

"Kyle I don't know what this mean but one of the men stated that while they searched the woods, they lost his scent, but there were no dogs with them."

I stood there silent for a moment, trying to piece things together. She went on telling me while on her way back she felt someone was following her. When she turned around no one was there. She went back to her cabin to get her camera when she thought she heard a knock at the door.

She went to check because she thought it was me and no one was there; she walked outside and headed towards the celebration dinner when she bumped into someone. A man she had never seen before but his eyes were mysterious and very cold. She thought he was a total weirdo because he sniffed the air and said he liked her perfume.

She had dropped her bags on the ground, but the stranger just stood there looking at her.

Elsha's voice trembled as she spoke. She said she felt that this man might be who the security team is looking for.

I asked her did he do anything else, she by the time she picked her bag he was gone. She turned around in complete circles and started running. Elsha is very strong and fearless, but whoever this man was gave her quite a scare.

There is definitely something going on here but I had a feeling we all were going to find out. Before going inside I asked Elsha if she was okay and if she needed a few minutes. She said she was just a little shaken up. There was more she wanted to tell me but we were pressed for time. I told her we would talk more after the dinner.

Then Big John and Benjamin approached us. I had wondered how much they had heard. By the look on their faces it was more than enough. Big John looked at Elsha with concern.

"Little lady are you okay, we were worried about you."

Elsha pulled her shawl over her shoulders I guess she didn't realize her attired needed adjusting.

"I'm fine, just bumped into someone that startled me. I'm okay though, thanks."

Benjamin removed his hat, approaching her as well.

"Sorry pretty lady we couldn't help but over hear your conversation, tell us what did this man look like?"

Elsha described him as six feet tall, very muscular, long dark hair and creepy. She said there was something about the way he looked at her. And as she stood before him he sniffed the air around him. She thought he was a pervert the way he acted. Benjamin asked if he said anything else and Elsha told them no, just as quick as he appeared he also vanished.

Big John and Benjamin gave each other long hard stares as if they were reading each other's minds. They told both of us to go on inside and enjoy ourselves. As we walked in the mom and dad were very worried.

"Is everything alright? Is anything wrong?

"Yes mom, everything is fine."

Elsha quickly took over the conversation; she didn't want them to worry.

"Yes, Mrs. Green you know how we girls can be I couldn't find the right shoes to match my dress."

Mom looks at Elsha and smiles, giving her a compliment.

"Well honey you look beautiful."

I had to agree, Elsha's dress was a beautiful shade of jade green with rhinestone trim. Her diamond necklace was gorgeous complements of her mother. She wore a hair in a French twist and I could barely keep my eyes off of her.

I never thought I would see her dressed up so well. But this was a formal occasion. We had a wonderful dinner, and Tony was busy stuffing his face.

After dinner we all helped ourselves to some delightful desserts, cakes, pies, ice cream you name it they had it. Becca was having fun making ice cream sundaes.

The next phase of the ceremony Chief Spearhorn came forward again along with Ms. Creed after the dancers to make an announcement. I wondered where Eric was I really wanted to see him. Chief Spearhorn talked about unity among the tribes and how it was good for everyone to come together.

When he had finished his speech, Ms. Creed came forward to acknowledge a few students from the school where she teaches and of course we had to stand and take a bow. Then she said each student that attended the dinner tonight names were placed in a secret drawing to participate in a sacred tribal dance. This would be a dance that has been passed down from generation to generation.

We all looked at each other with great surprise mom and dad was very excited. Becca thought it was so cool.

"Did you know about this son?"

Looking at my dad still surprised I could barely speak.

"No dad I had no idea. I'm just as surprised as you!"

I couldn't believe she called my name, what a coincidence. Or could this be a set up.

Ms. Creed walked over to a box filled with names; she placed her hand inside pulling out a piece of paper and I heard it.

"Kyle Green!"

She shouted my name. Everyone cheered and then people in native masks came to our table and took me away. They lead me to a room where I was to be given a thirty minute lesson in native dance. I was so nervous; I hoped and prayed the dance lesson was an easy one to follow.

The head instructor entered the room and introduced himself, he said his name was Timothy Sands of the Cheyenne tribe and he was honored that I was chosen for the Kiowa dance. I had to know what the meaning of the dance was.

"Kiowa dance? What does that mean?"

As Timothy explained the dance, I couldn't help but be a nervous wreck. He explained to me that the Kiowa dance is a fast paced dance that tests the endurance of the dancer. He also explained how the dance represents great strength, and the pride of our people. Though many tribes have different names for the dance, it keeps us linked together.

He was very nice and said it is always an honor to teach the history of our people to young ones. He said it is very important that we continue the tradition of our ancestors by dancing and showing our appreciation for the creation of life and well as the land.

After my history lesson he wished me luck and said the dance instructor would be in shortly to teach me the dance, and that I was to wait for the preparation team with my dance clothes. Shortly after he left they entered the room. They congratulated me and showed me the clothes that I would be wearing.

One of them gave me dark brown pants made with cowhide decorated with white diamonds stitched down each side. Of course I didn't want to get dressed in front of a bunch of strangers so I changed in a nearby room. I don't know how they knew my size but the pants were a perfect fit.

The next step was to place a beaded breastplate that covered my chest and even a pair of Moccasins. The painted my face and arms with very familiar symbols.

The symbols were the same as the man with the crystal blue eyes in my dreams. A small mask was placed over my head only leaving my eyes visible so I could see.

Once the team was done getting me ready for the dance, I was told to wait for my escort. They were pretty serious about all of this. As I waited I checked myself out in the mirror. I looked like a true warrior, doing different poses being silly I heard a sound coming from the back of the room.

"Hello, is anyone there?"

No answer, I called out again.

"Hello, is there anyone there?"

I could hear someone back there so before I could find out she emerged from behind a bookshelf.

She was a very beautiful young woman, but she seemed just as nervous as I was. I asked her if she was okay, but she had this look of fear in her eyes. She kept looking around as if someone was watching her or she was hiding from someone.

"Are you okay, is there something wrong?"

Looking around the room, I assured her I was the only one there. I asked if she was my escort and she said no.

However she did tell me that I looked like a true warrior but my outfit was not quite complete.

She handed me the head piece which was a headdress that was filled with red and yellow feathers that flowed down my back.

"Who are you?"

I just had to know, and I wanted to know why she was hiding. She played it off, totally ignoring me she fixed my head peace and kept her focus. She asked if it was too heavy or uncomfortable and I told her a little, she said to pretend I was as light as the feathers. Then she stared at me for a moment as if to ask me something.

She leaned closer to me, and spoke in a whisper.

"Forgive me for staring but I've heard a lot about you. Is it true what they say, that you are one of the chosen?"

At first I didn't know how to respond. I looked at her very strange and asked her why she wanted to know. She stepped away from me looking embarrassed, and then she pleaded to me.

"Please tell me, I need your help I heard you survived the attack, the spirit guides would not have sent you back if you were not the chosen one."

I was stunned, something was troubling her and she was desperate to get answers. First I needed to know who she was.

"What's your name? And why are you so troubled?"

Lowering her head in shame, she began to apologize to me. She said she should have never bothered me. I wanted to know what or who was bothering her. It was clear to me that something had her scared.

"My name is Nai'okah Reed I am of the Seminole Tribe. I'm sorry to trouble you. The dance will start soon; and your escort will be here soon to take you to the bonfire. She was shaking like a leaf,

I felt sorry for her but she was desperate.

"After the ceremony can you meet me later? I will tell you everything then."

I heard the door opening behind me and she played it off by congratulating me wishing me good luck with the dance.

The instructor came in with the escort party with a few others carrying drums and asked if I was ready to begin.

He introduced himself as Wind Dancer along with his staff they welcomed me. Since I was fully dressed he wanted to see how well I did wearing the clothes. As my lesson started I spotted Nai'okah watching through a window.

"Focus, young man focus, we don't have much time here."

Wind Dancer encouraged me to embrace the drums and move to the beat, everything else would come natural. I was very nervous, and when the lesson was over it was time to perform. The escorts came and ushered me out. As I walked I met with others dressed up in their native clothes and some carried drums made from thick deer hide.

They walked me down to the field where I could see the flames burning in the night sky. The moon was silver like a coin and huge, it looked like it had come close to earth. One could almost reach out and touch it. The music was playing and the workers put a lot of effort in building a platform. I was beyond nervous by now, I would have to ask later who and why was my name given and out of all the students why me.

My mind was filled with many things, about why Nai'okah wanted my help. Evidently news traveled about the attack. I looked around and there was another person dressed up in attire similar to me. I could not tell who he was because his identity was completely shielded.

I spotted Elsha and my parents down front seated next to Ms. Creed and Chief Spearhorn. I prayed I remembered the dance, how hard could it be. The crowd cheered as we approached. I stood on the left in the front and the other dancer stood on the right.

The drummers took their positions and it was time to dance, I coached myself how to begin and what not to forget.

"Left foot hop twice, right foot hop twice, feel the beat of the drum, dance with the wind."

Then the native calls rang out from the crowds, the drummers banged on the war drums and the dance began. I put my right arm behind my back, closed my eyes and danced. Meditating on the beat of the drums and the singing, instantly I went into a trance. The wind was my partner and I was light on my feet. I could feel myself gliding across the platform as I became one with the music.

The sky was filled with twinkling stars, the moon set right above us; I crossed the other dancer and locked arms with him, then spun around as we synced our dances again. Chief Spearhorn sat with his arms folded nodding his head with the music. My soul became one with the night; I could hear the sounds of wolves singing out in the distance. As I danced it became like slow motion, as if someone slowed down time.

Power surges ran through my body, my eyes fixed on everyone, I scanned the background and the fire even appeared to be dancing. A figure stood nearby watching. I couldn't tell what it was. But every move I made, it watched me. At the end of the dance everyone cheered and applauded. They shouted and rejoiced with us, we both stood there masks still on waving at everyone. Chief Spearhorn stood up raising his hands to quiet the crowd.

"*You have witnessed the dance of our people; truly you both are warriors at heart, the spirit guides rejoice with us as we celebrate the coming together of our people. For centuries our people have danced this sacred dance. When young warriors are ready to face the next phase in their lives we teach them to listen to the sound of the drum, using the elements and moving with time. These young warriors have represented well, by combining their spirits as one, synchronizing the dance becoming one with each other."*

Chief Spearhorn spoke so highly of us, I felt ten feet taller. Once he finished his speech he asked us to turn and face each other. We extended our arms out to each other to greet. Then Chief Spearhorn asked us to remove our masks. As my masked was removed from over my eyes I stood there and didn't move. I felt like I was staring into a mirrored image of myself.

Both of us were very surprised to see each other, we turned to face Chief Spearhorn and bowed. The crowd continued to cheer and my heart raced, I didn't know how to feel. But yet I was a little confused as to why Chief Spearhorn would arrange us to meet again like this. My parents had never met my brother so now is the time to give a proper introduction.

Chief Spearhorn excused us from the platform and smiled the whole time. I could not thank him enough for arranging this. I have to give to the old guy; this was a pretty smooth move. Eric and I embraced each other hard, patting each other on the back. Mom and dad stood applauding along with everyone else. I introduced Eric to everyone and mom and dad said they could not tell the difference.

Eric laughed as he stated he was the better looking twin.

There was more to do more to see, mom and dad took Becca to a Powwow for a free lesson. Elsha Tony, Eric and I went to tackle the big Ferris wheel. We had so much fun that night, I even enjoyed listening to Elsha scream as we rotated upside down.

After that I tried my luck at winning her a prize by throwing baseballs at one of the game booths.

Tony and Eric had something in common, food. They were having a competition on who could eat the most hotdogs. Watching both of them was too funny.

Elsha watched my every move; she stood off glaring at me.

"I swear there is something about you that has changed."

She walked over to me touching my abs and shoulders.

"What have you been doing working out? I mean seriously look at your frame, it's getting bigger!

I had no idea either, though I did enjoy her touch. I just played it off like nothing was going on. She said she couldn't believe how much my brother and I resembled each other. She was certain that I wanted to spend time with him since there was so much for us to catch up on. But before doing that I wanted to spend time with her.

Elsha asked if she could take Becca to see a few venues. She wondered if my mom and dad would mind, and I told her that I didn't think they would.

"Elsha I don't want you to worry about Becca, she is not like any other kids. She just lost her parents; she's a scared little girl."

Elsha sighed shaking her head at me.

"You act like I don't have sympathy for her or something, come on Kyle give me some credit."

I didn't want to start and argument with her, however I did want to spend some time with her so I could tell her how much I felt about her. Then I felt those impulses again, a surge of energy running through my body. So I thought that there was no time like the present.

I looked at her telling her how beautiful she looked and how I valued our friendship. She told me that she knew how much I cared about her and that's what friends are for, to be there to care. I don't think she heard me so I got her attention again.

Only her cell phone rang so I had to wait.

"Hi mom, how is Rio?"

Her mom has some timing. Here I am ready to pour my heart out to this girl; well I will just have to wait. Once she finished she told me that her mom would be home in a few days and that she had something very important to discuss with her.

I really wanted to tell Elsha how I felt about her. Looking at her my heart raced, and palms sweated. Her slender curvy body hugged every inch of the dress she was wearing. Her silk black hair nicely caressing a French twist, she made me want her more and more. My staring at her must have caught her attention.

But I could also tell she seemed a little disturbed.

"Kyle, why are you looking at me like that?"

Uh no I'm busted.

"Nothing, I'm admiring your body, I mean your dress, I just can't get over how beautiful you look."

Whew! Almost lost it there for a moment I don't think she bought it though.

"Kyle, are you feeling okay, you're acting a little weird."

I really wanted to tell her how I felt, but now would be a good time.

"Elsha, ever since the day I bumped into you I liked you, I mean I had kind of a crush on you. The day you went missing, I felt a piece of me was gone, I was empty inside. But when I found you I was determined then to keep you safe. So right now while the stars are out and the moon is full I will keep that vow that no harm comes to you."

There I said it, what a weight off my shoulders; then again I can't believe I said it. Elsha crossed her arms and then she kind of laughed a little.

"Oh Kyle, I like you to, you are a good friend. I never knew you felt that way."

I thought she would be shocked or speechless perhaps she didn't see me the way that I saw her. I just had to know she felt about me.

"Hey, hello did you hear what I just said?"

She responded by telling me that she did, however she also reminded that when we first met she was not looking for a relationship. She asked me how I could be in a relationship when so much is going on around me.

I responded by telling her that sometimes I need something else to take my mind off things. And how I did not want her worrying about the things she doesn't understand. Elsha just brushed it off, I asked her why push people away when they want to get close.

Then she sharply turned her head around at me, uh oh, I knew that look. Here comes the attitude.

"Look Kyle, I don't push people away alright! Look I know how you feel but I'm not ready for a relationship, just not yet."

I didn't mean to upset her, I apologized but she just walked away from me. I was so busy focusing on my feelings about her I had no idea something was bothering her. I beat myself up for doing that. I followed her to apologize again, but Eric and Tony cut me off.

"Hey bro what's the hurry, come on lets go have some fun."

Looking to see which direction Elsha was going, I told them to go on ahead and I would catch up with them later. Eric would not hear of it, I wanted to spend time with him also. Elsha's a big girl, and tough, I decided to give her space and catch up with her later.

Eric wanted me to join him at the next event for the tomahawk throw; he made jokes about me using my muscles.

I really wanted to make things right with Elsha, Eric saw that I had a worried look on my face; I didn't have time to bring him up to speed. He asked if I was having girl troubles, I told him no, I was just concerned. He told me how crazy things have been around the reservation. He said Uncle Benjamin gave him photos of our parents, and explained to him how they died.

He also said that Benjamin has visited him as often as he could. Eric said he always wanted to know about his past but learned of it through his dreams. He continued to tell me about his dreams of how AdSilah and Charley visited him once, telling him that he must follow the stars. He said at first he didn't know what they meant but his gut feeling told him something else.

I too knew what he was talking about, there is something definitely going on here and my gut still tells me. The more Eric and I shared stories, the closer we became. Although we have not been around each but our twin like minds did think alike.

After the tomahawk throw, we all decided to attend an ancient story telling session down by the bonfire. One of the Elders from the Cheyenne tribe was telling stories about our ancient ancestors and how they came together.

I also couldn't help but think about Elsha, a text message from her made me feel better that she was with Becca and my parents.

While we sat waiting I noticed Nai'okah sitting across from me on the other side, she nodded her head at me and got up and walked away. Ms. Creed was also there, I didn't want to seem suspicious so I told everyone I would be back in a moment.

I followed Nai'okah around the corner away from the bonfire. She apologized for taking me away from the festivities. I told her it was no problem.

"So what's bothering you?"

Nai'okah was nervous and scared.

"Everything, Kyle it's everything!"

She looked at me with tears in her eyes, and just cried.

"I can't eat, I can't sleep, sometimes feel I'm being followed, but when I turn around no one is there! I'm going crazy out of my mind."

I placed my hand on her shoulder to give her some comfort. I told her she was not crazy and to start at the beginning.

Nai'okah said when she was little she used to be haunted by bad dreams. Her mother and father would say sacred prayers so she would be safe. She went on telling me how sometimes in certain parts of her home she of could see dark shadows moving and she could sense she was being watched.

She would close her eyes and say a few prayers and hope that it would go away, sometimes it did and sometimes it didn't. At night in her sleep she could feel a presence hovering over her. She described it as the eyes being very deep, and dark, and then she turned away from me.

"What's out there Kyle? I mean what's hiding in the dark? What does it want with us and why doesn't it strike? What is it waiting for? I wish it would just kill me instead of torturing me."

I stood there motionless, but I knew I had to do something to help her.

"Have you told anyone else about this?"

She just shook her head.

"I've told no one, I didn't think anyone would listen to me."

With tears still streaming down her face, something moved from within the forest and she jumped.

"How can I tell anyone about this, something is happening here, people are dying? Some creature that uses the night to devour its victims has his mark on me. I feel there is no escape."

I suggested we return to the bon fire before we were missed. But she didn't care; her will to do anything was gone. I asked her to talk to Chief Spearhorn or someone about it, but she interrupted me.

"How did you survive? What did you do to escape it?"

Placing my hands on her shoulders to calm her down, I told her that I didn't know the spirit guides helped me. I explained to her how my nose alerts me to where they are. Even though I can't tell if they are near or far I can tell by the smell.

Nai'okah questioned me about this.

"Smell? What smell?"

I took a deep breath; I didn't want to relive this but for sake I had to.

"The smell is like burnt flesh, one you will never forget. I can sense when they are near and sometimes I can feel when something is not right. The balance between our world and the spirit world has been stirred."

Nai'okah's eyes widened as I spoke. I could see fear gripping her even more; I asked her if she was okay she asked me to continue.

"None of us are safe. Only those in the bloodline seem to be the target. I often wonder myself why I am still alive, but my destiny has brought me to this point and I am just as scared as you so from now on we must stick together."

I wanted her to know that I was on her side and that she didn't have to go through this alone. Although Nai'okah was scared she told me something was definitely happening and I couldn't help but to agree so I had to be sure she stayed safe.

"You are right something is happening here. I suggest we find my uncle Benjamin and get you to safety he will know what to do."

I asked her to head back to the counseling center and wait for me there. I made it back to the bon fire just in time to learn more about our people. I chatted with Ms. Creed and Eric and it was very interesting how legendary stories were passed down from generation to generation. Each one the same as the next but told from different tribes.

I know just how Nai'okah felt; my gut told me something big and it was close. Now was the time for me and Eric to share some of our stories together as well. Once the legendary storytelling was over, I asked my brother to take a walk with me. I wanted to ask him about his survival in the woods.

He told me he was out on a hiking trip in the east canyons; he was a head of his group and was to meet them at the next check point. But he never made it.

He said from what he could remember it was a pretty good day, but when you are out in the wilderness your days can turn to night very quick. He said he had a strong feeling something was going to happen but he didn't know what. The wilderness was alive that day until he fell into the mine shaft.

Chapter Seventeen

DARKNESS CALLS

He didn't know how long he was unconscious but he could remember what happened before the fall. As he walked on one of the trails, he thought someone was behind him perhaps one of the other students but no one was there. He said he kept walking and thought he saw movement behind one of the trees.

He talked about a dark shadow hovering over one of the trees, as he walked staring at it, that's when he fell. As he fell, hitting his head, Eric landed on his leg and was knocked unconscious. He said he had very odd dreams of a place that was very dark. He heard many voices but couldn't make out who they were.

He also said he thought he saw someone but his vision was blurry so he couldn't make out who it was. There were whispers all around him, and he felt like his spirit was leaving his body.

When he had awakened a sharp pain in his leg hit him like a ton of bricks. Then he noticed his leg was twisted underneath him.

He cried out in pain, he couldn't climb out but he knew he couldn't move.

"Being in that underground cave it felt more like a tomb."

I had to stop him for a moment.

"Wait a minute, a cave? I thought it was a mineshaft."

Eric laughed a little.

"No brother it was a cave, the mind shaft was a cover story to keep people away."

I can see how it made sense for them to do that, it is better to keep people away especially during a time like this. Eric continued.

"I thought my life was over, I saw things down there that I have never told anyone about." The sounds I heard were horrible. I knew grandfather would come looking for me but I stayed close to the opening where I fell in."

Now this I just had to know. I asked him to give me the details and he did.

Eric continued telling me how the drawings on the wall were of a blue painted man with all sorts of symbols. He said the drawings show him standing on a high mountain underneath a full moon.

Below the mountain was a huge bonfire with people dancing around it. Eric said he had seen this man in his dreams before. Somehow watching over him keeping his protected from danger. He said he also felt someone was with him in the cave.

I asked him how he knew this and he said because when he woke up the food and water was next to him.

It seemed very odd and strange to be in a dark place with no light, but the sounds he heard terrified him. He couldn't tell if they were close or faraway, he just focused and cleared his mind.

He said he studied the drawings, and pulled his silver stone from his pocket. He wanted to test it to see if it would light up and it did. Eric shook his head and let out a sigh.

"I thought I was going to die, I have heard many stories of this dark skinned man. There are many rumors that this man in an ancient one who was granted eternal life to walk the earth watching over the chosen. And from what I have learned he is not the only one."

This really blew my mind, how could all of this all be possible.

"I too have dreamed of this man, and each time he has saved my life but only in my dreams."

Eric spoke with such reassurance that I could not doubt him. I asked him if I were in any of his dreams and he said yes. He said he had a dream he was standing over me telling me the bloodline was strengthening and I needed to wake up. The more Eric spoke the more he confirmed; I stood there reliving my nightmares all over again. I'm glad we had this time to talk so I questioned him even more.

"What else did you see while you were in the cave?"

The look in his eyes, spoke for him and I understood, Eric didn't have to open his mouth. I could see the picture in his eyes.

"Brace yourself Kyle; we are headed for a war. One of the drawings showed eyes in the flames, watching those around it. Another drawing revealed a man transforming from a man to beast."

I had to agree with him, that we are headed for a war, and from now on we must stick together. I told about Nai'okah and how terrified she was, she too knows something is after her I explained to Eric how I told Nai'okah to meet me later to ensure her safety I wanted her to talk to Benjamin.

Eric said there are others around who have said the same thing, so I questioned him again.

"How much do you know about the Suhnoyee Wah?"

Eric quickly replied.

"Everything and more, I know enough that something is going to happen, and we must prepare ourselves for what's coming."

He steps closer to me looking into my eyes. His look sent shock waves through me.

"I dream of a woman giving birth to twin boys, the elders take them away, then I hear screams coming from the village, shifters killing everyone insight, and just before I can escape a dark skinned man with crystal blue eyes emerges and covers me in a white smoke.

They can't get to me, but they want me. Part of me wants to know who this woman is and what the link is between those boys and. I know the Suhnoyee Wah is real.

Eric turned his head from side to side looking in all directions.

"And I know they are here, watching, biding their time to strike."

My body throbbed with emotion, and my blood boiled. I started breathing heavy and I gripped a tight fist until my knuckles cracked.

My senses sharpened, and suddenly I could hear everything around me, voices moving in the wind, growls and snarls. Eric was saying something to me but I couldn't hear him. Something triggered inside me, part of me wanted to run and hunt down every one of them.

A sharp sting across my face snapped me out of it.

"Eric slapped me and told me to snap out of it. Do you always do that?"

Rubbing my face I nodded my head.

"Yes, something is wrong we need to get back."

Eric agreed. As we walked the buzz in my pocket meant another message a phone call. I checked my cell I saw that it was Tony calling me.

"Hey, what's up?"

"Dude we need to talk where are you?"

The panic in his voice startled me.

Quickly Tony responded.

"Hey something weird is going on here, and I mean weird!"

Eric looked at me wondering what was happening. I began to walk faster.

"Stay there I'm on my way!"

I must have been walking too fast; Eric was trying to keep up with me.

"Slow down! What's going on?"

I didn't want to alarm him so I told him to keep up. As we made it back to the bonfire we ran into Mrs. Creed.

She must have seen the look on my face and quickly asked me if everything was alright. Eric was also asking. Looking around I walked away and waited for Tony. With both of them following me Ms. Creed wanted to know.

"Kyle the last time I saw that look on you it meant something serious now what is going on?"

Ms. Creed was very serious and she wanted an answer fast. Eric was getting agitated.

"Yeah bro what's going on, who was that on the phone?"

Before I could answer Tony rushed up behind me all out of breath. He looked liked he had seen a ghost. Ms. Creed and Eric looked at each other very puzzled. After Tony was able to speak, after breathing so hard, everyone wanted to know what was going on.

As Tony took his time gathering his thoughts, Ms. Creed suggested we go to a more private place to talk. We walked away from bonfire, and found a secluded place, near a huge water fountain.

Ms. Creed asked Tony to explain what was going on, and he looked at me as if he didn't want to. But she encouraged him to go on. Tony looking over his shoulder making sure no one followed him started telling us what was wrong.

"I don't know what's going on around here but it is big, I saw you uncle and Big John run into the woods as if they were chasing after someone. Shortly after that more men entered the woods following behind them."

Eric was just as curious.

"Did you see who they were after?"

Tony continued.

"No, I walked over to an empty booth and hid so no one could see me. All I know is something big is happening here, talks of a mysterious man, apparently he was sighted following a young woman earlier, and now she is missing."

My heart sank deep into my chest; and I softly whispered her name.

"Nai'okah."

Ms. Creed clutched her silver stone. Eric just like me needed more answers. We were going to find the others and find out, but Ms. Creed ordered us to stay put. She asked if Tony heard anything about the missing girl and he said only she was one of the dance instructors. And from what he heard she was last seen walking with someone on the trail.

I tried to call Elsha and did not get an answer, everyone agreed to go with me to my parent's cabin to see if she was still there. We cut across the campus into the entrance of the camp. The lights were still on so I hoped everyone was there.

When we arrived we found Elsha and Becca asleep on the couch and my parents were gone.

I asked Elsha where they were and he said they wanted to see more of the festivities so she agreed to baby sit.

She sat up on the couch and stared at all of us trying not to disturb Becca she approached us.

"What's going on, why are you all staring at me like that?"

Ms. Creed stepped forward.

"Nothing, don't worry we just wanted to be sure you are safe that's all.

Elsha did not buy it.

"You wouldn't just come in here asking questions like that; now tell me what's going on."

I looked at Eric and he nodded at me to tell her.

"One of the dance instructors is missing, she was last seen walking with someone, and she hasn't been seen since."

Elsha went pale, Ms. Creed asked her if she has noticed anything strange tonight and she said only when she bumped into a stranger and he sniffed the air around her.

Eric whispered under his breath clutching a tight fist.

"Trackers, I knew it!"

Ms. Creed turned to him with a concerned look.

"What do you mean trackers?"

Elsha wanted to know who was missing. Ms. Creed took over the conversation.

"First thing first, we don't know who is missing and what do you mean by trackers!"

Eric didn't want to alarm Becca so he looked over to see if she was still asleep.

"Trackers are people who worship evils spirits. They believe that they will be granted passages to the spirit world by selling their souls to the Suhnoyee Wah. In order to be spared they will sacrifice their own kind just keep from getting killed. They worship them by chanting, allowing the evil spirit to use their bodies as guides."

Eric looked at me again only this time is he was serious. Walking over to me he whispered.

"You're going to have to get your family out of here, whatever you do make up some excuse get them off this reservation."

As I figured out what to do, Becca mumbled in her sleep, Elsha walked over to her and then she let out a scream.

"No, no, no! Por favor, por favor! "Aléjate de mí!"

Ms. Creed ran over to help Elsha with Becca. She was sweating, and she felt hot. Elsha ran to the bathroom to find a first aid kit. When she returned to the room, Becca woke up. She was breathing heavy and coughing. Tony ran to the kitchen to get her some water. Ms. Creed touched her forehead.

"Honey are you alright, let me check your temperature, you may have a fever. You're alright now we're here."

Becca was afraid, whatever was in her dream must have really scared her. Tony gave her a glass of water and Ms. Creed told her to take her time. He hands shook as she tried to drink water.

I sat next to her putting my arms around her, she was still shaking. I told her everything would be okay, and she was safe. But Becca did not think so.

"We all must leave this place; something is going to happen I know it. I just do!"

With tears streaming down her face, she told us her dream and how was she was running and something was chasing her. She fell down and a huge wolf like man stood before her. His eyes peering through the night just staring at her, she said there were many of them, and they looked like they were planning for war. Many of them gathered, lined up ready for battle.

Stars were flying across the night sky as people were swallowed up by the darkness.

Eric stepped forward, to also comfort Becca, but she continued to warn us all.

"We must leave now, it is not safe here. People are going to die."

Ms. Creed asked me when my parents were due back, and I told her soon. She encouraged us to stay together. She was going to find Chief Spearhorn but Becca told her not to leave. Before she could ask why my parents walked in, looking at us wondering what was going on. I approached them with concern for Becca.

"Mom, dad Becca is sick; I think she is running a fever or something. You guys should take her to a doctor.

Mom walks over to Becca checking her temperature.

"She is quite warm."

Dad also checked her, and agreed.

"Hey kiddo, what's going on, fever bug got ya."

Becca brushes her hair back and tells them that she was feeling bad earlier so she took a nap. She thought if she rested a while she would feel better. Mom and Dad thanked Elsha for keeping an eye on Becca.

Then she turned to Ms. Creed and said it was good to see her again. Ms. Creed smiled at mom and told her it was good to see her as well.

Mom asked if she was missing something, earlier everyone was gathered as if there was meeting. Ms. Creed told my parents that they stopped by to see if we're going to attend the closing ceremony. Dad stepped forward with a disappointed look on his face.

"Son, I'm sorry we are not going to make the ceremony, I have to get back home and take care of a few things."

I didn't want them to leave so soon, but it was a good idea. Mom smiled as she walked toward me.

"Honey we have had a wonderful time here."

Mom turns to Ms. Creed.

"You must tell Chief Spearhorn, thanks for his hospitality. But we must be getting home now."

I felt my parents were hiding something from me. I asked to speak to with them alone.

"Mom, dad, a moment alone please?"

We walked into the kitchen, and I closed the door.

"Okay, now tell me what's really going on, both of you are acting strange."

Dad started first by telling he didn't want me to worry.

"Son everything is fine, we just have to cut our trip a little short, but you don't have to. Stay here with your friends and enjoy the rest of the festivities."

I wanted to believe him, my gut told me otherwise. Mom said I should stay awhile and catch up on things with Eric. I hope this did not bother them. Though they are parents I want them to be as far away as possible.

I loved them both but perhaps and the more I thought about it would it was a good idea for them to leave. Becca's premonitions are very strong; perhaps it would be safe for her to leave as well.

"I'm a little worried about Becca; perhaps she is coming down with flu or something. Maybe she needs to see a doctor it could be serious."

Becca must have heard me she ran into the kitchen hugging my neck.

"No, no, I don't want to go I want to stay here with you." I'm all better now, really I am!"

I didn't want to disappoint her but it was better if she left with mom and dad. Mom explained that she needed to take her home dad also agreed. While they packed to go home, I took Becca outside for a moment. I wanted to let her know that I was going to be just fine and she did not need to worry about me. I really needed Becca to trust me on this but she would not listen.

"Something bad is going to happen, I know it! Why don't you believe me?"

I wanted her to trust me, and I did believe her. I just wanted her to be safe. I touched her on her forehead and she was quite warm, her cheeks started to get rosy.

Eric joined us on the porch inquiring about Becca.

"Hey little sister how are you feeling?"

Becca brushed her hair out of her eyes.

"I'm doing okay, I guess. I just feel a little weird."

She told Eric she did not want to leave. And he told her that she was very brave and strong and everyone wanted her to be safe.

Becca replied.

"Just like you?"

Eric laughs as he responded to her.

"Yes, just like me."

Mrs. Creed and Elsha joined us to check on Becca, while mom and dad were still packing. Mrs. Creed tried to break the ice a little and asked Elsha did she enjoy everything so far. But Becca was way too smart for that. Ms. Creed also wondered if Becca should be outside.

"I know what you all are trying to do, but it is not going to work. I know something bad is going to happen. Please come home with us, don't stay here."

Ms. Creed comforted her, and asked why she thinks something is going to happen. Becca looked at everyone first, then she told us the demon told her in her dream. She was very scared. Mom called out to Becca and she went inside. I looked through the window and watched mom put a sweater on her. I took what she told me very serious, I didn't doubt her for one moment.

Tony, Eric, and I helped dad put their bags in the car. He told me not to worry about Becca. Ms. Creed wondered if Becca should be seen by one of the doctors on the reservation. But under such circumstances she wasn't so sure.

Mom thanked everyone and I told them I would see them when I got home. I'm glad they had no idea what was happening but I wanted them to hurry and get moving. Elsha walked Becca outside and put her in the car. As we watched mom and dad drive away Elsha unleashed.

"Will somebody please tell me what's going did I miss something here?"

Elsha moved toward my direction, she had every right to be upset. Before I could respond to her my uncle Benjamin arrived with a guest, he had a grim look on his face.

"I'm glad you're still here. We have a problem and I'm hoping any of you can help out."

Ms. Creed asked him was there anything wrong and Benjamin didn't want to alarm anyone however he was very hesitant but his guest spoke instead.

"My name is Adam Reed, we have a situation and I need to ask you a few questions."

Elsha stepped away from me looking at me very strange.

"Kyle what's going on?"

Adam pulls a photo from his wallet and showed me a picture of Nai'okah, my heart sank to my feet.

This is my niece, her name is Nai'okah, and she is missing. She was last seen with you about an hour ago and has not been seen since. I need your help in finding her.

Benjamin asked me if I saw her and I told him yes, right before the war dance. I explained how she appeared nervous about something. Not that I would hide the truth from anyone but from what she told me I feared for her life.

Adam was very worried along with Benjamin, and both of them wanted answers. Ms. Creed asked if Nai'okah disclosed any details about herself that would help in locating her. I looked at everyone and asked them to come inside and sit down first Adam disagreed.

"There is no time, please tell me what you know, I'm not here to accuse you of anything but if she told you anything please help me."

The look in his eyes, sent chills through me; I looked over at Benjamin and he encouraged me to talk. Elsha was just as anxious to know more just as everyone else. So I didn't waste any time. I began by telling everyone how I met Nai'okah and she questioned me about my survival. When I got to the part about what she was experiencing her uncle clutched his fist. Not knowing if he was getting angry at me I took a step back.

I continued telling him, how Nai'okah asked me to meet her later, and I explained how frightened she was. Adam wanted to know why and I told him she thought someone was following her. Clutching his fist on his chest, he uttered a few native words.

"U-ne-qua, great spirits guide her to safety."

The word he uttered meant great spirits another name for the creator. Benjamin asked if there was anything else, I told him yes. I explained how Nai'okah saw things that make her scared. I explained to my uncle how I told her to go to him and wait that he would know what to do.

Eric placed his hand on my shoulder asking if I were okay, I told him no. I somehow felt responsible; I should have told her to stay with me. I told my uncle I would help to locate her. He suggested I stayed put, then Elsha asked about the strange man she had encountered, and wondered if it could be the same person.

Benjamin addressed everyone.

"At this point we don't know, I suggest you return home and leave the reservation, we will take it from here."

Elsha was very stubborn, and in her defiant mode she refused to listen. Benjamin told her she didn't have much of a choice. I apologized to Adam and my uncle, I felt really bad. Ms. Creed told me not to feel guilty about anything; there was nothing I could have done.

I wish she was right, the very thought of someone missing brought me back to when Elsha went missing. I looked at her with pitiful eyes, and walked away, I just couldn't stand around any longer. The more I thought about Nai'okah, my guilt turned to anger, this fueled my emotion so much everyone knew I was upset.

Elsha followed me as I headed back towards the bonfire.

"Kyle, wait up where are you going?"

I ignored her, the more I walked, I thought about what Eric saw when he was in the cave. I whispered out loud as I headed back toward the bonfire.

"Eyes in the flame he said something about the eyes in the flames. Images of a burning man flashed before my eyes."

I stopped immediately frozen, unable to move. Elsha caught up to me along with Ms. Creed and the others.

Benjamin, Eric, Adam, all looked at each other as if they knew what was happening.

Elsha pleaded with me.

"Kyle, please tell me what's wrong? I don't like the way you are acting."

I turned my head towards her; the look in my eyes caused her step away from me. I could feel my muscles tightening, and my heart pumped faster than ever before. I did not feel like myself, something about the way I felt was different.

Everyone stood there looking at me; my eyes looked beyond them but focused on the woods. Ms. Creed tried to console me.

"Kyle, honey I know your upset about Nai'okah, don't do this to yourself they will find her."

I kept my focus on the woods; I scoured everything, and just listened for the obvious. Not one sound was made. I looked in Tony's direction and he was startled.

"Dude, you are acting very weird, what's happening to you?"

I didn't waste any time responding. Speaking to him without making a move softly uttered.

"Get Elsha out of here now. Get to the counseling center as fast as you can and don't look back."

There was not time to explain. Elsha went to speak and just as I swiftly turned my eyes toward her she looked at me as if she saw a ghost. Tony took Elsha away and I encouraged Ms. Creed to leave as well. Although she refused, I never took my eyes off the woods.

"Kyle, tell me what do you see? What's out there?"

Never looking at her, I kept my focus and said.

"Death, death is out there, now get out of here!"

Clutching her silver stone, she knew what I had meant; Eric stood next me and didn't move either. Ms. Creed said she was going to find Chief Spearhorn Adam stopped her.

"Ms. Creed don't leave just yet, wait here for a moment."

Adam and Benjamin approached me slowly, and wanted to know also.

Son, please tell us what do you see. Never taking my eyes off the woods I kept my focus.

"It's not what I see, uncle, it's what I don't hear."

Eric didn't move a muscle, as Adam and Benjamin stood with us, Ms. Creed grabbed Benjamin's arm. She whispered to us.

"Someone please tell me what's going on here, I don't like this."

I couldn't move from my position, something was out there watching and waiting. I asked everyone to clear their mind and focus. We stood there motionless; there was a dead silence all around us. It was as if time stood still, the woods were very quiet, and nothing moved or even made a sound.

Eric and I glared at each other for a moment; there was no wind, just a dead calm in the air. Benjamin and Adam moved in front us and stood motionless for a few seconds then he ordered us to walk backwards.

"Move toward the truck now."

Ms. Creed moved first, the look of horror was all in her face, then Eric moved, and then I moved. But Benjamin and Adam did not. We watched from the truck, I had no idea what was happening but it felt like whatever we couldn't see was definitely watching us.

A sound from my cell phone made all of us jump. It was Tony, he said the animals were going crazy and wanted to know what was taking so long. I told him I would be there soon and he was not to move. Tony was ready to leave the reservation fast, he ordered me to hurry. I told I would, and then he was very persistent.

"Kyle, something weird is going on here, I just overheard a couple guys saying for no one to leave the building, something about wild animals on the loose."

I asked if Elsha was okay and he said yes, she was sitting with a couple of kids, and he said she was worried about me. I was more worried about them instead.

Benjamin walked back to the truck and we took off toward the bon fire. Ms. Creed demanded to be taken to the counseling center to find Chief Spearhorn. Once we arrived, we were met by a team of men although they didn't say much; the expression on their faces told me that they knew something.

Adam was the first to speak.

"Any word on my niece, has there been any news."

One of the men stepped forward; he was a medium tall, and very stocky. He said his name was Joseph. He stated everyone was out looking for her but no sign of her yet. Then someone ran up to him and stated that there was someone at the bonfire that may knowledge of her whereabouts.

Benjamin suggested Eric and I stay while they went to investigate. Both of us refused, I somehow felt responsible for Nai'okah's disappearance. I should have told her to stay with me instead. Soon after we took off toward the bonfire, Guards were posted outside of the counseling center, no one in and no one out.

By the time we arrived there was a crowd of people. The Elders stood around a little boy who said he saw Nai'okah walking toward the counseling center when a man approached her. He said he was running up the trail and that's where he saw them. One of the Elders asked why he was running, and he said because he heard strange noises so he hid behind some bushes.

Although the boy was very scared, Chief Spearhorn asked him his name and he said Tanner. He was also wanted to know who found him. One of the men stated they heard noises coming from the woods and that's where they found him. Chief Spearhorn comforted him and asked him to clear his mind. Everyone else around was to do the same. We all sat on the ground in front of the bonfire, and the drummers beat their drums softly.

Chief Spearhorn asked Tanner to continue.

"While I was hiding, I saw a lady walking. She kept looking behind as if someone was following her. Then a man came out of nowhere and took her away."

Chief Spearhorn asked if he saw the man's face, and she said it was too dark and he couldn't tell because of his hat. Adam kneeled down next to Tanner and asked him could he show them which direction he took her in. Tanner was a little hesitant, the look in his eyes was very familiar.

It was the same look Becca had the night I found her in my home. I asked if I could reach out to him. Chief Spearhorn nodded and told me to proceed.

I sat down next to Tanner and asked him how he felt, and he said he was scared. He said he didn't want to go back to that place because it was very scary. I told him how scared I used to be when I was his age. I explained how the darkness can be a scary place, even when you see things that scare you.

As Tanner looked up at me, something in me shifted. The fear in his eyes told the story that he saw more than he is telling everyone. Adam asked him again if he could take us to the place where he hid.

Tanner started to cry.

"Please don't make me go; I don't want to go back there it is too scary. The dark thing will get me. Please, please, don't make me go."

Chief Spearhorn saw how this bothered him, he told Tanner he would be protected and no harm would come to him. Chief Spearhorn suggested that Tanner be taken to the counseling center where his parents were waiting for him. But before they did I put my arm around him and told him to be strong. One of the men took him away and Chief Spearhorn said told Big John to alert the men right away.

He looked at me and then Eric; he told both of us, that though these are perilous times, it was now time for us to join in a sacred call for help. He told us how he could feel a strong shift in the atmosphere and the spirit of a young woman was tugging on him.

As more men arrived, Chief Spearhorn summoned the drummers and the dancers to take their places, he asked Eric and me to sit next to him and clear our minds. He told us not to focus on anything, no family, no friends, nothing.

With his calm voice he told us to keep our minds clear, and let the elements speak to us.

We were to let the sound of the drums, take us to a serene place, I wanted to question him as to why we were doing this when a Nai'okah was missing. Chief Spearhorn must have seen the concern on my face.

"I know you are questioning the reason for this, but in few moments you will see."

He placed his hand on my chest, my heart beat was fast.

"Calm your spirit young one; although you have the urge to run, sometimes it's best to wait until the storm passes."

Looking around, with his head toward the sky, he closed his eyes. The look on his face was a powerful one and his countenance changed. As others arrived, everyone took their places. All of the Elders sat opposite each other facing different directions, Chief Spearhorn explained that we must summon the spirit guides to help us find our missing daughter.

More wood was added to the fire, Big John pulled a pouch very similar to mine out of his pocket. He placed his hand inside the pouch and tossed something onto the flames which shot clear up into the air. It was like nothing I had ever seen before, the flames seemed to dance.

With the sound of the drums I tried to clear my mind, it was not easy. I wanted so much to find Nai'okah and fast. Chief Spearhorn's words burned in me deep. I did want to run; I felt the need to run as fast as I could.

More people arrived dressed in their native colors, all from different parts of the country; they each took their place as Chief Spearhorn led the sacred prayer.

"O Great Spirit, who art before all else and who dwells in every object, in every person and in every place, we cry unto Thee. We summon Thee from the far places into our present awareness."

I tried to control myself but I just couldn't something was building up in me and it was very powerful. I started to hear very familiar sounds, coming from every direction around me. As the Elders prayed in their native language, the dancers moved in circles around the fire. I tried to focus, but it was too hard, I kept my eyes open and watched.

Looking up at the sky, the moon was so big, and full it lit the sky for miles. I closed my eyes for just a moment then I saw her.

Nai'okah's face flashed before me, Eric must have seen it to, because he quickly jumped to his feet. Then I heard a voice crying out from the wilderness something was going on out there and we both knew it at the same time.

My gut told me to run, Eric snapped out of his prayer, he looked at me and turned his head in the same direction.

"Remember brother, trackers will kill their own kind for protection from the shifters. The war is beginning; there is no turning back from here. Use your instinct and follow your gut."

I didn't have time to talk about what I already knew. Nai'okah was out there and she needed our help. Immediately Eric and I took off running, we moved so fast it was amazing how we kept up with each other. Fear tried to grip me but I shook it off.

The snapping sounds of tree limbs surrounded us, ripples in the night and a far too familiar smell hit my nose. I knew we were getting close. Eric slowed his speed, placing his hand in front of me.

I stopped running, I asked him why did we stop and he told me to just listen. The sound of wolves howling up in the hills gave me the chills. Then we heard it, a loud scream coming from the direction of the wolves.

The louder the screams, the louder the wolves howled as if they were trying to cover the sound. Part of me wished this was a dream but this was very real. The more I thought about it, I started to have a feeling of déjà vu. I have been here before only there were wolves running beside me.

Eric crouched down on the ground, and called upon the great spirits of the earth.

He suggested I do the same. I sat down and focused my mind on the sound of the drum. No matter how much I tried only my attention was distracted by something else. Ripples in the night, it was darkness moving on either side of us. Eric called out to me again.

"Brother, I need your help now!"

Kneeling down next to him I closed my eyes. Simultaneously we called upon the great spirits. I could hear movement all around us and felt a cool breeze the north. The sound of voices in the wind began to speak to us. It was too much to take in at once, if I was going to die, I'd rather do it with my eyes open.

As I opened my eyes, I stood there frozen, panic kicked in quick. Quietly I called out to Eric. He opened his eyes, slowly and rose to his feet, a huge white wolf stood right before us. With its eyes glaring at us, neither one of us moved, deeper within the woods we heard the screams again.

I was convinced that those screams were from Nai'okah. The wolf turned its head toward the night sky, howled, then turned and ran toward the direction of the screams. It stopped for just a moment looking back at us.

Something in the eyes of the wolf spoke to us to follow it. This was definitely déjà vu, and one could only pray the spirit guides has answered our prayers.

Chapter Eighteen

DARK VISIONS

I don't know how long we ran but it felt like hours, strong power surges ran through my body. Out of the corner of my eye I could see that Eric and I were no longer alone. As we followed the wolf, something else was following us. The dark shadows moving fast through the trees were kept pace with us.

The wolf stopped up ahead and howled even louder this time, and then seven white wolves emerged from the woods. Another one ran between us and I felt compelled to keep going.

We ran right by them and turned around to see what was about to happen. The wolves began to growl while they stared into the darkness. The smell of burnt flesh hit the air. Eric said we must keep moving, he said the wolves are our protectors. He said they would hold the line until we returned.

This could not be happening, how I could know what the wolf's intentions was; something about it spoke to me and connected. What is going on I asked myself.

We could hear chanting coming from a few yards just ahead beyond the trees. Eric and I moved in to get a closer look. The smell was getting to me, I felt sick all of a sudden. I looked around to see if there were any glowing eyes.

There were none, but we did see something else. Nai'okah was lying on a flat stone, several pots lay beneath it. Her hands and feet were bound with twigs and rope she was crying and begging for her life.

"Please don't kill me! Please let me go!"

A group of people danced around her chanting a very familiar name. Each of them called out to Liwanu, the great god of the night.

Then a man appeared from the darkness dressed like a shifter. He wore bear skin, holding a huge knife in his hand. Something in me jumped, Eric turned to me placing his fingers on his lips, telling me to keep quiet.

His body was covered in ancient symbols; his chest was painted black with two large eyes right on the front.

We watched him as he turned his head toward the night sky and spoke out.

"Our great god of the night, we have brought you the enemy of those who took your life so long ago. We offer up her blood as a sacrifice to you to devour her soul."

Then he took his knife slicing her wrist. Blood began to flow as she screamed out again. He picked up a bowl and let the blood drain into it. I couldn't sit there and do nothing; he was going to kill her. We had no weapons, and we didn't even have a plan. But little did I know something else had plans for us.

The sound of a stick breaking behind me got my attention. As we both turned around were face to face with a huge white wolf.

My heart nearly jumped out of my chest, looking at each other we didn't know whether to fight or run. A white mist wrapped around the feet of the huge beast as it stared at the man with the knife. Revealing its teeth and huge fangs something about this wolf was different.

If we were the enemy it wouldn't have waited, it would have attacked us while our backs were turned.

We were not the targets, Eric and I moved out of the way and watched at others appeared. We had to get Nai'okah out of there and fast. This must have been the Jeremy Hawk that was inquiring about us, scared Elsha and kidnapped Nai'okah.

Though this no dream with everything that is happening now I know there is a war coming, but the fight was about to begin. As Jeremy held up the knife, he asked for the warrior spirit to enter his body. As the fire raged a dead calm hovered over us, not one sound was made. The ripple movement in the darkness I saw was sign enough, Liwanu was here.

The dark figure moved toward Jeremy as he invited the spirit to enter his body. As I picked up a stick I felt an adrenaline rush hit me. I wanted to charge at him quick, I did not want to watch Nai'okah die like this. As I went to make a move I heard a voice speak to me.

"Wait Kyle, don't move."

I turned around to see if anyone else was there or if the wolf was talking. Then I heard it again.

"Don't move, wait for the wolf."

Eric was still watching and waiting, I noticed he pulled a knife from his jacket. I touched his shoulder telling him to wait and watch the wolf. As the big beast moved in closer, others joined in. A thick heavy dark mist swarmed around Jeremy consuming his entire body. The painted eyes on his chest seemed to glow, the people around the fire kneeled with their faces to the ground.

They worshipped the great warrior as he now hosted the body that belonged to Jeremy Hawk,

Nai'okah screamed out in such fear, I couldn't take it any longer. Eric was ready with his knife in hand we stood up at the same time.

The look on his face was just as serious as mine. What was he waiting for, why doesn't he just get it over with. It was only then when I saw the blood; I knew what was going to happen next. To know if your enemies were true, he would taste their blood, he held up the bowl and began drinking her blood.

I could see her eyes, slowly opening and closing, she was losing a lot of blood, if we didn't act now she was going to bleed to death. I looked around and the wolf was gone. Sounds from different directions and wolfs howling it was time to get ready.

I heard the voice speak to me again.

"Wait Kyle, wait for the wolf."

Eric and I hid behind two trees, as others arrived huge beast arrived, they laid low as if waiting for a signal. Then a sound so loud, hit the atmosphere, it sounded like the sky was cracking open. As the dark entity drank Nai'okah's blood it was moving in for the kill.

Then all of a sudden something big and fast ran between the trees where Eric and I stood. As the shifter moved in on Nai'okah, a wolf two times as big as the one I saw earlier jumped on the shifter. The people on the ground began to run, but only to be cornered by the wolves.

Then Eric and I moved in for the rescue. Quickly we untied her hands and feet, she was barely conscious due to the loss of blood. We needed to get her out of there as fast as we could. Eric tried talking to her to keep her conscious.

"Nai'okah, can you walk?"

She just moaned, she was too weak to even stand. I felt we needed to get out of there as fast as we could and not look back. Eric grabbed her legs and I held her upper body and we ran with her. Sounds of screams were behind us, I dared not look back. The wolves were in a fight that I did not want to witness.

Eric and I Just ran, we carried her to the edge of the woods beyond the clearing. We needed to get Nai'okah back so she could get medical attention. The sounds of the trees snapping over us told us we were being followed or hunted. Wolves ran alongside us for added protection.

A white mist also guided the way back to camp. There was no time to be afraid, my adrenaline rush was so strong, and Nai'okah felt light as a feather as we carried her back.

Once we reached the first part of the trail, we stopped to catch our breath. Moments later, the smell of burnt flesh hit my nose. Eric quickly grabbed a stick and drew a circle around us. He looked at me with a grave look on his face.

"There is no time brother, I need your help."

At first I didn't know what to do, but then I remembered the pouch my uncle gave me. Quickly I removed it from my pocket and opened it. It felt very empty, as I looked around something was headed towards us very quick. Running wolves were swallowed by the night. Eric called on me again.

"Anytime now brother, anytime now!"

They were almost upon us; Nai'okah was still bleeding, and unconscious. A huge wave of dark matter headed in our direction with eyes glowing in the night. This was it; I knew we were going to die. No time to call for help, I had to act fast.

I placed my hand in the bag and grabbed a handful of what felt like powder and tossed in the air above us. It covered us in what appeared to be white sparkles. When the shifters hit it the sound was like a truck hitting a concrete wall. Whatever this stuff was, it created a barrier that completely surrounded us.

When the shifters got too close to the barrier it would burn them. The sound it made was as something was frying.

Eric then pulled out his pouch and sprinkled some fragments on the ground.

"This will hold them off until we cross the barrier."

I wanted to know how we were going to cross the barrier without stepping out from it. Eric looked at me and said.

"As I drop the stones on the ground you carry Nai'okah, they won't touch us as long as we in the barrier."

I asked him how this could be. He replied.

"How do you think I stayed alive in the cave, I knew I was not alone, so I used the pouch with the stones. There is a lot you have yet to learn my brother; if we stick together we will survive this."

The sound of something being deep fried was getting to me; we walked until we reached the clearing. Once we crossed the barrier I knew we were going to have to run for it. The only place was to the bonfire where the Chief Elders were.

Eric gave me the signal, once we crossed the barrier, he quickly grabbed Nai'okah's legs and we ran. The protective barrier held the shifters long enough for us to escape. Not daring to look back Eric yelled out.

"Were almost there, keep going!"

As we ran back to the bonfire, we could hear loud screams. Running as fast as we could we were met by a group of men. They were standing side by side at the edge of the woods. Each of them holding staffs in their hands.

Men who guarded the reservation met us and immediately took us to the chief elders. As they did, the shifters went on the attack. The night swallowed them as if it were a black hole. Screams rang out from all around. The elders stood their ground, as the shifters moved in closer.

We could see others up ahead; Adam and a few other men took Nai'okah to get her to safety. She had lost so much blood Eric and I were covered in it. We were so tired; we tried to catch our breath. So much was happening around us; it felt like a whirlwind of chaos. I really hoped Elsha, Tony and everyone else were safe.

How can you fight something you can't see? How can you defeat something that uses the night as its skin? This was madness, one by one I saw men snatched into the night. The light only holds them off for so long.

One would have to become one of them in order to defeat them. The sounds of the drums increased even louder, loud enough to cover the screams. I felt my body shifting from side to side.

Nearly jumping out of my skin, Eric was leaning over me.

"He bro you okay? You spaced out for a moment."

I stood up and looked around at everyone. My heavy breathing and scared look startled everyone. I turned around in circles looking at everyone staring at me. Benjamin approached me to calm me down.

"Nephew, just calm down, slow your breathing, your fine."

I wanted to believe him but what I just saw was so real, I tried to gather my thoughts. Did I just have another vision? I looked down at my hands and whispered.

"No blood, there's no blood."

I looked at Nai'okah's uncle quickly approaching him.

"Nai'okah is she still missing!"

He hesitated for a moment, and then he looked at Chief Spearhorn. Chief Spearhorn nodded at Adam to respond to my question.

"Well is she, is she still missing?"

Adam trembled, placed his hands on my shoulders and said.

"Yes, she is still missing; now tell us what you saw."

I looking around at everyone, I told them what they already knew. Glaring over at the Chief Elders with an angered look my blood began to boil.

"Gather as many as you can, we don't have much time."

I pointed eastward toward the mountains and stated that is where Nai'okah can be found. Immediately Adam and a few other men gathered themselves to start the search. I cautioned them to wait. I told him that Eric and I would go along to show them the way.

As I spoke I could hear the fire crackling loud behind me. The smell of death was in the air. Somehow I felt taller as my body filled out. Not knowing what was happening behind me the look on everyone's faces was evident enough I started to change.

My body mass filled outward as if I was a weight lifter. I couldn't stop what was happening to me. But as I started to change there was no more time to wait. I knew she was out there and needed to get to her. Then the wind blew strong and voices cried out that everyone could hear.

Then I heard her loud and clear.

"Kyle, help me!"

I looked over at Eric and before anyone could move, a dark shadow hovered over us. Eyes peered through the darkness, long sharp claws became visible. Long sharp teeth began to appear. Wolves howling in the woods drew in closer to us. We were surrounded.

I had to do something quick to get to Nai'okah. The Elders started speaking in their native languages; everyone circled themselves backs towards each other. Then there was a dead calm. The night became still as I became sick to my stomach, I could no longer stand the smell.

No one moved but everyone was on guard, my ear was ringing with Nai'okah's cries for help. I looked over and saw Eric removing his pouch from his pocket, then another voice from within telling me to wait for the signal.

Chief Spearhorn looked over at me and nodded, speaking with me through his eyes. I heard him tell me to run as fast as I could.

The Suhnoyee Wah was everywhere, growling and snarling at us, Chief Spearhorn raised his hand pointing his finger toward the woods. Ripples in the darkness look liked black silk; Chief Spearhorn looked at us one last time.

"When I make my move brave warriors run, let the spirits guide you I will be there as well. Whatever you see, and whatever you hear do not stop."

Then Chief Spearhorn raised his staff and the eagles head glowed bright as the sun. A cloud of a shimmering light surrounded him taking the form of an eagle. Exposing the Suhnoyee Wah, he blinded the night shifters then Eric and I ran as fast as we could.

As soon as we entered the woods, we could hear screams, very loud screams. That sent chills up and down my spine. We just kept running in the direction as I saw in my vision. As I looked over at Eric, I saw something moving next to him, and then it moved in between us and took lead.

A huge white wolf as big as I have ever seen led us deeper into the woods. Then more joined in with us and some ran alongside of me and Eric. Screams rang out and the sound of wolves, but these howls were strange, more like the ones Mr. Peterson described. Eric and I were headed right for it. If this was my destiny and my calling, then this is something I must face.

As more joined in with us, I swear I saw something shift from man to wolf. We made it to the clearing and nothing could have prepared me more for what my eyes saw.

Up ahead I could see something moving in the dark, glowing eyes formed a line and waited for us. We could not stop running but to only run into them. Stars shot across the sky so fast, they hit the ground transforming into huge beasts.

Increasing my speed, there was only one thing to do, keep going and don't stop. My night vision increased more and more, along with my senses, sounds so sharp and clear pierced my ears.

Eric kept his stride with me, as we saw the dark ripples ahead, the night shifters emerged from the darkness, teeth bared and claws extended. I never thought I would be running to these ghastly beasts, in my dreams I'm running away from them. But this time was different; voices began speaking to us telling us to take out our pouches as we approached the line. They were waiting for us, closer and closer, we yelled out as if to face death itself.

Then it happened, this is impossible, how could this be? Could this be real? Surely my eyes were deceiving me but they were not. This all makes sense now, I feel that I am about to cross paths with my destiny so let the battle begin.

To be continued...

Printed in the United States
By Bookmasters